GRANT MY DESIRES LACHLAN & HALEY PART III

STEELE INTERNATIONAL, INC. - JACKSON CORPORATION A BILLIONAIRES ROMANCE SERIES CROSSOVER BOOK 3

CHARMAINE LOUISE SHELTON

CONTENTS

FREE BOOK!

PREQUEL
NEVER
RELEASED!

EXCLUSIVE FOR SUBSCRIBERS!

A Trilogy of Desires Roger & Leonie Parts I-III

A Trilogy of Desires Malcolm & Starr Parts I-III

Series Extras

Series Playlist

STEELE INTERNATIONAL, INC. - JACKSON
CORPORATION

A BILLIONAIRES ROMANCE SERIES CROSSOVER

Tempt My Desires Lachlan & Haley Part I

Tease My Desires Lachlan & Haley Part II

Grant My Desires Lachlan & Haley Part III

Intrigue My Desires Harris & Kat Part I

Decode My Desires Harris & Kat Part II

Honor My Desires Harris & Kat Patt III

A Trilogy of Desires Lachlan & Haley Parts I-III

A Trilogy of Desires Harris & Kat Parts I-III

Series Extras

Series Playlist

ABOUT STEELE INTERNATIONAL, INC. - JACKSON CORPORATION A BILLIONAIRES ROMANCE SERIES CROSSOVER

Welcome to the titillating world of the multibillion-dollar global companies and the love affairs of the families that controls them.

STEELE International, Inc.- Jackson Corporation is a series of interconnecting Billionaire romance. Follow the Steele and Jackson families as they fly around the world chasing the women they love and their happily ever afters. Get ready for glitz, glamour, and steamy romance books. What's better than that? The Jet-set Lifestyle has never been hotter...

The Desires Series is not for the tea set; it's for the top-shelf vodka straight up in a pretty crystal glass coterie!

Don't miss any of the sizzling romance books in the STEELE International, Inc. - Jackson Corporation A Billionaires Romance Series Crossover:

Tempt My Desires Lachlan & Haley Part I

Tease My Desires Lachlan & Haley Part II

Grant My Desires Lachlan & Haley Part III

Intrigue My Desires Harris & Kat Part I

Decode My Desires Harris & Kat Part II

Honor My Desires Harris & Kat Patt III

A Trilogy of Desires Lachlan & Haley Parts I-III

A Trilogy of Desires Harris & Kat Parts I-III

Series Extras

Series Playlist

Visit CharmaineLouiseBooks.com for the complete list.

ABOUT GRANT MY DESIRES LACHLAN & HALEY PART III

Grant My Desires Lachlan & Haley Part III

Welcome to the titillating world of the multibillion-dollar global companies and the love affairs of the families that control them.

Will sexy as sin Lachlan finally claim shy-cum-feisty Haley Steele The One he's always loved? Or will their complicated past interfere with their fairytale future?

Find out if fate grants Haley's desire of a life of love, marriage, and a baby with her childhood crush Lachlan in the last part of their sizzling, second chance billionaire romance.

Close your eyes and make a wish as Lachlan charms his

Haley around the world from his Scottish castle to the top of the Eiffel Tower to the beauty of Bali.

Anthem: "All For You" Janet Jackson
https://www.youtube.com/watch?v=J551f-TyqjY

Playlist:
https://www.youtube.com/playlist?list=
PLXwYvn0e218CntwCpmdYKP-8npGhh5YvO

Visit CharmaineLouiseBooks.com

"I never thought I'd say this to you. I always figured it would be Lachlan I'd have to curse out—hell, even beat my best friend's ass—over you. But oh, no... Haley, *you* messed up, didn't you?"

My eyes widen at my brother's declaration.

Sebastian Steele, the eldest of The Big Four—as I nicknamed my overbearing brothers. Or The STEELE Quaternity as the media dubbed the multibillionaires for being the most sought-after of the world's eligible billionaires. Their near-limitless wealth, power, and good looks attract women like bees to honey.

Well, three of them are out of the lineup, including Baz with Lola, then Malcolm *The Enforcer* with Starr, and Roger *The Responsible* with Leonie. My fraternal twin, other half of the Dynamic Duo, and youngest of the four, Harris, still clings to his playboy card like a life preserver in a tsunami.

Baz pins me with his platinum gray eyes—a Steele trait along with ebony hair and olive skin tone. As I stare back at my handsome brother, I can agree with women finding them attractive. At six feet, four inches with a muscular frame, he towers over me, and I'm no petite woman at five-eight. An Alpha Dom who oozes sex appeal with no effort whatsoever, women can't help but to vie for his attention.

However, Lola—his petite spitfire wife—snagged him. Her Independent Woman-cum-sub proved too much for Baz to resist. Their passionate love affair started with a meeting for her luxury lingerie company, Lola's Coterie, then had its fair share of setbacks. So he can speak from experience about relationships with trials.

"You know how I know? Lachlan's been evasive for weeks. At first, his excuses of work made sense to prepare for time away during your honeymoon. But when he didn't have time to see me while I was at STEELE Aberdeen—in your own backyard—I knew shit was fucked up. Even then, I assumed he was at fault. But now, paying more attention to you, I can tell you're the one at fault, Haley. What did you do?"

Effortlessly, Baz shifts between older brother and leader. An ability he's cultivated over the years as the leader of our siblings. Then most recently as the CEO of STEELE International, Inc. It's our family's multigenerational, multibillion dollar luxury real estate development and management company based in New York City with global offices and properties.

After his retirement a few years ago, our father,

Morgan, trusted Baz to carry the legacy into the future. My brothers and I respect him and accept his leadership. Each sibling works at STEELE: Malcolm president of the Entertainment Properties Division; Roger, president of the Residential Properties Division; Harris and I, as the tech wizzes coder and hacker, respectively, co-founders of our subsidiary STEELE Technology and Cyber Security.

Our mother Michelle—known as Shelley by those closest to her—runs STEELE Foundation that builds and manages attractive, affordable housing for urban, lower-income families. The name is a play on the house foundation, being strong and supportive like steel. The annual fundraiser at my parents' beachfront mansion within our family's compound—Steele Southampton Village—marks the end of the summer season. It's a well-attended event that generates millions each year.

She met our father when she was a shopgirl at a STEELE retail property. A native New Yorker with an independent streak and a feisty personality, she captivated our father who's ten years older and an Alpha Dom. Married for almost forty years, my parents have a relationship to strive for.

Baz and Lola, Malcolm and Starr, Roger and Leonie, Lachlan and me.

Lachlan, my teenage crush turned first and only lover now husband. Well, at least for now...

It's been six weeks since Lachlan left our penthouse flat in Aberdeen, Scotland after a major disagreement.

Sixteen years ago, when I was sixteen and he was

twenty, I realized I was in love with Baz's best friend and our cousin. That summer, my mind finally admitted I couldn't deny my attraction to Lachlan.

With gorgeous movie-star looks similar to the debonair Cary Grant, his rugged masculinity and charm leave women breathless. A six-foot-four-inch well-formed frame and blazing emerald green eyes, thick, sable brown hair slicked back from his chiseled cheekbones, and strong jawline with a cleft chin adds to his allure. Not to mention a swoon-worthy Scottish lilt lessened by years spent in the United States. Jackson. Lachlan Jackson.

Best friend or cousin no longer mattered to me.

Cousin since our mothers are best friends who formed a closer bond than they have with their blood siblings and relatives. Blood isn't always stronger. It's those who treat you with respect and love you that count above all.

Lucinda—aka Lucie—as fate would have it, also married a billionaire ten years her senior and an Alpha Dom, Connor Jackson. She ran away from a less than stellar life in New Orleans to New York City and became a bartender in one of their pubs. Jackson Corporation's— their Aberdeen-based, multigenerational, multibillion-dollar global company—repertoire includes fine dining, distilleries, and vineyards worldwide.

The Jackson's Irish and Scottish family created the finest single malt Scotch Whiskey and became billionaires years ago. King James VI titled the Jackson family as Marquess of Huntly with their family seat—Jackson Castle —in Banff, Aberdeenshire.

To go from a regular working girl to the Marchioness of Huntly is just plain ole wow! Another fairytale like my parents' romance.

Aside from Lachlan the first son, and the heir to the family seat with the title Earl of Aboyne, they have Lydie the eldest, Lucien *The Sexy Chef,* and Laurent. All of them take after the Jackson clan with green eyes and dark brown hair. And like The STEELE Quaternity, they refer to the boys as The Jackson Trio for their multibillionaire, power, and bachelor status.

With Connor as the CEO, each sibling works at Jackson Corporation: Lydie, Overall Vice President and Vice President of the Board; Lachlan, President of Liquor and Second Vice President of the Board; Lucien, President of Jackson Corporation Restaurants/Bars/Lounges and Third Vice President of the Board; Laurent, Director of Jackson Corporation Cigars Division and member of the Board.

Lucie runs Jackson Foundation that operates alcohol treatment centers for lower-income individuals and support for their family members. The annual fundraising gala is the highlight of Aberdeen's social calendar. Patrons from across the United Kingdom and the world attend.

The Steele and Jackson Matriarchs being best friends carry beyond us being cousins into our family businesses. STEELE serves and sells Jackson products in STEELE properties around the world, as well as in Jackson restaurants, pubs, stores, and businesses.

Just thinking about how close we are makes my heart clench with sadness.

Before Lachlan left me, he dropped the gauntlet: *"It will either be a vow renewal or a divorce. The choice is yours, Haley."*

Some days it feels like six months. Others six long years. I miss him so much I ache. A hole sits in my chest where my heart belongs. I rub the spot as Sebastian speaks. In hopes the new habit I developed will ease the pain.

Although, as Baz stated, this time I fucked up. Big time.

Despite my teenage crush, neither Lachlan nor I acted on our feelings. It wasn't until three years ago I learned his view of me as Baz's kid sister and a little cousin morphed into an attraction that summer too. He wasn't the one to make the move, though. I did.

After a year of bliss, where he insisted we keep our relationship a secret to prevent Baz from losing his mind and ending their friendship, or worse, I couldn't accept second place and left. Lachlan and I spent a year apart, during which I reconnected with a classmate from Harvard Business School—our family's legacy school, along with Harvard undergrad.

Callum Graham, Duke of Montrose. Another handsome Scottish billionaire with green eyes and long blond hair whose father is grooming him to lead his family's Graham Energy, Oil & Gas Company, based in Aberdeen. He's also an Alpha Dom four years older than me who could have had my heart if it were not for Lachlan.

During our time apart, Fiona Ridel—Princess Fiona the Fair of the enchanted violet eyes and ash blonde waist-length hair—continued her crusade to capture my Lachlan and his ring. The thirty-one-year-old Scottish heiress who his father wanted to make Lachlan's bride and mother to his heirs…

Despite almost a year with Callum, I couldn't help but to go back to Lachlan when he professed his love for me in front of our families. The Big Four were none too pleased. But I could not care less. Lachlan Jackson was mine without hiding from our families.

On a trip to Sorrento, we encountered a crowd of people dressed in white heading to Chiostro di San Francesco. A mass wedding was about to occur. In the spur of the moment, Lachlan dropped to one knee and proposed.

Once again, we shrouded our relationship in secrecy. Only our families knew of our nuptials. At my insistence. This time it was my need to make the perfect impression on Scottish society, nobles, and royals. I agreed with Mom Lucie's suggestion we have an engagement party, then have my fairytale wedding at Jackson Castle and announce it as a vow renewal. Which led to Callum still pursuing me and Fiona sidling up to my Lachlan even though she and Callum claimed to be a couple.

Six months later and three before our public wedding, Lachlan lost his shit when Callum—who trapped me outside of the ladies' room at a fundraising gala in Aberdeen—asked if I was married to Lachlan. I denied it. They fought. We left. We fought. He left.

All of this time, I continue with the wedding preparations and working as though nothing is amiss. I decided not to tell my family—not even my girls Lola, Leonie, and

Starr or Blair and Billie Lola's CMO and COO, respectively—because the reality was too painful.

It hurt less not to face the fact Lachlan left and wouldn't answer my calls, text messages, emails, smoke signals with more than one-word responses.

I stayed at our Aberdeen penthouse flat for two weeks. But Lachlan didn't come home and refused to tell me where he was staying. A trip to his office provided the news he was out of the country on business with no return date available.

So I returned to our newly remodeled duplex penthouse in The STEELE Tower on Billionaires Row at Fifty-seventh Street and Fifth Avenue in New York City. Absence makes the heart grow fonder and all that, I suppose. But then again, I guess not since I had no idea Lachlan returned to Aberdeen according to Baz. So my husband doesn't miss me. At. All.

No one found it weird Lachlan and I weren't together since I travel to work with my clients in their offices around the world directly. He's not involved so much in our wedding planning since Sergeant Shelley and Lieutenant Lucie run it with some of my input. Easy peasy…

At least I thought I was doing a pretty good job of being normal. Until now. Obviously my ruse didn't work since Baz all but glares at me. Damn.

"Oh, Baz," I wail as I slump back against the leather sofa in the living room. My dove gray eyes fill with tears.

He moves from the silk-upholstered chair to sit beside me. One arm wraps around my shoulders to pull me to his massive chest while a hand sticks a loose tress of my waist-length ebony hair behind my ear.

Patiently, Baz waits for me to let it all out. I sit back with a hiccup and dab the wet spot on his black cashmere v-neck sweater. He shoos my hand away with a chuckle.

"I don't think that will do it, Hal," he says. Then he goes to the bar and pours two Waterford Crystal snifters of Jackson Special Blend Scotch. "It may be three in the after-noon. But I think this situation requires more than tea. Wouldn't you agree?"

I nod, and he hands a snifter to me.

"Now, fess up," he commands all Alpha Dom.

I take a gulp of the fragrant amber liquid for courage, then cough. It may be smooth, but not a toss-back liquor for my alcohol-consumption level.

Baz laughs and shakes his head.

"Go on," he says. His request not to be denied.

Knowing I can trust my brother to not make me feel like a fool—albeit I am one—I confess the whole sorry tale of that horrible night. As expected, he gives me sage and to-the-point advice.

"Get your ass back to Aberdeen and fix this shit, Haley Jackson! Now."

An hour later, I'm aboard my Gulfstream G650ER private jet bound for my husband.

LACHLAN

"*Lachlan. Baby. I'm so sorry. Please forgive me, my love. I miss you more than you can imagine. Please, My Lord. I love you, Lachlan Jackson.*"

My wife's warm breath skims across my cheek as she whispers words of love and forgiveness. Moisture dots my skin as her tears fall to my face. A soft sob escapes from her full lips.

With the hungry growl of a beast deprived of his mate for weeks, I grip her hips and roll her lush body beneath me. Soft curves meld to firm angles—including my suddenly rock-hard ten-inch cock—as our bodies align on the bed. The too large for only me king-size bed.

My wife's sob turns into an equally hungry groan as my mouth crushes hers. A shudder wracks her body as my tongue forces its way past her parted lips to taste every inch of her warm, wet mouth.

Our tongues duel for dominance. But the Alpha Dom in me will have none of it. My sub will obey. I growl, and she shivers. A nip to her plump lower lip and a tweak of her beaded nipple has me swallowing her moans of carnal pleasure.

My bare cock twitches against her belly.

Fingers trail along my flank, across my v cuts to seek out my heavy arousal. The wandering tips barely touch my thick shaft when I growl and yank the arm over her head. One sizable hand pins both of her wrists against the white silk sheets. She gasps into my mouth. I swallow it.

Still in need of a deeper connection between us, her legs part to cradle my pelvis to hers.

I allow the mischievous behavior. The warmth at the apex of her thighs welcome me. I grind against her groin as I purr in carnal delight.

"Oh, Lachlan... Do you forgive me?"

Sh pants as I suckle the sensitive skin behind the shell of her ear.

"Tell me... Do you?"

My mouth trails down her neck as my mind remains oblivious to her questions.

"Wait, Lachlan."

She wriggles beneath me. Her arms push up on my palms.

My biceps flex to tighten my grip on my wayward wife.

"Wait!"

Her sharp cry snaps me out of my lust-filled haze.

"Lachlan... Are you even awake?"

I shake my head to clear it further.

Awake?

What does she mean? I'm—

"Lachlan, baby. You're still sleeping."

What the bloody fuck?

My eyes pop open.

They take a moment to adjust to the darkness. But I don't need my vision to sense Haley. Imprinted on my brain, her elegant perfume fills my nostrils. A delicate yet intense floral scent of jasmine, orange flower, and musk blend harmoniously. The contrast like my woman—sensuous yet innocent.

Except she's not innocent.

She lied.

About me.

About us.

To Callum Wanker Graham, of all fucking people. Her ex-boyfriend. My archenemy.

Fuck. Me.

I sit back on my haunches and run my hands over my three-day stubble and through my tousled hair. Then tug the strands. Perhaps the pain will help clear the last vestiges of my wet dream from my muddled head.

Haley scoots back against the headboard and stares at me.

I stifle a groan at my aching blue balls as I climb off the bed to turn on the nightstand lamp. Without glancing in her direction, I stride towards the en suite bathroom.

Time for my millionth and one cold shower…

Minutes later I return to the bedroom in black, low-slung sweatpants. My muscles ripple as I pad barefoot across the floor.

Haley still sits on the bed with her arms wrapped

around her bent knees. The luxurious curtain of her ebony wavy hair covers her face as her cheek rests against her forearms.

Again, I don't have to see her fully to know exactly what she looks like. Gorgeous. My beautiful Baby Girl, sub, wife. Long, thick lashes brush her cheeks with her dove gray eyes closed. The dimples in her cheeks not pronounced until she laughs. Flawless skin on a heart-shaped face. Cheeks that bloom a beautiful pink when she screams my name in ecstasy or crimson when angered. Kissable moist lips—and not just on her face.

I shake my head again. Get ahold of yourself, Lachlan, I chide.

But it's been much too long without my wife. I miss and love her more than *she* can imagine. Yet, I refuse to give in. Too much secrecy again and again. It's not good. For her. For me. And definitely not the best for our fledgling marriage.

Sure, I went along with her and my mother to keep the truth about our marriage under wraps until the wedding. I damn sure don't want to make it difficult for my wife to join society that extends beyond Aberdeen to nobles and royals throughout the world. God knows I've hated being bothered with it all my whole life. But one does what one's wife wishes. And I plan to make every single wish of Haley's come true.

Even if it means time apart.

She needs to get her head together. There comes a point when one can no longer deny the truth. Case being

Graham taunting her about the veracity of our marriage. I thought my head would explode when she answered no.

Instead, I walked away. Best to have space than an all-out end. Although I gave her the options. If her words hold truth, then it's vow renewal and not a divorce.

"It's best we have this conversation in the living room," I tell her as I head for the bedroom door and open it.

The rustle of fabric precedes Haley walking through the doorway ahead of me. An oversized off-the-shoulder sweater and leggings can't hide her curves from my eyes.

My arms ache to pull her close to my chest and bury my face in her hair. Not yet.

She settles on the sofa. I take a chair. She frowns at my seat choice. Not yet.

"Lachlan, did you hear what I said to you before we kissed?" She asks as she fiddles with her fingers on her lap.

In the light of the living room's lamps, I take a moment to absorb her beauty. Damn, I missed this woman. It's just so dumb we wasted six weeks apart over nonsense. My hesitancy makes her bite the corner of her mouth as she tries to hold back tears glistening in her dove gray eyes.

"I thought I was dreaming. So kindly repeat what you said," I respond, wanting to be certain with no doubt of her feelings. Plus, she needs to repeat her apology. Again and again.

I sit back and fold my arms over my bare chest. Then smirk when her eyes widen at my bulging muscles.

Aside from countless cold showers and working nonstop, I hit up the Scottish Arts Center training in

Historical European Martial Arts even more than usual. A hefty Highland broadsword and targe certainly amp up my upper body. While the footwork strengthens my legs. Plus bare knuckle fighting and free weights…

Not that I was a shrimp before. Hell naw. But five times a week will boost any body to the next level. And Haley is beyond impressed, I chuckle to myself. Then flex.

She blinks and clears her throat.

With a determined expression, she rises from the sofa and kneels before me. Her left hand reaches for mine. The Jackson Emerald glints in the low light. It's our most important family's heirloom. The thirty-three carat, flawless, pure green, Colombian emerald has an octagonal step-cut set on a diamond platinum band.

Along with other traits, an emerald can signal unfaithfulness if it changes color. A glimpse of it shows the deep green hasn't changed a bit. Not that I expect Haley to cheat on me. She didn't for a year during her time with that bloody wanker.

I take a deep breath and give my hand to her. The sight of Haley on her knees makes me want to throw her to the floor and ravish her until the sun rises, then some more.

"Lachlan, I'm so sorry. I was wrong to deny our marriage. It doesn't matter what anyone says. They can go fly a kite! I miss you, baby, and I love you even more. Please forgive me," Haley states with imploring eyes as she squeezes my hand between both of hers.

I close my eyes as waves of emotions roll over me.

The weight of her body as she climbs onto my lap

makes me open them. She cups my face between her palms. Our gazes lock.

"I love you, Lachlan Jackson. You are my man. Mine! Now forgive me so we can put my madness behind us. Do you understand?"

I laugh out loud at her use of my Alpha Dom question I put to her. She flipped the script. But again, I allow —conditionally.

She squeals when I flip her over onto her belly, yank her leggings down to her knees, and rip her lace G-string off. The tug against her sensitive flesh elicits a yelp and her attempt to close her legs.

Not happening.

I wedge a leg between hers and place both of her wrists crossed against the small of her back.

She tosses her long hair over a shoulder and growls.

"Lachlan! Wait!"

I chuckle wickedly.

"Oh, no, Naughty Girl. You *will* pay the price for your unacceptable behavior," I say. "Did you think your words of love and forgiveness would be enough for your transgression?"

She sputters, then gasps as the first of many spanks land on her round ass in quick succession. Her hips gyrate as the pain morphs into erotic delight. The tips of my fingers smack her pussy lips and come away soaked. She hisses and bucks.

The room fills with the squelching sound of my hand smacking her wet pussy and her wails. The musky scent of her arousal blooms all around us. It increases when I thrust two thick digits inside of her core. The inner walls clamp around them greedily.

I purr.

My Naughty Girl undulates against my cock caught between her hip and my eight-pack abs. It strains against my sweatpants, forming a tent beneath the soft cotton. I ignore my carnal needs.

Her punishment continues until she lies spent over my thighs. Gasps and sobs fall from her mouth as her tears drip to the floor.

I remove her leggings and flip her around to straddle my legs. My hands knead the heated, swollen flesh of her ass.

She whimpers and buries her face in my neck as she wraps her arms around my shoulders.

"I—I—I'm so sorry…" she croaks.

My purrs soothe her.

Moments later, I speak.

"Haley, you are my wife, and I love you beyond measure. Let this serve as a lesson for both of us. No more secrets, and no one comes between us ever again."

She nods.

I rise and carry my wife to our bedroom where I strip the sweater and her lace bra off, then place her on the mattress on her belly. A hand to her lower back keeps her still. I go to the en suite bathroom and return with a moistened cloth and a tube of cooling gel. I wipe her face and smooth her bottom before I kiss both and tuck her in the bed.

"But Lachlan, we need to talk—"

I hush my wife as I spoon behind her and groan when my groin connects with her hot ass.

"Later in the morning after breakfast," I say.

She yawns and nods, sleepy from the intensity of her erotic spanking.

I wrap my arms around her and bury my face in her fragrant hair.

My Baby Girl is home at last.

Where she belongs.

LACHLAN

"**W**hy didn't you tell me, brother?" Baz asks.

We're on the terrace of his and Lola's duplex penthouse at The STEELE Tower. My Baby Girl and I flew in yesterday for Lola and Starr's joint virtual baby showers viewed via giant screens Haley and Harris installed. Starr has hers in the garden at her Benedict Canyon Drive mansion in Beverly Hills.

The family split attendance at both, with Starr's parents present too. Along with My Baby Girl and me, Blair and Luc Montaigne—Lola's mentor and the Parisian multibillionaire head of his family's multigenerational Banque Montaigne empire—gather on the terrace. The others sit in the garden with Starr and Malcolm.

Lucien provided the mamas' favorite dishes from his restaurants in both cities for their lunches. One of his pastry chefs created lifelike and tasty cakes in the shape of a cradle. Of course, they oohed and aahed over them. He's such the charmer.

During a break in the games Blair led, Baz takes the opportunity to question me. More than likely since I avoided him over the last few weeks, not wanting to out-and-out lie to my best friend. Hell, it was bad enough being evasive with my mother, who seemed to pick up on My Baby Girl's absence.

I shake my head and sigh.

"Do you tell me everything that happens between you and Lola?" I ask, then continue when he shakes his head. "Well, Haley is my wife, and I don't go around discussing our relationship with anyone, either. Not even to my best friend."

Baz stares at me for a moment, then nods in under-standing.

"I can respect your decision," he says. Then his eyes slide to Lola, where she sits with My Baby Girl. "I have to tell you, Haley was a disaster these last few weeks. She thought she could hide it from me, especially since she traveled a lot. But I know my baby sister. She was stressed and unhappy. I got the truth out of her and told her she was wrong this time."

I follow his gaze.

She glances up as though sensing me. A broad smile spreads across her face, making her dimples appear. So gorgeous my heart aches. When she winks at me and sticks her tongue out at Baz, we chuckle.

"Yeah, she's much better… Obviously," he adds drolly.

Then turns to me and asks, "And you?"

My thoughts go back to the morning after my wife returned home.

"Oh, Lachlan, I'm so glad you forgive me!" She exclaims in between bites of the omelet I made for our breakfast. "And to feed me in bed! How you spoil me, your Naughty Girl, Sir."

Her jubilant laughter tinkles around our bedroom.

I scoop another forkful into her mouth and respond, "You will thank me properly as soon as you have a full meal in you. You will need your energy, Naughty Girl."

The light in her dove gray eyes dims, and she slows her chewing. Her gaze drops to my lap where my erection tents the sheet. After she swallows, she clears her throat.

"Lachlan, I um..." she hesitates when I cock my head with a raised eyebrow. "Promise you won't get mad. Okay?"

I growl low in my throat. My wife had better not have done anything sexual that would make me need to promise such a thing. Meanwhile, I've been self-medicating.

She rushes on with her hands up, palms pressed together.

"Nothing bad. Well, not that bad I don't think," she hedges, then continues. "I want us to wait until our vow renewal wedding night to make love again."

My brain short circuits. Unintelligible words sputter from my gaping mouth.

"I mean, it's tradition and such an important night. I know we're already married and had our first wedding night. But this is after our fairytale wedding. Please, Lachlan?" My wife asks with her hands clasped together tightly.

I shake my head to clear it and stare at her beautiful, heart-shaped face and wide, beseeching eyes.

She continues to murmur please until I nod—anything to keep my wife happy—and she launches herself across the bed at me. We fall back against the headboard as she straddles my thighs. She peppers my face with kisses, and my cock leaps at the close contact. With a gasp, she scrambles backwards as though electrified.

Six more weeks of cold showers and hand jobs. Damn.

I glance over at Baz and laugh out loud. If only he knew.

He sits back, surprised, while the girls jump at the unexpected outburst.

"All good there, Jackson?" Luc asks with a twinkle in his dark denim blue eyes. "Perhaps I need to join the two of you for a drink instead of re-folding these onesies!"

Everyone's laughter gets interrupted by a commotion from Starr's baby shower. She's gone into labor, and they rush her to hospital. Their excitement and the party tire Lola. So we bid her and Baz good night and leave.

Once My Baby Girl and I enter our duplex penthouse a few floors below on the fiftieth and forty-ninth floors, she sighs wistfully.

"What's wrong?" I ask.

She shrugs and continues to walk down the hallway to our bedroom suite. As we walk past a guest suite closest to our rooms, she pauses, glances over her shoulder at me, and opens the door.

I follow her inside.

She and Leonie designed each guest suite differently. This one has a sitting room with a yellow floral decor leading to a bedroom in shades of cream with yellow accents and the en suite bathroom in travertine. It's a tranquil atmosphere.

My Baby Girl stops in front of the double doors of the bedroom and stares at me.

I raise an eyebrow questioningly.

"This would make a lovely nursery. Leonie says it won't take much to convert it," my wife says and pauses. She bites the corner of her lower lip before she continues. "What do you think, Lachlan?"

Her top teeth worry her lip again, and I want to suck it into my mouth.

Instead, I frown.

"Um… I don't know, Haley. Don't you think it's a bit soon to think about kids? I mean, we're just getting back together," I respond.

Her head snaps back as she blinks rapidly.

But before she can answer, I rush over and swoop her into my arms, nuzzling my nose against her neck.

"I'm only teasing! Of course, this would make a fantastic nursery, Mrs. Jackson. In fact, let's fill each guest suite with a baby. The more the merrier!" I exclaim. Kids? With My Baby Girl? Hell yeah!

She wraps her arms around my shoulders and buries her face in my hair.

I turn the knob on the double doors and kick them open as I carry her to the king-size bed. Lying down on my back, I pull her half across my body. Her head rests over my heart with her hand on my chest and one leg between mine. My hands stroke her arm and back.

"That many, huh?" She asks, giggling.

I nod vigorously, overjoyed by the thought of our babies running around.

"Absolutely! We'll make our own clan, enough for a polo or rugby team. How's that?" I respond.

She laughs some more as her fingers play at my cashmere sweater.

"Well, my last birth control injection was a couple of months ago. My doctor tells me it can take a few months to get out of my system," My Baby Girl says. Then she rises onto an elbow and stares down at me. "Wouldn't it be amazing if we get pregnant on our vow renewal wedding night?"

Her dove gray eyes glimmer in the light from the setting sun outside of the wall of floor-to-ceiling windows.

I reach up and slip a lock of her ebony waves behind her ear, then cup the back of her head to bring her face closer to mine. My mouth covers her soft, full lips. She moans into my passionate kiss. I feast on her until she's breathless.

"Oh my, My Lord. A girl couldn't ask for a better response than that one," she says.

My eyes flick between her kiss-swollen lips and obsidian eyes, pupils blown with lust. Slowly, I run the tip of my tongue across my lower lip to collect the taste of her sweetness.

Her gaze tracks my movement. Unconsciously, she mimics me. Her little pink tongue pokes out to swipe over her luscious lip.

I growl.

"If you keep looking at me so fuckable, Little Temptress, I won't be able to wait until our vow renewal night to fill your womb with my seed."

A soft gust of warm breath slips between her parted moist lips.

My cock twitches with the need to be in her mouth.

With a herculean effort, I roll off of the bed to tower over her.

"Look what you do to me, Little Temptress," I say as I point to the increasing bulge in my jeans. My cock punches against the restrictive denim painfully. "Six more weeks of this. Up! I need to take a cold shower. Again."

For a moment, she remains on her elbow, staring up at me with sultry eyes. The flush of arousal colors her cheeks a pretty pink. Beneath the silk wrap dress, the outline of her peaked nipples visible clearly. While the soft fabric rode up to expose her long, toned legs.

It would be so easy to give in to the carnal temptation. But I promised my wife we would wait. And so we shall.

I extend my hand to her. She blinks at it, then slips her hand into mine with a resigned sigh.

"Need I remind you, Mrs. Jackson, this was your bright idea. Tradition you claim," I say as I lift her from the bed to her feet.

She wobbles and clutches my biceps to steady herself. Then shakes her head.

"Of course not, Mr. Jackson. However, you prove temptation personified, My Lord!" She rejoins.

I throw my head back and laugh heartily.

"Touché, Mrs. Jackson. Touché!" I say between chuckles.

We leave the guest suite soon to be the first nursery and head for our rooms. I take my much-needed shower while she changes.

When I exit my dressing room in a t-shirt and slouchy sweatpants, I notice she's chosen a tank top and cashmere robe with matching lounge pants. I laugh to myself at her attempt to hide her bodacious curves. Nothing can detract from her sensual allure. Forever My Little Temptress.

We settle on the sofa in the sitting room. As she scrolls through her mobile, I check my calendar for the upcoming week. My administrative assistant scheduled meetings for me to attend while I'm in New York City.

"Oh, Mom Lucie asks if you need any help with our honeymoon."

I glance up to find My Baby Girl staring at me. She's trying to hide her excitement. For weeks, she's tried to get out of me our plans. But I told her it's a surprise. Now, I see she's gotten my mother involved.

I cock my head and narrow my eyes.

My Baby Girl squirms, knowing she's cold busted.

"No, thank you," I respond. "But nice try, Naughty Girl."

Her eyes twinkle with mischief as she giggles and shakes her head. She returns to her mobile, and her fingers fly across the screen. When she finishes, she fills me in on the latest developments with the wedding planning. Her excitement proves contagious.

We spend the next two hours looking at sketches, seating charts, the guest list, activities, and more. Sergeant Shelley and Lieutenant Lucie—with the help of the planners—do the heavy lifting. It's perfect since I'm not that keen on selecting colors, going round to shops. No thanks. I set my boys with their tuxedos while my father, brothers, and I have new kilts, along with custom tuxedo jackets and accessories already taken care of. I have My Baby Girl's Jackson clan sash, too.

After the ceremony, the charitable polo match ranks high on my list. We plan to split the proceeds between Jackson Foundation and STEELE Foundation.

My siblings and I play as a team since we could pick up a mallet. Our father—a top player for years—insisted my brothers and I learn the sport of kings. It was our mother who demanded Lydie learn too, or none of us would. And in typical Lydie fashion, she strove to prove to our father she can do as well—if not better than—as her brothers. It was the best decision since we are always the team to beat.

After a while, My Baby Girl and I decide to order Thai food and watch a film on Netflix in the media room downstairs. I love how she enjoys action films like me. Her having four older brothers has its benefits. Sometimes.

As the credits roll, she sits up from resting her head in my lap and stares at me.

"What?" I ask.

She takes a deep breath.

"Are you nervous about getting married to me again?"

Now my head snaps back, then I scowl. Where the hell did that come from?

I must have spoken the question aloud because she blushes and swipes at the bridge of her nose.

"We've been through so much… I—I just want to be sure you're still okay with everything. That's all," she mumbles, with her head hanging.

I place my index finger beneath her chin and raise it to bring her eyes on a level with mine. They search her face for any sign of her being nervous. That would finish me off. Fortunately, I only see her concern about my feelings.

With a shake of my head, I respond, "No other woman exists for me but you, Haley Jackson. Never have and never will in this lifetime or in the next and any thereafter."

I lean forward and brush my lips over hers as I press our foreheads together. We inhale each other's breath before I continue.

"This is a ceremony for *you*, my love—your fairytale wedding at Jackson Castle. For me, our marriage happened in Sorrento eight months ago. So, no nerves whatsoever. Do you understand?" I ask.

Her eyes fill with tears as she nods.

"Words, Mrs. Jackson. I will have your words."

A breathtaking smile spreads over her face as her cheeks pinken.

"Yes, Mr. Jackson, I understand completely. And I love you beyond measure," she responds.

I pull her onto my lap and bury my face in her hair.

"I cannot wait to marry you again, my love," I murmur.

"Haley, you are so lucky! The weather is simply perfect for your wedding celebration. I can't believe we'll have five days of clear sunny skies and unseasonably warm temperatures just for you! And to kick it off with the polo match couldn't get any better. I just saw some friends from London, Paris, and New York. So many people came from all over the world for you."

Blair's enthusiasm—not to mention my fairytale wedding finally being here—makes me grin from ear to ear.

I can't contain myself and bounce on the balls of my feet.

"I know! It's incredible, and we couldn't be happier!" I exclaim as I clap and shimmy my hips.

The time is here at last, and Lachlan and I can proclaim we're husband and wife for all the world to hear.

I glance over my shoulder towards Jackson Castle's

polo pitch, where he stands beside his string of ponies with Lydie, Lucien, Laurent, and their horses. They look so professional in their gear—not to mention how sexy my man's muscular thighs appear in his white polo pants. He tosses his head back and laughs at something Laurent says. The sound carries over to Blair and me, where we stand beneath the canopy with the other guests who mill about.

"He's in a chipper mood. No nervous groom, huh?" She asks with a knowing smile.

I giggle.

"Why should he be nervous? He's marrying the lovely Haley."

Blair and I glance up to find Luc smiling down at us as he hands us flutes of Mimosas. He's a handsome man in his early fifties—the epitome of a silver fox. Or as Leonie and Lola call him *Le Renard Argenté*. His dark blue eyes glitter like sapphires as they flick to Blair.

She takes a sip from her Waterford Crystal flute to hide her blush.

"*Merci, Luc!*" I say, as I tip my flute to him in salute.

"There you are, *chérie*! So many people, and we couldn't find you!"

Leonie with Daphne in her arms sweeps past the other guests to double kiss my cheeks before she greets Blair and Luc. Roger close behind her with Rodolphe and Gaspard by the hands grins as he says hello.

"Do you see *Oncle* Lachlan with his polo ponies? That'll be you soon, my loves," I say in French as I pick The Twins up on each hip. "See him over there?"

They jabber on about the ponies excitedly, and I promise to take them over once the match ends. Already they've gone riding at their grandparents' ancestral estate in Paris, just as their mother did before them.

"I love your dress, Haley, honey. All white everything for your nuptials extravaganza!"

I turn and smile at Billie, recognizing her Savannah accent instantly. The petite Southern Belle hugs The Twins and me at once as they giggle.

"Polo? What happened to a good old rugby match? The sport of real men!" Patrick states as he greets me.

Everyone laughs.

We're soon joined by my parents and parents-in-law. The Moms tell me it's time to welcome everyone and announce the start of the match. We make our way to the edge of the pitch, and Lachlan strides over. He wraps his arm around my waist and pulls me to his side.

"Thank you for joining us to support Jackson Foundation's alcohol treatment centers for lower-income individuals and STEELE Foundation's affordable housing for urban, lower-income families." Mom Lucie starts.

She hands the mic to my mother, and she continues, "Our families also welcome you to the start of the celebration of Lachlan and Haley's nuptials. Enjoy your time!"

Lachlan squeezes my waist, and I glance up at him. He bends down and kisses me softly. I whisper good luck, and he winks as he strides back to his team.

"Come on, sweetheart. You're swooning," my mother laughs as she loops her arm through mine.

Mom Lucie takes my other one, and we make our way back beneath the canopy. Several guests stop us to offer their congratulations and to chat about the foundations' endeavors. As I head towards the tables laden with foods Lucien's team prepared, someone touches my elbow.

"Hello, Little Lass."

Callum.

Damn.

I knew he and Fiona—along with her family—RSVP'd to attend the polo match as it's open to the public. But I hadn't expected him to waylay me. Mom Lucie did not include them on the guest list for the wedding ceremony with the excuse of space limitations within Jackson Castle's chapel. However, they will attend the reception. Best for society relations and all.

Now, I gird myself by tightening the belt on my crochet-trimmed linen and ramie maxi shirt dress and pivot to face him. As it turns out, Princess Fiona the Fair and the rest of the Ridels stand beside Callum.

Great. The gang's all here. Just great.

"Hello, Callum"—I nod at the others—"Hello. Thank you for supporting the foundations. Enjoy!" With a practiced smile, I parrot what The Moms said. Then shift back towards the food, although I now have a twinge in my stomach. Ugh!

"Congratulations, *Countess*."

I swallow a sigh and glance around to find Fiona's sneering face. Her violet eyes shoot flames of magical purple fire at me.

"Hey, sis! We're missing you."

I send a silent prayer up in thanks for Harris. As he places his hand on the small of my back and guides me away, he nods at Callum and the Ridels briefly.

"How good of you to come," Harris smirks over his shoulder. Then he leans down and whispers in my ear. "Give me a fucking break already. Didn't Mary J. say no more drama?"

I nod and giggle in response.

Thankfully, the rest of the match proves just that—drama free!

"Now, stir the mixture with gentle strokes of your spoon. Excellent... Well done... Oh, you have a knack for this..."

Lola nudges my side and whispers, "*The Sexy Chef* is on a roll today, huh?"

I agree with an eye roll and a giggle.

He's got the women eating out of his hand—no pun intended—as we take part in his cooking demonstration with wine pairing. So many women—and a few men—RSVP'd it became the most popular of all the wedding activities. Bailey and his event planning team had to move it to the castle's main kitchen.

Lucien is in his element. At six feet, three inches, he's super handsome with sable hair cropped on the sides and long at the top, bottle green eyes, and dimples on his clean-shaven face. His millions of followers on social media adore him just as much as those present. But he isn't only a good-looking guy. He's a talented chef with tons of Michelin stars. So he can get away with little innuendos and, being a flirt while he teaches us his spin on the traditional Scotch Pie.

Lola, Anita Green—our friend, yogi, and wife of Norman Green the world heavyweight champion turned gym owner—and I decided to participate. Lola and Anita are foodies who love to cook, and I need to up my game. The other girls chose to spend the afternoon shopping in the local villages for "cute souvenirs," as Leonie says. And just as well, since she's known to burn water...

We'll meet up later for my bachelorette party. They won't tell me what it is except no stripper to prevent Lachlan—not to mention the guys—from going ballistic. They're doing something for Lachlan too, after his Jackson Scotch tasting activity this evening.

Last night was our rehearsal and dinner afterwards with family and close friends. Tomorrow is the Big Day! My fairytale wedding takes place at long last.

Goosebumps rise on my arms at the thought. I can't help a little shimmy and giggle.

"Ooookay... What's got you all Shakira?" Lola asks with a smirk. "Could it be you're thinking about your man?"

"But of course! I still can't believe we're only one day away from being official, official," I say with a cheesy grin. Then I lean closer and whisper so only Lola can hear. "Especially the wedding night. I asked Lachlan to forego any sex until then. It's been *forever*!"

Lola splutters on the spoon she licks as her eyes widen in surprise.

"I know, right! Plus, I hope we get pregnant that night," I continue with a sigh. "We want to start our own little family. Well, big, according to Lachlan! Being around you guys makes us eager to get started."

"Oh! I'm so excited for the both of you! I was so anti-baby, wanting to focus on Lola's Coterie's expansion. But I'm so thankful Baz stuck it out with me and made me realize what's most important in our lives," Lola says with a wink. "Leonie, me, Starr. So you're next, Haley!"

Lola bumps her hip against mine and giggles.

"Aaah, Mrs. Steele, Countess, do we disturb your private party?"

We bite back our laughter as Lucien towers over us, tapping a spatula against his palm. The Alpha Dom's eyes glitter with mischief.

"Shall I report your misbehavior?" He asks with a raised eyebrow and a knowing smirk.

Lola and I glance at each other at the same time and bust out laughing.

"Duly noted, ladies," Lucien says as he moves to view the progress of the next participant.

The pies turn out well—even mine. While the rest of us drink wine, Lola has iced lemon ginger tea since she breastfeeds her twins—Sabrina and Stella.

With a grin, Lola lifts her glass and nods.

"Soon you won't be able to drink liquor, so enjoy it while you can, sister. You'll join us Hot Mamas with iced lemon ginger tea—perfect for soothing nausea and as a mocktail," she says. "You can thank Leonie for it."

I grin and tap my glass of Jackson Cabernet Sauvignon to her tea glass.

"Here's to Leonie, her iced lemon ginger tea, and to me needing lots of it. Soon!"

We toast and finish the rest of our tasty meal while we chat about marriage with an Alpha Dom, pregnancy tips, and the joys of babies.

"THAT'S IT, Haley! Use your inner thigh muscles. Squeeze like it's Lachlan between them!"

"Yeah, baby! Show 'em what you got, girl!"

"*Chérie!* Look at you!"

I grin at my girls as I hang upside down, gripping the stripper pole between my legs. No male strippers. But a few female ones and burlesque dancers make my bachelorette party a blast!

It was Leonie's idea. She did a surprise burlesque dance at LEVELS Paris for Roger the night of their wedding. Granted, he was less than pleased she was nearly naked in front of others. But she aced it thanks to a world-famous Las Vegas burlesque performer who offers private lessons Billie introduced her to. The dancer helped Leonie to choreograph her routine. Now, my girls flew the performer and some of her dancer friends over to teach us.

Mom Lucie had Bailey turn one of the outer buildings into a plush club, complete with poles, giant champagne glasses, ballet barres, lounge sofas, and a fully stocked bar. A barefoot bartender dressed in a black half-face mask, suspenders and pants serves a signature cocktail Billie crafted for the occasion. She wouldn't reveal the ingredients, only that it's sweet and powerful like me. She calls it Temptation. A DJ—dressed similar to the bartender—spins music that blares out of hidden speakers strategically placed to heighten the hedonistic vibe. A videographer and a photographer—both female—capture the happenings and will give each of us a video and an album as keepsakes.

"OMG! My boob!" I laugh as my D-cups overflow from the white bandeau top.

I'm not concerned the guys see anything since Bailey made sure to hire men who prefer to ogle men and not my tits. So I don't let the mishap stop my show.

When the instructor tells me to round up and grasp as high up the pole as possible, I just do it. Better than Nike any day! Once upright, I pull my top back in place, kick out my legs parallel to the floor, and throw my head back with a whoop. Gracefully, I drop to a squat and bow my head.

The girls stomp and clap while the DJ hypes me up over the mic.

I hug the instructor, and she tells me how well I perform. She even says I can make a guest appearance at her show in Vegas whenever I'm in Sin City. I don't hesitate to accept her invitation, knowing Lachlan would get a kick out of it as long as I wear a mask and a wig. Well… maybe. But it would be loads of fun!

With stars in my eyes, I give the stage to Maribelle

Hayes—my gym buddy and friend from New York. She hops up and does a few stretches they showed us earlier to limber up. Her eyes shine bright with enthusiasm as she tightens her high ponytail.

We applaud when she grabs the pole and swings herself up onto it.

The bartender comes around with another tray of cocktails and iced lemon ginger tea. We snag glasses and root Maribelle on. I do a wolf whistle with my fingers in my mouth—a trick I learned as a kid from Malcolm.

My grin widens at the thought of my brother. He's here to celebrate my wedding with me as he promised—wheelchair and all, a snazzy aerodynamic version. He and Starr arrived with their newborn twins—Selina and Elio—her parents, and nanny. I'm so proud of my brother and all he's accomplished after his horrific motorcycle accident. A coma and partial paralysis *cannot* stop a Steele!

"Go on, Lola! It's your turn, *Chérie!*"

"Yeah, Lola!"

Leonie and Starr rouse me from my musings as they catcall Lola. The petite spitfire takes the challenge and leaps onto the stage.

"I'm ready to outdo all of you!" She boasts good-naturedly.

We whistle and whoop to encourage her performance. And she dazzles us with an upside-down split. When she finishes her routine, she throws her arms up in victory.

The instructors place Swarovski Crystal embellished crowns on our heads. Mine has bride written on it in green stones like my engagement ring. I laugh and hug each of my girls as I thank them for making my night so special and unforgettable.

We dance and drink until after midnight. Then we pile into Mercedes-Benz G-Wagens for the ride back to the castle. More hugs and we part for our suites.

My mobile rings as I place it on the nightstand after a shower. I smile when I recognize Lachlan's ringtone and accept the call.

"Good night, My Baby Girl. I'll see you tomorrow. I love you," Lachlan says softly over the line.

Tradition bound again, I asked we not see each other after midnight.

"Good night, My Lord. I love you more," I whisper past a yawn before I end the call.

My eyelids droop closed as dreams of my fairytale wedding play in my mind. Haley Jackson, Countess of Aboyne, wife of Lachlan Jackson, Earl of Aboyne. The corners of my mouth tilt up as I sigh contented. Part two of my happily ever after comes with the dawn. Then Part three, our babies.

Soon.

"So, we're on the eve of you being hitched, joining most of us in the loving beauty of marital bliss—"

"Aw, man! Give us a break with the gushy gushiness of being tied down to one lass!"

"Exactly! No thanks!"

I laugh as Laurent and Harris interrupt Norman's speech. The youngest of the Jacksons and Steeles refuse to give up their playboy ways. No matter how much we tell them there's nothing better than a stable relationship with one woman you love and who loves you. One with whom you can build a life.

We're at my bachelor party Baz organized in the lodge on Jackson Castle's lands my brothers and I use as our hangout. With its open floor plan great room with massive fireplace, kitchen and games areas, four bedrooms, and five bathrooms, the lodge has ample space. Baz gathered the

Jackson and Steele brothers, Borya and Anton Alexeyev—the Russian cousins and former MMA champion and VP of Development for Malcolm's division, respectively—Luc, Patrick, Ewan, and Calvin Hayes, the husband of My Baby Girl's friend.

Just as I decreed no strippers for my wife's party, she said the same for mine—not that I want them, anyway. It's a night of poker, billiards, cigars, and Scotch. And of course trash talking.

"You can keep a bloody relationship, Champ. I'm for dominance and a shag with a different sub a night at one of my LEVELS clubs kind of lad," Lucien adds as he blows smoke rings with his Jackson Cigar.

Laurent and Harris—along with Borya—raise their glasses in agreement.

"I know I'm new to you guys. But I was a player before I met my Maribelle. She took my breath away and knocked me sideways with just one glance," Calvin says as he nods at the others. "Love will catch you when you least expect it. So, gloat, fellas. For now."

"Amen, brother!" Baz agrees. "Look at me and Lola. That fiery, hazel-eyed vixen bumped into me literally, and she floored me. Now, happily married to the love of my life with three beautiful babies!"

"Nothing beats a wonderful woman who sticks by your side through the good and the roughest of the fucking rough," Malcolm adds in a voice gruff with emotion.

We turn to *The Enforcer* who—despite being in a wheelchair paralyzed from the waist down—still commands a room. He's Baz's doppelgänger at only two years apart and, being a rebel, fought their resemblance and his place as the second son. Now once again, like his brother, Malcolm—the former playboy Alpha Dom—has a woman who loves him immensely and has twins. So if anyone can express his about-face on no commitments, it's Malcolm.

"Hear, hear!" I say as I stand and raise my snifter high. "A wonderful woman eclipses a romp in the sack with an unknown lass any day!"

Cheers go up from those of us in relationships while the singles hiss and boo.

The bartender refreshes our drinks, and the server offers more of Lucien's game night snacks. Refueled, my boys and I set to rowdy games of cards and billiards for the rest of the night. Roger *The Responsible* calls an end to the evening to avoid me having a hangover during the wedding. I thank them for a great send off to marital bliss. Then duck from a handful of nuts thrown by Laurent.

Once we're back at the castle, I head to a guest room. My Baby Girl insists we not see one another after midnight. Something about jinxing our marriage. I gave in to make her happy. But I can't resist hearing her voice before I go to bed.

The butler confirmed the girls arrived back from her party. So I call her on my way to my room. She answers with a sleepy voice, and I smile.

"Good night, My Baby Girl. I'll see you tomorrow. I love you," I murmur.

"Good night, My Lord. I love you more," she responds as she yawns, then ends the call.

"Dream of me, my love," I add, even though she's no longer on the line to hear.

* * *

"TELL ME, bro, do you Scots go commando underneath your skirts?"

Harris asks while trying to keep a straight face. Then chuckles when he hears Patrick's rumbling growl.

"You Yanks will never learn! A Scotsman wears a kilt, not a lass' *skirt*. The idea of being bare under it started with the military centuries ago, not what every Scotsman does per se," he responds with a shake of his head. "But if you ask me, I'd tell you yes with your girlfriend's shade of lipstick."

Harris stares blankly, then throws his head back and laughs. The rest of us join in, and I slap Patrick on the back.

"Good one, mate!" Ewan exclaims.

"Pardon me, gentlemen. It is time to leave for the chapel. Lachlan and groomsmen, kindly follow me to your G-Wagens. Ushers, my assistant will escort you to the Sprinter."

We turn towards the door to find Bailey and one of his assistants.

My heart skips a beat, knowing I'll see My Baby Girl soon.

A hand on my shoulder draws me from my thoughts.

"Lach, I've got the jewelry and the sash. Do you need anything else, bro?" Baz asks. His platinum gray eyes search my face.

"No, only to get to my woman," I respond confidently.

He grins broadly and claps my shoulder.

"The Twins are ready for ring bearer duty," Roger adds as he swoops Rodolphe and Gaspard up on his hips.

They're adorable in bespoke tuxedos that match the groomsmen and resemble miniature Rogers. They lift the pillows with ring replicas in the air.

"*Oui, Oncle* Lachlan!" They say in unison.

I chuckle and thank them for their service with a promise of ice cream later. They grin happily.

"You're a natural, bro," Roger says with a smile. "This will be you soon."

I smile so hard my cheeks hurt. I *cannot* wait for My Baby Girl and me to have our babies!

"Well, let's get going! My twin awaits her Little Lord Fauntleroy!" Harris commands.

We file out of the room converted into our dressing room and to the trucks. As we approach the lane for the chapel, the wedding decorations appear in the Jackson clan colors: emerald green for the rolling lands; navy blue for the Don and Dee Rivers and the North Sea; silver for the mica in the gray granite; amber for Jackson Scotch. Wreaths and garlands of local flowers and leaves, along with notes from the villagers, adorn decorative trees wrapped with silk.

When we arrive at the chapel, the sight of it takes my breath away. The cloudless blue sky allows the sun to shine on the stained-glass windows while more flowers and trees line the path to the wrought-iron double doors. The sound of string music and the voices of an angelic boys' choir filter through them. It's a magical fairytale moment.

Bailey leads us to a side room where we wait until the ushers—Ewan, Norman, Patrick, Borya, and Anton—seat the guests. My parents and mother-in-law enter the room and hug me while they offer words of delight. The Moms assure me My Baby Girl is here and eager to renew our vows. Then it's time for the processional.

Baz and I extend our arms for our mothers and escort them from the room and down the aisle. First Mom Shelley with Baz, then my mother and me, followed by my father. I notice the guests barely. So many faces watch as we pass them. Once we seat our mothers and my father, Baz and I take our places at the altar with the officiant. We turn to face the aisle.

The Twins stroll down with the rings pillows aloft as they smile at the guests, who oooh and aaah over the handsome pair. Harris with Lydie, Malcolm with Starr, Roger with Leonie, Lucien with Blair, and Laurent with Billie follow. The women are elegant in gowns in shades of green, amber, and platinum. Lola enters, and my heartbeat speeds up.

My Baby Girl comes next!

The music changes, and the air crackles with electricity. The guests rise.

Like a vision, Haley appears at the doors. The sunlight filters through the stained-glass windows to highlight her ethereal beauty.

A veil covers her face but can't hide her radiant smile. It's more brilliant than the Jackson Coronet atop her head. The multitude of diamonds adorn the intimately shaped platinum with a giant emerald in the center. The stones flash in the sunlight.

The exquisite princess ballgown has a neckline and corseted bodice that accentuate her full breasts and narrow waist. Slips of sleeves drape off of her shoulders, leaving ample space from her swan-like neck to the tops of her breasts. It serves to showcase my collar with rows of different cut diamonds and a giant one in the center, surrounded by two rows of smaller diamonds. Layers of tulle topped by appliqués make a full skirt that sweeps the stone floor. A bouquet of white flowers completes her fairytale princess look.

Heart-stoppingly gorgeous.

A hush comes over the guests as they marvel along with me at Haley's beauty. Her eyes never leave mine—nor mine hers—as she walks down the aisle on Dad Morgan's arm. I'm so enthralled by her, it's not until the pressure of a hand on my back rouses me to step forward and accept my bride from her father.

When the officiant asks who gives this woman to this man, Dad Morgan pins me with his intense stare and announces he and his wife do. The breath I didn't realize I was holding escapes in a soft whoosh, and he smiles warmly at me as he shakes my hand.

Then My Baby Girl is in my grasp. She beams at me as we step onto the altar. Neither of us has eyes for anyone or anything else as the officiant starts the ceremony.

The guests murmur in surprise when he welcomes them to the vow renewal of Lachlan and Haley Jackson. They're shocked again when they see the wedding jewelry I place on my wife's left hand.

A diamond eternity band on her middle finger connects to a removable custom hand harness of varying shaped and sized diamonds that end in a delicate bracelet around her wrist. Her engagement ring sits on her ring finger and her diamond paved Cartier Love Bracelet rests above the diamond bracelet.

Haley is more than a princess. She's my wife who I will shower with more than just jewels. I will give her my all.

Tears fill her eyes, and I use my thumb to swipe them away gently as I murmur words of everlasting love.

Once she places my platinum wedding band on my finger, I feel complete.

Baz hands the Jackson clan tartan sash to me, and I pin it on Haley as she smiles up at me lovingly.

"There you go, *Mo Chridhe*," I murmur. "Now, you are officially of the Jackson clan."

"*My heart*," she whispers.

The officiant announces us husband and wife, and I swoop her off of her feet into my arms as I kiss her possessively. Our wedding party laugh and clap. When I put a stunned Haley back on her wobbly legs, the officiant introduces us as Lachlan Jackson, Earl of Aboyne and his wife Haley Jackson, Countess of Aboyne. The guests rise and clap.

I take my wife's hand and stride back up the aisle, nodding at those who wish us well. She does the same ever so graciously. I damn near drag her into the waiting room and shut the door as soon as we're inside. My mouth crashes onto hers for a toe-curling kiss I pour all of my love and need into. She's equally passionate and grips my biceps to hold on.

A knock at the door forces us to part. Breathlessly, we stare at each other, then grin like Cheshire Cats.

"Mrs. Lachlan Jackson, I love you."

"Mr. Lachlan Jackson, I love you more."

I tuck her into my side just as the door opens. My mom pokes her head in to tell us it's time for photos. Fortunately, they won't take long since we did separate shots before the ceremony. A makeup artist and hairstylist enter to freshen up my wife. I adjust my burgeoning erection surreptitiously.

After the photographer and videographer declare they have enough images, Bailey escorts my wife and me to a horse-drawn open-top carriage. It's time for our ride from Jackson Castle through the village and back to the reception. It's the first marriage for a Jackson since my parents wed. The streets line with people who call out their best wishes to us and throw flowers before the carriage. My wife waves like a princess as she beams at them. I can't take my eyes off of her.

"Oh, Lachlan! This is magnificent! Way beyond my dreams of a fairytale wedding! Thank you, *Mo Chridhe*. I love you so much," she says as we leave the village.

I lean over and brush my lips over her smiling mouth, then lean my forehead against hers.

"You are my fairytale, *Mo Chridhe*," I murmur.

She sighs and tilts her head to kiss me.

We ride along holding hands and recounting our parties and the ceremony. As she bobs her head and moves her hand in her enthusiasm, the jewels glint in the sun. Fifteen months ago, I vowed she would wear my collar and wedding rings, too. Now, there's no mistaking Haley Steele is Haley Jackson. Mine. All mine.

Moments later, the emcee introduces us, and we enter the ballroom to cheers. I raise my wife's hand high, and she sashays alongside of me. We grin and wave to our guests as we make our way to the dance floor.

The opening strains of Frank Sinatra's "I've Got You Under My Skin" begin. I surprised my wife with the selection since it reminds me of our trip to Las Vegas and how much she loves Ol' Blue Eyes.

She peeps up at me with her dove gray orbs and smiles knowingly. Then she gasps when the soulful voice of Michael Bublé fills the room. She swivels her head to see him as he strides onto the stage where the band plays. He nods in greeting as he serenades us.

I wrap my arms around my wife and pull her close. Her

arms reach up and around my neck as she whispers the words to me, eyes shine with tears. I tried not to give in, but the temptation proved too much. No warning voice can keep My Baby Girl from me anymore.

Our parents join us, followed by the rest of our wedding party, then guests. When it's time for the toasts, Baz rises and takes the mic.

"Lachlan, we've been best friends since we were toddlers. Thanks to our mothers being best friends, our families are extremely close. Sixteen years ago, you almost tipped your hand to reveal your love for my little sister. Lucky for you, I ignored the inkling," he says with an arched eyebrow. "But just as lucky for me, you proved to be a man worthy of Haley and of her love that never wavered for you. So I didn't lose a best friend, I gained a brother."

My wife gasps and sobs. I have to bite my lip to hold back a cry of my own. Baz's words touch me deeply. I nod and raise my Champagne flute in salute as I wrap my arm around her shoulders.

Her friend Maribelle takes the mic from Baz. She gives Haley a moment to collect herself before she starts her toast.

"Haley, so many times I tried to play matchmaker for you. Insisting you go out since you rarely went on a date"— Maribelle pauses and smiles at me—"All along, her heart belonged to you, Lachlan. I am so happy for you, Haley, my friend. Your wish came true, and I hope the rest come to fruition, too."

My wife mouths her thanks and raises her flute to her friend. I smile and do the same.

The rest of the evening is a dream. Even when I catch sight of that wanker Graham dancing with Fiona. Their presence can't diminish the power of our wedding or of our love for one another. I chuckle to myself when I wonder how they must feel, having heard Baz and Maribelle's comments about there being no one else for either Haley or for me. Hopefully, Graham and Fiona got the message.

"I am proud of you, son."

My father's voice draws my gaze from my wife, where she dances in a white lace mini dress with her girls. He smiles and claps me on the shoulder.

"Haley is your perfect match. Now, you must complete your responsibility to your family by taking the helm at Jackson Corporation."

"Dad, I—"

He raises his hand to stop me.

"We will not discuss it further during your wedding. But know the time has come, Lachlan," he says. Then claps me on the back and walks away.

I shake my head. Again, I won't let anything take away from this moment. However, it's time for us to make our exit. I need to be alone with my wife. And have her make good on her promise of a wedding night I'll never forget.

"Excuse me, ladies. But it's time for my wife and I to leave," I announce as I reach her and the girls.

They cheer and push her in my direction.

She blushes at their suggestive jokes and waves over her shoulder as she takes my arm.

Once we're in a G-Wagen—after being stopped by countless well-wishers—I cup her face and kiss her breathless. She sighs and leans into me.

"Where are we going?" She asks as I start the engine.

I wink and tell her it's a surprise.

She giggles and adjusts in her seat to peek out of the window for clues as we drive through the estate's grounds. When we near the coast, she swivels her head to me with wide eyes.

I grin but don't say a word.

"Oh, Lachlan! I can't believe it!"

Before us stands the ancient watchtower, restored from crumbling ruins to its former splendor. Lit up outside by torches and inside by candles. It's a beacon on the open field with the dark expanse of the North Sea in the background and millions of stars in the inky sky above.

Ten months ago, My Baby Girl and I rode horses out here, and she told me a secret. As a kid, she became enchanted by it and would pretend she was a princess in her tower, where the fairytale always had a different theme. Her love would save her from the mean duke, or her husband would return from fighting abroad. But what made my heart soar was me always as her hero.

I vowed to repair the watchtower for her. It makes the perfect gift and magical place for us to spend our vow renewal night after our fairytale wedding. I stop the truck and hop out to carry her through the door.

The bottom level is an open space with a high ceiling perfect for a lounge, stone fireplace, kitchen, and a bathroom. A spring landscape of the watchtower I commissioned from my wife's favorite local painter hangs above a caramel leather tufted sofa. Stairs lead to the upper floor, where a vast bedroom with a king-size canopy bed in the middle, an enormous stone fireplace opposite it, and an oversized copper tub sits before one window overlooking the sea. The roof is all glass through which the moonlight filters down to the bed, making the white silk bedding glow.

"Oh, Lachlan, this is unbelievable. I—I don't know what to say," my wife whispers in awe as I lay her on the bed.

"Mrs. Jackson, you do not have to say a word other than my name as I make sweet love to you until neither of us can move, *Mo Chridhe*."

HALEY

"Oh, My Lord!"

"Yes, I am."

Lachlan's wicked chuckle blows his warm breath across my wet, swollen folds.

I shudder as another orgasm—I've lost count since he woke me—shatters over me. My back bows from the sweat-soaked bed as I try to grind my pussy against his face. But I can't move far since white silk cords bind my wrists and my legs attached to a spreader bar draped over his muscular back.

A keen falls from my parted lips and rises to the glass ceiling of our watchtower. The dazzling morning light sparks behind my shuttered eyes. Through the open windows, the sound of crashing waves on the rocks below joins my cries of carnal pleasure. The scent of sex and pheromones mixes with the salty sea air.

Our night of passion only broken by a few hours of

sleep during which My Lord woke me from my slumber to ravish me repeatedly. Just as he does now as the sunlight fills our bedroom high atop the watchtower.

Glorious!

After he feasts voraciously, he prowls over my belly with his lust-filled eyes more obsidian than emerald green locked on mine. A trail of open-mouthed kisses marks his path to my heaving chest, where he engulfs my breast before he pulls back to suckle on the plump nipple. Hard.

Another wail pierces the bedroom as I buck beneath him from the erotic pain.

His tousled sable haired head moves between my breasts as he continues to dine on my flesh. Low, possessive growls slip from his wicked mouth. His massive girth thumps against my inner thigh.

"Oh, My Lord!"

I can't control myself as another climax overtakes me. My head tosses from side to side as I squeeze my eyes shut.

A nip at my throat precedes his sensuous mouth crashing over mine for a dominating kiss. My toes curl as I bend my knees to press my heels and the spreader bar into his back. I need him closer. I need him inside of my throbbing pussy.

My pleas fall on deaf ears as he swallows my words.

At last, one of his hands grips my ass cheek while the other fists his turgid cock. In one swift thrust of his hips, he impales me on his ginormous dick.

More erotic pain morphs into pleasure as he pistons in and out of my quivering core. I scream his name again and again as he brings me to heights unknown. My pussy walls clamp on his thick length, and he roars.

"MINE! MINE! MINE!"

His chant fills our bedroom and bounces back from the stone walls.

My Lord lifts my hips to suspend me in the air as my arms remain stretched overhead. He sits back on his haunches and pounds into my wrecked pussy as he chases his release. His feral grunts and groans draw a series of orgasms from deep within my core.

Then he stills.

His dick swells, and the first pulse of his cock shoots his hot seed into my womb. He throws his head back as he yells my name, and his balls empty inside of me.

Time stands still as the sensations course through my body.

With a groan, My Lord lowers my hips and leans over to unbind my wrists. As he rubs them, sweat drips from his forehead to my lips.

I poke the tip of my tongue out to gather his salty taste into my mouth.

He groans and slants his mouth over mine. I hum in satisfaction as he kisses me possessively.

After a much-needed soak in the giant copper tub, we dress and leave our enchanted watchtower. As we drive away in the G-Wagen, I glance back over my shoulder and sigh wistfully.

"Don't worry, My Lady. We will return to your watchtower again and again," My Lord says as he squeezes my thigh. "No one will disturb it aside from the maid. Only you hold the key."

"Thank you, My Lord," I whisper as I lean over and kiss his smiling lips.

"Now, let's make brunch quick so I can get you away for our honeymoon," he says with a wink. His emerald green eyes twinkle with mischief before he slips his Tom Ford aviators on to his movie-star face.

My husband is one handsome devil!

"Yes!" I exclaim as I pump my fist in the air.

We arrive at the castle where a footman helps me from the truck as another opens the door for Lachlan.

"Good morning, My Lady Aboyne," the footman says.

Still not used to being formally addressed, I stifle a giggle and greet him.

"Good morning, My Lord Aboyne," he says as Lachlan rounds the front of the G-Wagen.

He greets him with an easy smile and takes my hand.

"You'll get used to it," he whispers in my ear.

I smile up at him and ask, "How did you know?"

He smirks.

"I've told you one before. I know everything to know about you, Baby Girl. Remember that," he says.

"There you are!"

"We were about to send Lucien for you!"

We glance up to find The Moms hurrying towards us with Lucien. He rolls his eyes and stifles a yawn. Undoubtedly, he was up late with the redhead he was flirting with last night. Lachlan chuckles.

They lead us to the banquet hall where our family and guests gather for the post-wedding brunch. Lucien excuses himself as one of his staff rushes over while everyone claps and offer greetings. Harris waves us over to a table where he sits with Baz, Lola, Roger, Leonie, and Laurent. Malcolm, Starr, Borya, Anton, Luc, Blair, Patrick, and Billie sit nearby.

On our way, we chat with guests and thank them for coming. The more formal of them refer to me as Lady Aboyne or Countess. Each time, my heart skips a beat.

Before we reach our table, a polite cough draws our attention. Lachlan growls low and tightens his hold on my hand. I glance around.

Callum. And Fiona.

Great. I forgot we invited him as his station of duke requires, according to Mom Lucie. Fiona and her family with her father a baron, no. But she's Callum's plus one, naturally…

"Good morning, and I'd like to wish you the best," he says as his emerald green eyes flick from me to Lachlan. "Let's move on. Shall we?"

I wiggle my fingers to get Lachlan to ease his grip. But I wait for his response.

He narrows his eyes.

Callum inclines his head. Fiona stares at me.

"Thank you. My wife and I turned that page already. Enjoy your brunch," Lachlan says.

Then he nods. Without an acknowledgement to Fiona, he places his hand on my lower back to guide me towards our table. I nod in general. While inwardly jumping in the air and cartwheeling in delight.

Booyah! Mic drop!

As promised, my husband has us stay at brunch for less than two hours, then whisks me away to the Castle's helipad. We board his Sikorsky S-92 Executive Helicopter bound for the airport. He still won't tell me our destination even as we buckle up in his Gulfstream G650 private jet, and his pilot confirms a fifteen-hour flight time.

Lola and Leonie went shopping for me and packed my luggage. So I don't even know what type of clothes I have to wear. They giggle about my bespoke Lola's Coterie lingerie trousseau and assured me I'll thank them later.

As the jet climbs into the sky, the adrenaline ebbs away like the wispy clouds around us. The stress of being apart from Lachlan, nerves about the impression I'll make on society, the excitement of the wedding, and our long night of lovemaking hit me all at once.

I must have fallen asleep because I awake in the jet's bedroom hours later when a soft chime rouses me. Lachlan's warm body wraps me in a comfortable cocoon I don't want to leave.

"Come, Mrs. Jackson, we land in thirty minutes," he murmurs in my ear before he presses a kiss behind it and rolls from the bed.

I groan in protest. Then remember I'll finally see where we'll spend our honeymoon. I stretch languorously, and Lachlan groans when my tits pop into view. I giggle and toss back the covers.

"No time for hanky-panky, Mr. Jackson. We have our honeymoon for that," I tease.

He smacks my bare ass and growls.

I yelp and skip past him to the bathroom.

Before we land, he ties a blindfold over my eyes with a wicked chuckle. It's not until we're in another helicopter about to land that he removes the blindfold.

I gasp.

Before us, a five-hundred-foot megayacht that looks straight out of a James Bond movie floats in sparkling turquoise waters off the coast of a tropical island. The sunlight glints off of the glossy, jet black, sleek hull. Four white tiers with banks of windows sit atop it. An incredible bank of three-deck-tall windows command the megayacht's center. Cutouts on its sides offer multiple areas to enjoy. Aptly named *Temptation*, it's impossible to resist its allure.

The helicopter alights on the pad at the rear of the third deck.

Lachlan hops out and helps me to the deck. He grins like the Cheshire Cat and gestures with his arms wide.

"Welcome to the Indonesian Islands aboard your wedding gift *Temptation*—as you will forever be for me, Mrs. Jackson. We'll cruise around Bali, Gili Meno, Gili Air, Gili Trawangan, Java, Nusa Lembongan, Nusa Penida, Moyo Island, and more for two months. Just the two of us —aside from the crew—alone at last!"

Lachlan's enthusiasm is infectious, and I jump onto him, wrapping my arms and legs like a little monkey around his powerful torso. He laughs and carries me from the helipad. I barely wave at the crew dressed in pristine white formal uniforms lined up to greet us as his long legs stride past them. But I make sure to grab two bottles of Dom Pérignon Rosé Champagne from a tray a steward holds. She smiles, and I grin like a loon.

"The boat has ten oversized staterooms. We'll start with the primary suite, then christen each one. Not to mention the sun decks, pool, salons… Sounds good, Mrs. Jackson?" He asks as he takes the elevator to the topmost tier.

"Absolutely, Mr. Jackson!" I respond, then kiss his lips. Our tongues dance until the elevator doors open.

When his eyes light up, I glance over my shoulder. The suite takes my breath away.

A U-shape bank of floor-to-ceiling windows comprises three walls of the open floor plan. A bedroom area marked by a plush carpet where a king-size platform bed covered in sumptuous white with black piping linens plus heaps of pillows sits close to the windows facing the bow. Two separate areas for a salon with a bar and a dining table with chairs in the middle on more plush carpet and a glass-enclosed white marble bathroom with dressing room sit towards the stern finish the space. Strategically placed ceiling pots and lamps light the various areas. It's superb.

Without a word, my husband crosses the entry area's marble floor to the bedroom. He stands me beside it and places the Champagne on the nightstand. His sizable hands cup my face as he angles it for a kiss. The slow burn builds as frissons of erotic energy roll down my spine to my clit. I moan into his mouth with need. His kiss turns scorching as he grinds his massive erection against my lower belly. I tremble.

Deftly, he disrobes me and tosses me onto the middle of the bed. I bounce amongst the luxurious linens, then raise my arms to him. His clothes drop to the floor. As he crawls across the bed, I part my thighs in welcome.

As this morning, my husband makes a meal of my pussy until my voice is hoarse from my passionate cries. He lifts me up and lies down on his back, holding my hips so my dripping pussy hovers above his thick, rigid shaft.

I lean forward to brace my palms on his firm pecs with my fingers gripping his shoulders. My waist-long hair forms a curtain around us as I lower my head to capture his mouth for a toe-curling kiss. I whimper when he drags my wet pussy lips back and forth over his bulbous tip. My juices mix with his pre-cum.

My head lifts to stare at him with pleading eyes.

"Ride me, Baby Girl. Take what you need."

I cry out in wild abandon when his hips snap up as he yanks me down onto his velvet-covered steel. Immediately, my greedy pussy tightens around him like a vise. My inner muscles flutter along his shaft to pull him in deeper. When my ass meets his groin, we groan in unison as he stretches me.

Then we stare at the juncture of our intimate connection. Transfixed, we can't look away as I rise on my knees. Slowly, his ten-inch dick reappears. I bite my lower lip at the sight of it coated with my arousal.

My husband growls deep in his chest.

I slam back down.

My head falls back at the burn of the stretch as his massive cock fills my pussy.

"So fucking tight," he grunts.

I continue with slow drags and fast drops with swirls of my hips. The angle changes as I lean forward to make his tip hit my G-Spot or back with my hands gripping his muscular thighs to stroke my engorged clit.

I lose my mind to our carnal dance. Time has no place.

Sweat drips down my spine and beads at my hairline. My heavy tits bounce with each move. The muscles of my inner thighs protest the constant clenching as I ride Lachlan towards our climatic finish line.

His thumb presses against my clit, and I explode.

My pussy clamps on his throbbing cock. His roar punches the air right along with my screams of pure ecstasy. A torrent of his cum fills my womb. Aftershocks rock us.

Too drained to remain upright, I slump over his sweaty torso. In my haze, I feel my skin tingle from his gentle touch as he strokes my damp back to soothe me. Amorous sighs slip past my parted lips.

"So good, Baby Girl… So good," he says in a raspy voice.

I hum in the back of my throat, then know no more once a state of sheer euphoria claims me.

LACHLAN

"*H*aley Jackson! I did *not* marry you nor bring you on our honeymoon to *lose* you! Let's not do this, Baby Girl! HALEY!!!"

My heart leaps into my throat, and my stomach drops as I watch helplessly. My bride just jumped off of a cliff at Devil's Tears—of all the bloody names.

We anchored *Temptation* off of Nusa Lembongan and took a tender to the shore. It's thirty minutes before sunset since the crew claim the tide pools have incredible reflections as the sun lowers on the horizon. The point was to enjoy the vista at a local beach bar while we eat dinner.

But no.

My wife overheard some guys talking about the amazing jumps they had off of the cliff, and their plan to return to the tide pools one more time. Naturally, being the sister of Alpha males—and having Malcolm the biggest thrill seeker amongst them—she asked if she could join them.

Me? I freaked out, not because I'm a wuss. But because it's dangerous as… Well… Hell! Devil's Tears, my ass!

Did she listen to me? Aah… No.

Two of the guys stayed in the water to help if necessary while I tried to hold her back.

She laughed.

And jumped.

I grab fistfuls of my hair as a string of obscenities pour from my mouth and lean over to see the end result.

Waves.

Guys bobbing.

Panicked, I yell her name and begin to jump. But the other two guys tell me to wait so I don't land on her. I glare at them and growl with my teeth bared. They raise their hands palms out in surrender and back up.

Just as I turn to jump in after my wife, her giddy laughter floats up on the breeze, along with cheers from the guys below.

Fuck. Me.

"Come on, Lachlan! Jump!" She calls up as she waves both arms overhead where she bobs next to the guys.

No way will I let some long-haired, jobless, hey dude wankers who show off for googly eyed women all day impress my woman.

Hell nah!

I give her the thumbs up, check the waves, and jump.

It's exhilarating to flip through the air. All sound seems

to stop as the air whooshes past my body. Then splash as I cut through the turquoise water's surface. My wife's smiling face the last thing I see and the next when I kick up from the depths.

"My Lord!" She squeals as we swim toward one another.

The guys cheer and wolf whistle.

"You, Naughty Girl, deserve a spanking," I growl as I snatch her by the waist and pull her body flush to mine.

And fuck me if my cock isn't as hard as steel. The adrenaline pumps through me. I could drill a hole into the cliffside. Instead, I crash my mouth to hers and kiss her possessively. I catch her plump lower lip between my teeth and tug with a growl.

She whimpers.

I give her the eye, cock my head to go, and swim towards the tide pools. Splashing lets me know she's behind me, then beside me. Out of my peripheral vision, I notice her peeping nervously at me every few strokes.

Yeah. Be worried, Naughty Girl.

"Lachlan, don't be mad at me. Please," my wife says as I help her from the water. "I've done cliff diving before with Malcolm, Lucien, Borya, and Anton. I know what I'm doing."

Wordlessly, I take her by the elbow and guide her back to the trail for the bar. The guys catch up to us and jabber on about the jumps and where we should go for more *rad stuff.* I nod while my wife bites the corner of her mouth, doing her best to keep up with my long strides.

"So, what? You're not going to speak to me forever, Lachlan?" She pouts when the server leaves our table. "I'm sorry. Okay? It just looked like so much fun, and I wanted to brag to the guys about it!"

I set my glass of ale on the table and trace a circle in the condensation.

From beneath my eyelashes, I see her flick her wide eyes from my hand to my face. After a moment, I glance up at her.

"Haley, I am well aware of how many daredevil excursions you went on with *the guys*. And I know you are capable of taking care of yourself and will not put yourself at risk—in your mind," I say slowly. "But you are my wife and will bear my children—you may already be pregnant —and I cannot sit back and watch you put yourself in harm's way. Not even for bragging rights. I am in no way controlling you but telling you reality. Do you understand?"

Her mouth opens and closes as she blinks.

I raise my eyebrow.

She huffs and throws her hands up in exasperation.

"Fine! I didn't think about it like *all* that, *Lachlan*," she responds. "And you know how much I want a baby. I would *never* do anything to harm our child. That's not fair."

She sniffs and turns her head towards the setting sun.

I sigh, knowing I took my fear for her safety out on her. I scoop her from her chair and sit back on mine. She squirms to get off of my lap. But I band my arms around her and bury my face in her neck.

She shudders as my warm breath blows across her damp skin.

"Baby Girl, I don't mean to sound harsh. But you scared the piss out of me. One minute you're next to me on the cliff, and the next you're flipping over the bloody edge. Not cool," I say as I stare into her eyes. "Can you see it from my viewpoint?"

She tugs at the corner of her mouth as she reflects on my words. Her gaze returns to mine, and she drapes her arms over my shoulders.

"Yes, My Lord," she answers as she grips my hair to angle my head for a spine-tingling kiss.

"Attaboy, mate!"

"Woot woot!"

My Baby Girl giggles against my lips as the guys—not really an awful bunch—tease us for our PDA. I groan as my cock weeps against the fabric of my board shorts. It thumps along my inner thigh at the loss of My Baby Girl from my lap.

She curtseys, and everyone applauds.

I shake my head and gulp down my ale.

The server arrives with our plates of fresh grilled seafood and green salads. We dive in—no pun.

My wife's hum of pleasure after she takes a bite of shrimp goes straight to my cock. A bead of buttery seasonings sticks to the corner of her mouth. I lean across the table and lick it off with a low growl.

"Later, I will eat you just as deliciously after I spank that ass red, Naughty Girl," I rumble. "Next I will put more of my seed deep in your womb in case you shook up the last batch to make our first of many babies."

She grins like the temptress she is, winks, and blows me a kiss.

I shake my head and take a bite of my flaky fish. A contented groan matches her hum as the local flavors burst over my tastebuds. Good. But still not as scrumptious as my wife.

* * *

"I CANNOT BELIEVE two months passed so quickly! It feels like we only arrived yesterday, Lachlan. Let's run away for another month!"

I shield my eyes to glance at my wife as we lay naked on an oversized sunbed sipping cocktails and watching the islands in the distance from the upper level of *Temptation*. She barely has any tan lines since I didn't allow her to wear clothes or bikinis for most of our honeymoon. Not even the sexy lingerie she showed me. Nice, but unnecessary.

It's been weeks of lovemaking—all over the megayacht, in the water, on secluded beaches only accessible by a tender—excursions onto the islands, and plain old time alone. Pure heaven.

I don't blame My Baby Girl for waiting to stay longer. We'll have to add at least three trips a year here. The rest of the time, our family and friends can use *Temptation*. It'll be another boat added to the Jackson-Steele fleet. While the others docked off of Banff, in the Mediterranean Sea, and in the Caribbean Sea, this will be the first in Asia. A bonny addition, for sure.

But duty calls for both of us.

My wife will meet with a few clients in Hong Kong and Tokyo on our way back to Aberdeen.

I'll drop in on some of our Jackson Corporation's partners while we're in those cities and in Los Angeles. With a trip to see Malcolm, Starr, and the twins. Already my father scheduled a meeting for my first day back in the headquarters at Jackson Town House. He and my mother will fly in from New York City a few days before Haley and I arrive. I'm mentally preparing myself for that battle.

"You're almost as glum as I am."

My wife's words rouse me from my musings. She leans over and cups my cheek as her thumb brushes over my lips.

"What's bothering you, my love? You've been a bit quiet since yesterday," she says with a crease between her eyebrows.

I tell her about the meeting with my father, and how upset Lydie will be if I take over Jackson Corporation instead of her. Haley understands as does everyone else since they're all aware of my father's outdated belief men should run the company regardless of who's the eldest or wants it the most.

Not that I don't want to replace him as CEO and Chairman of the Board when he retires. I love my job and work hard to make my division the most profitable of them all. Especially since it's the foundation of our family's business. But I will not hurt my sister for my gain. No.

"Oh, babe. That's a tough one. Could you and Lydie co-lead like Harris and me? Split the responsibilities and offices like you do now?" Haley asks as her dove gray eyes soften with concern.

"It's a possibility. I'll wait to see what my father says before I counter. There's never been two CEOs before. So I don't know how that would work. But it's an excellent solution," I answer. A quick shake of my head clears it, and I prowl over her luscious, sun-kissed body. "Enough talk of business. We have a baby to make, Mrs. Jackson."

She purrs when my lips meet the back of one knee, then her inner thighs as I bend her legs to reach her shoulders.

"Absolutely, Mr. Jackson," she sighs as I part her moist flesh with the tip of my tongue.

All thoughts of meetings, business, and my father fade away as I feast on my wife's sweet nectar. No distractions will keep me from making her cum again and again on my tongue, in my mouth, on my fingers and on my cock. My intense release obliterates my mind. All vestiges of work blow away.

For now.

LACHLAN

$\mathcal{M}$y mind flips through various scenarios as I stride across the executive floor of Jackson Town House on Union Street in Aberdeen. Despite me being the only full-time Jackson at our corporate headquarters, my father, mother, and siblings keep a suite of offices each spread throughout the floor for when they're in town. I'm on my way to my father's office for the talk.

Even though I focus my mind on the battle to come, I can't help the sense of pride that fills my chest. It increases with each glance of past generations who founded and helped to continue the legacy of Jackson Corporation immortalized in portraits. Starting with the founder who created the finest single malt Scotch Whiskey and set us on the path to the most renowned liquor company in the world. Then successors of each generation follow with my father last. The spot next to him remains blank. His expectation being my portrait will fill the void. Not Lydie's image.

Always hyperaware of office activities, my gaze moves around as I stride towards my destination at the other end of the building. The executive floor has offices for our legal, finance, operations, and technology departments, along with various conference rooms. Our other divisions have designated floors below. As always, the productive employees move about busy at their tasks for the day. The hum of their conversations and activities mixes with the soft classical music piped in through the surround sound system.

The decor highlights the Old World feel of the landmark property built by our founders of the famous Aberdeen granite. Jackson Town House is the second largest granite building in the world. A palette of caramel and Bordeaux hues with gold accents reminiscent of our Scotch and wines blend with the dark mahogany woods and leather furniture, crystal light fixtures, and original artwork. The reception area has a spacious desk. Three attractive receptionists with headsets in their ears and custom-tailored caramel-colored dress suits and skin-tone heels that serve as uniforms sit behind it.

With a nod and a smile, I greet them by name as I pass silently on the Aubusson rugs. I make it a point to know everyone I come in contact with daily. It boosts employee morale when they experience recognition from top management. And our staff ranks high on our list.

My steps continue until I reach the outer portion of my

father's offices comprising a reception area, conference room, and desks for his Aberdeen personal and administrative assistants. They flank either side of his inner office. Like the others, he maintains assistants in New York City and here rather than have them travel with him from one office to the other. Plus, each set of assistants keeps them aware of happenings in both locations.

My father's admin states he's waiting for me and asks if I'd like some tea or coffee. I decline. Had she offered a snifter of Scotch, I would have accepted it. Lord knows, I may need a drink or two after this conversation.

I rap on the door twice and enter when he calls out.

"You appear well rested and satisfied, son. I take it your honeymoon went well," he says as he rounds his desk and opens his arms for an embrace.

"I am, and Haley and I enjoyed our time together. A pleasant respite from our day-to-day lives," I respond.

My father claps me on the shoulder and gestures with his hand for me to take a leather guest seat opposite his desk. I unbutton the jacket of my suit and sit. As he lowers himself into his chair, his intense emerald green stare never leaves my face. He sits back and steeples his hands beneath his chin.

A handsome, distinguished man in his late sixties, he stands as tall as me at 6 feet, four inches with the same thick sable brown hair, only cut shorter. We're so much alike as Alpha males—and I assume Doms—it's like staring at my reflection in a mirror.

We both feel passionately about our family's multigenerational company and want only the best for it—including its future growth and legacy for the next line behind us. I can appreciate he's for tradition, but not at the expense of placing me at the helm as opposed to Lydie simply because she's a woman. She's busted her ass for Jackson Corporation and has the skill to move it forward. No different from me.

I await his opener for the meeting. So, I sit back and cross an ankle over the opposite knee. My face remains blank. I learned negotiations from the best—Connor Jackson.

After a moment, he nods as though his observation of me proved positive and worthy of the start to our meeting.

"Lachlan, no need to drag it out. The time has come for you to take the lead of Jackson Corporation. I plan to retire in four months and need to announce you as my successor. Plus acclimate you to the full role of CEO and Chairman of the Board," he says, then pauses to lean forward.

His gaze scans my face again for any sign of disagreement since he knows my thoughts on overstepping Lydie.

I wait.

With a squint in his eyes, he sits back.

"I know your concerns about your sister. But I made her aware of my decision after your wedding."

It takes an effort. But I remain neutral even while my surprised mind attempts to explain his words. Lydie has mentioned nothing to me. True, Haley and I returned only two days ago. But Lydie could have given me a heads-up. How must she feel? Damn.

"So, no need for you to concern yourself with that detail," my father continues. "She handled it better than I thought she would. But your sister is strong. But a woman, nonetheless. And a male heir has always run Jackson Corporation, typically the first male of the current leader."

I take a deep breath to control the timbre of my voice. Or I might yell at the top of my lungs at him for his sexist bullshit.

"Dad, with all due respect, that's a crock of crap"—I hold my hand up when he opens his mouth to respond—"This is not centuries ago when women were not trained for leadership of a company. Lydie and I have the same education and experience at Jackson Corporation, as do Lucien and Laurent. She's successfully run the company overall as your number two for years, while I handled the largest and most profitable division. So we are equally qualified for CEO and Chairman of the Board."

When he mentions her being a woman and having responsibilities in the home, the simmer in my veins turns to a boil.

"Father! If she were a man, who would you announce as your successor?"

He shakes his head and pushes back from the desk to rise and pace the floor.

"Lydie is not a man. So your question is irrelevant, Lachlan," he says as he turns to face me. "Focus on the reality and not on some hypothetical scenario."

I stare at him in disbelief for a moment. What the fuck?

Dismayed in his outdated mindset, I rise from my chair and head for the door.

"Where do you think you are going, Lachlan? Our meeting is not over," my father's voice booms across the space.

I hesitate at the door with my hand on the knob. Another deep breath, and I pivot to face him.

"Father, this is not the way I want to succeed you. I will speak with Lydie, Lucien, and Laurent. In one month, I will give you our decision. Until then, I will hear no more of Lydie being less than because she doesn't have a cock."

I leave him with his mouth agape.

"HEY, bro, thanks for taking my call during your lunch meeting. Shit is real."

I sit with my legs up on the tufted leather sofa in the sitting area of my office. Two fingers of Jackson Special Blend Scotch swirl in a Waterford Crystal snifter as my arm rests along the back of the sofa.

It's been a long day since the meeting with my father. I refused to let his nonsense get in my head and distract me from the work at hand. Finally, the day is over, and I can get Sebastian's input on the situation.

He's well aware of Lydie's daddy issues and of her desire to prove herself worthy of the lead role. He's been her confidante for years. Especially since they're in the same position: first born of powerful families and in the position to take over once our fathers retire.

The difference is Dad Morgan didn't harp on who has a cock. Baz was the natural fit. And even if Haley were to have wanted the position, I doubt Dad Morgan would have had the same antiquated thought process as my father.

Ridiculousness.

"No worries. You know, family first. Besides, the guy was a sycophant wanting to blow smoke up my ass to gain favor for a new retail project we're sourcing vendors. So what's up?" Baz says.

I recount the meeting, and he guffaws at my parting shot. I chuckle along with him now that I can reflect on it through the eyes of someone else.

"Well, damn, Lach. That's pretty ballsy of you, bro!" Baz says after his laughing subsides. "But in all seriousness, that's utter bullshit. Lydie is damn sure up to the task. As are you. So the bottom line is who's best between the two for Jackson Corporation. Take out all the other shit."

I take a moment to think about it while he waits in silence. Lydie and I are pretty much on par. Even though she oversees all divisions, I am involved in the final decisions. I would say I have an edge over her since I handle our core division intimately. Just as Baz still runs his Retail Properties Division—the core for STEELE International, Inc.—and his role as CEO and Chairman of the Board. It makes sense.

Lydie never ran an individual division. She wanted to focus on the overall aspects of the company.

I tell Baz as much, and he agrees I would be the best fit. But the question still remains of Lydie's role. Would she want to continue as Overall Vice President? Or would she want to co-CEO, as Haley recommended? And worse case scenario: Lydie would resign. And that cannot happen. At. All.

"The best thing is to speak with Lydie, and then we speak with Lucien and Laurent for their input. We always decide things together," I say. Then I take a swig of my drink and add, "I will not allow our father to steamroll us into his warped sense of succession. Is he even aware of the century we're in?"

Once again, Baz chuckles.

I can envision his platinum gray eyes sparkling with mirth as he strokes his five o'clock shadow and shakes his head.

"Man, I just don't know. Somehow, Uncle Connor is trapped back in time, Lachlan!" Baz exclaims. "I think it's a good idea to speak with your siblings. It's what I would do. And that's why mine respect me as their leader. I never make them feel less than me. We're a team. I make the final decisions. But I respect their opinions on matters."

I nod even though he can't see me and finish my drink. Sitting up, I swing my legs around and stand. I have to get going.

My wife and I have dinner tonight to celebrate our one-year anniversary since our marriage in Sorrento. I would have preferred a trip away. But we've had two months removed from our responsibilities already. I promised her we'll spend extra days after Malcolm and Starr's surprise wedding on Laucala Island in Fiji next month. We'll have the crew bring *Temptation* midway between Bali and Fiji and stay aboard for a week.

I tell Baz I have to head home to change for dinner, and surprised, he congratulates us. Everyone forgets My Baby Girl and I married long before our Aberdeen ceremony. I chuckle and thank him for his insight before we end our call.

After telling Gladys Sinclair and Isla Ritchie—my personal and administrative assistants, respectively—good night, I head to the executive floor's private elevator. My driver Theodore Doyle steps out of my Rolls-Royce Phantom Extended at the curb and opens the back door. I slide onto the sumptuous leather seat and sigh, thankful to be headed to my wife to celebrate the greatest day of my life.

In no time, we arrive at the penthouse, and I remind Doyle we'll be down at eight for dinner. It's after six, so I have time for a shower. I let the warm water sluice over my body to wash away the drama of the day. The steam helps to relax my muscles.

A cool breeze hits my back, and I glance over my shoulder.

Through the mist, I see my wife. A seductive smile plays on her full lips as she crosses the marble floor of the shower to stand before me. Then she drops to her knees gracefully. My head falls back against the shower wall and a groan slips from my parted lips as she takes the mushroom head of my cock into her warm, moist mouth.

"Oh, fuuuck, Baby Girl," I groan when she takes me to the back of her throat.

Her gag reflex kicks in. But she pushes past it to swallow my swiftly growing shaft. She hums in delight as she senses my girth increasing.

My fingers tangle in her ebony locks as my hips move in a slow, circular rhythm. Once she's adjusted to my sizable cock, I hold her head still and pull out to the tip before sliding back in to the hilt. Her breaths through her nose waft across my groin as her lips brush my skin.

My dick jumps in her throat.

She swallows, and I damn near cum.

I pull back slowly, then fuck her willing mouth. My gaze lowers to her face, and she smiles around my thickness. Her hand moves between her thighs as her fingers provide her pleasure. With a grunt, I thrust forward one last time and spill my seed in spurts down her throat.

She hums and cries out from her self-induced orgasm.

I reach under her arms and lift her to her feet. My cock pops from her mouth as she stares at me with hooded eyes. Quickly, I spin us around and pin her to the wall with my body as my mouth covers hers.

She laps at my tongue, and I groan as the musky taste of my jizz mixes with lemon from tea she must have drank.

"Your turn," I murmur as I break our kiss and lower to kneel before her.

One leg over my shoulder, I part her pussy lips with my thumbs and blow warm air onto the sensitive bud. She shivers, then mewls from my tongue lapping at her clit, mimicking her ministrations moments ago. Her juices flow for me to swallow and to suck for more until she's wobbly on one leg.

I cup her ass and stand, sliding her up against the slick marble wall until her pussy greets my erect cock. With a snap of my hips, I impale her onto my shaft.

We groan in unison. Eyes squeezed shut, hers from the stretch and mine from the tightness of her pussy.

Our slow grind—like a sensual tango—builds to an explosive climax. Double cries of pleasure resound in the shower. I lower My Baby Girl to the marble bench and bathe her with a sponge. While she leans back thoroughly sated, her hooded eyes watch as I soap and rinse my body. Muscles flex with each movement.

As I dry her hair sitting on the terrycloth pouf, she places a kiss on my lower abs and stares up at me.

My heart soars with love for my wife. I say a silent prayer of thanks for our bond and marriage. Then lean over and kiss the top of her head.

"Happy anniversary, Mr. Jackson. I love you," she whispers.

"Happy anniversary, Mrs. Jackson. I love you more," I murmur.

I send a text message to Doyle.

Mrs. Jackson and I will eat in tonight.

HALEY

"Bring your hands together at your heart center. Fingers press to fingers and palms to palms. Take a moment to feel the energy as it moves between them. On a deep inhalation, clear your mind of all but the sensation of your breath as it enters your nostrils… reaches the back of your throat… down your windpipe… and into your lungs evenly. Hold the nourishing breath in for a count of six… five… four… three… two… one. Slowly exhale at the same pace as your inhalation. Bring your focus to follow the reverse path of your inhalation. Hold the cleansing exhalation for a count of six… five… four… three… two… one. Once more… Now, breathe naturally as you bring your awareness back to your surroundings. Hear the white waves of the turquoise water as they roll onto the sandy shore and the seagulls as they soar high above us. Feel the warmth of the sun on your skin and the mat beneath you. Gently open your eyes… Namaste."

"Namaste," I respond with a bow to Anita.

It's the morning after Malcolm surprised Starr with a proposal and their wedding on the private Laucala Island in Fiji. It was a beautiful ceremony. But the highlight was Malcolm as he stood from his wheelchair and kneeled on one knee to propose to Starr. None of us had any idea he recovered from the paralysis. We cried and cheered at the same time. So incredibly thankful!

Anita offered beach yoga and meditation to help *us* recover from a long night of delicious food and magnums of Krug Clos d'Ambonnay Champagne—Starr's favorite. Lola, Leonie, Lydie, Blair, Billie, and I woke early and trudged down to the beach from our villas. Grumpy, now at peace.

Except, despite Anita's direction to clear our minds, mine still goes back to the visits I had with my gynecologist and primary care physician. I went to see them before Lachlan and I left Aberdeen. It's been six months since my last birth control shot and three since our vow renewal wedding night. But no baby, and I'm scared despite my doctors' assurances I'm perfectly healthy and pregnancy can take time for some women.

I glance around at Anita who has two children, Lola with three, and Leonie with three, not to mention Starr with twins. All of them conceived easily. What the hell is wrong with me???

A sigh escapes my mouth, and Billie glances at me.

"What's wrong, Haley, honey?" She asks as her Granny Smith apple green eyes widen with concern.

She tightens the hair tie in her wavy, medium-blonde balayage hair. Her pecan-colored skin flushed from the vinyasa flow. The sports bra and shorts show off her curves. Combined with being on the beach, she resembles Tyra Banks during a swimsuit photo shoot. But a petite version at five feet, four inches.

I hug my knees to my chest and glance out over the tranquil waters of the South Pacific Ocean. I don't mean to put a damper on everyone's fun times. So, I shake my head and tell her nothing.

"Yeah, right. Where's the twinkle in your eyes and the pep in your step, honey?" Billie teases as she nudges me with her elbow. "Your Prince Charming not loving you right?"

She giggles, and Leonie shifts on her mat to face us.

"*Non, chérie*! Anything but that!" She says dramatically.

The corners of my mouth curl up despite my glum thoughts. My girls always make me smile. I shake my head and switch to a cross-legged position.

"Oh, no. In fact, My Lord has plenty of skills. It's me," I respond.

Now all of their heads turn in my direction. Lola frowns, and Anita moves her mat closer. They question me at once, and I raise my hand to stop them.

"No, no, I'm fine. It's just that we've been trying to get pregnant for months now," I say, then swallow over the lump growing in my throat. "My gynecologist and my primary care physician assure me I'm in excellent condition. All parts in working order... But no baby."

Anita leans forward and clasps my hands in hers.

"Haley, as a doula, I can tell you many women take longer to conceive. And the more they stress about it, the more time passes without a viable pregnancy. Since your physical health isn't an issue, you need to focus on your mental wellbeing. You and Lachlan have been through a lot, and you need to relax. Enjoy your life. I can help you with a wellness plan. How would you like that?"

My eyes fill with tears at her kindness. She helped Starr —who was Leonie and Lola's doula—with her pregnancy and fitness. I know she can help me too.

"Oh, Haley! Don't cry!" Lydie says. "And I'm sure my father's rants about heirs doesn't help. You must take care of yourself first. A baby will come in time."

I nod and smile at my sister-in-law.

"Exactly!" Lola adds. "And I'm sure you're thinking about Leonie, Starr, and me. Sure we got preggie quickly. But that means nothing. Every body is different."

Of course, Lola would point out just what I was thinking. Over the years, she's gotten to know me so well.

The others chime in with words of encouragement.

My glum thoughts dissipate on the tropical breeze as my girls offer me support and tease me about various sex positions they guarantee to make a baby. I cover my ears and sing when my brothers' names come up. Lola and Leonie knew I would laugh once they mentioned intimacies with them. They never stop trying to tell me about their love lives. As if I want to hear about my brothers' virility. No, thanks!

"Before you and Lachlan leave for your getaway, you and I will sit down and create a plan for you. We can do Skype sessions," Anita says.

"Sebastian joins in on the yoga sessions Starr has with me, and especially while I was pregnant. Perhaps Lachlan will join you and Anita," Lola adds.

Leonie claps her hands and giggles.

"*Oui!* Roger did the same. Especially the yoga nidra. He falls into a deep sleep every time!"

We continue our conversation as we gather our mats, towels, and water bottles. It's almost time for the post-wedding brunch, and we need to shower and change.

By the time I return to the villa, my mind is finally at ease. I say a silent prayer of gratitude for the love of my girls.

* * *

"THANKS SO MUCH, Anita! That was an awesome session!"

"You persuaded me to take my first yoga class. And I must say, it's great to *tune into your inner self*. Thanks, Anita!"

"You're more than welcome! Remember to let go of things that are not in line with your harmony. The resulting stress of holding on to the negative impacts you on every level. Now, go snorkeling for me!"

We end our first Skype session with laughter. Then with whoops Lachlan and I jump off the second tier of *Temptation* into the sparkling Arafura Sea between northern Australia and southern Papua. We snorkel in the sea for another relaxing thirty minutes.

Once back aboard the megayacht, we make love in the shower before we eat breakfast on the third tier.

"It's so good to be back on *Temptation*," I say as my gaze moves across the horizon at the islands in the distance.

Lachlan chuckles wickedly, and I turn to look at him.

"I'm always on temptation, every chance she gives me," he says with a wink.

I tilt my head and frown.

"What?" I ask, confused. Then blush when I realize he refers to me—his Little Temptress. "Ha, ha, hilarious."

"I can't think of a more relaxing way to spend my time," he adds. "I wonder if Anita recommends leisurely love-making for inner harmony."

I roll my eyes at my silly man and pop a strawberry from my fruit salad into his mouth. My intention to hush him. But the sensual way he wraps his tongue around the strawberry and sucks it into his mouth makes my clit jealous. His groans of delight as the flavor bursts over his tastebuds harden my nipples.

As I pounce on him with a growl, I agree there is no better practice for inner harmony than to make love with my man.

LACHLAN

A smirk spreads across my face as I watch my older sister enter Jackson Pub. As always, Lydie strikes a powerful, yet sexy appearance with her waist-length sable brown hair in a bun at the nape and in a ruby red pencil skirt suit. Beneath the belted jacket a wisp of nude lace from her camisole peeks out as she reaches over to greet businessmen who leave the restaurant.

They glance with appreciative expressions over their shoulders to watch as Lydie sashays down the ramp to the restaurant's primary seating area. Her nude stilettos click on the tile with each confident step. The sound heard above the din of chatter and cutlery draws the attention of other diners. Men and women alike observe her.

Her emerald green eyes scan the room, then light up when she spots me. She waves like a queen and rushes towards me. Her long, toned legs make quick work of the distance. I smile and stand to greet her.

We're having lunch at one of the two restaurants—both run by Lucien and his team—in Jackson Building our New York City headquarters on Park Avenue between Fifty-second and Fifty-third Streets. I told Lydie I wanted to discuss our father's retirement and the impact on our roles. She agreed without comment in a neutral tone. But I couldn't gauge her reaction since we spoke on the phone.

Watching her approach me, Lydie appears her polished, well-kept, in control self who garners the utmost respect from hard-as-nails titans. She's a shark in the boardroom, a formidable opponent. But she's my sister and won't cut me to the quick as she would an outsider. So, I don't expect our discussion to draw blood.

"Hi Lach, forgive my tardiness—not a power play. My meeting ran longer than expected and traffic was a mess from SoHo to Midtown East," Lydie says as she double kisses my cheeks.

Her delicate floral perfume fills my nostrils. Again, the contrast between the strong Independent Woman and a feminine beauty becomes apparent. She balances both sides well.

"Hi, Lydie, I would never think it was a power play. I ordered your favorite dish and a glass of wine for you. The server will bring our salads out shortly," I say as I help her into a chair.

She nods and thanks me while she puts her black matte alligator Hermès attaché case in the seat beside her. When I sit, she leans forward with her palms on the table. Her eyes flash brilliant green fire.

"Our father is a male chauvinist pig!" She exclaims in a whisper yell aware of others around us and not wanting them to overhear her statement.

I throw my head back and guffaw, not giving a damn who I shock with my outburst. Lydie is bang on in her description of Connor Jackson.

She sits back with glittering eyes and a satisfied smirk. Then she unfolds the linen napkin and places it across her lap.

"I promised my therapist I would tell you when we met," Lydie says. "It's part of shedding my Daddy-approval cloak. A true process from years of self-indoctrination. But I've come bloody far!"

The server returns with our wine and green salads. Once he leaves, we eat while catching up since we last saw each other on Laucala Island. The conversation is easy-going and continues through our entrees. We decline dessert in favor of Jackson Scotch as a digestif.

"Dad didn't tell me he spoke with you after my wedding about his retirement and demand for me to succeed him. He mentioned me stepping into my responsibilities during the reception. But said we'd discuss it further," I start, then lean forward.

"When I returned from my honeymoon, he came to Aberdeen to meet with me. Let's say I didn't out and out call him a male chauvinist pig. But I did tell him he should not disregard you for the roles of CEO and Chairman of the Board simply because you do not have a cock."

Now, it's Lydie who throws her head back and snorts. I

join in until we're dabbing tears from the corners of our eyes. I share the memory of our father's florid face as I left him sputtering in his office. Lydie snorts with laughter as we continue to crack up.

Once we've sobered up, I tell her I want her perspective so we can make a decision and discuss the plan with our brothers for their input. I reiterate we're a team, and all opinions matter.

Lydie nods in appreciation and sits back in thought. After a moment, she smiles.

"Lach, that is exactly why you will make an exceptional CEO and Chairman of the Board for Jackson Corporation. You consider all parties involved and have a modern mind," she says.

I cock my head to the side, not sure I understand she's not wanting the roles anymore. When I begin to speak, she holds up her hand.

"I had an epiphany. I love our family's business and my work. But it's been too many years of me focusing solely on the betterment of Jackson Corporation and not on my own best life. I'm happy to remain as Vice President Overall and Vice President of the Board," she says, then pauses. "That is if you want me to continue as such."

A sense of pride wells in my chest for my sister and her grace.

"Thank you, sis. I truly appreciate your admiration and support. However, I do not believe VP is in your future," I respond.

Lydie blinks as her head snaps back. A crimson color

flushes her cheeks. Her mouth opens and closes soundlessly, unable to form words.

"As CEO, I want a new role of COO," I continue. "And I want you to fill the position. You know all the ins and outs of Jackson Corporation. No one else can meet my expectations. Deal?"

I lean forward and extend my hand to her as I grin like the Cheshire Cat.

Relief floods Lydie's beautiful face as the glitter in her eyes returns. She matches my grin and shakes my hand firmly.

"Deal!" She responds.

"Now, let's talk about the details before we speak with Lucien and Laurent during dinner," I say.

An hour later, I'm back in my office suite upstairs on the thirty-eight floor and fill Baz in on the latest. He agrees it's an excellent decision for all. Then we confirm squash for tomorrow at his Union Club of the City of New York.

I shoot a quick text message to tell my wife I love her while I start my video conference call. Her response of kissing smiley faces makes me smile.

Yeah, all is well in my world.

"WELL, I'm glad that's resolved. Bloody hell!"

"Exactly!"

Lydie and I glance at each other and laugh at Laurent and Lucien's reactions to me as CEO and her as COO.

I expected as much from them. Neither has an interest

in leading the company. *The Sexy Chef* enjoys being President of Restaurants/Bars/Lounges Division. Laurent is doing well as Director of the Cigars Division.

However, I can see him adding on my Liquor Division should the CEO role prove too demanding. The two divisions align well and with his personality and skills. I keep that thought to myself as I smile at my siblings.

"Now, can we eat? I am starved!" Laurent says as he rubs his stomach exaggeratedly.

"We wouldn't want you to go without a meal, little brother..." Lydie responds with an eye roll. "Lucien, what do you have for us?"

He claps his hands and jumps to his feet.

"A new dish I'm working on. I won't tell you the ingredients. Just tell me how you like it," he says, then raises an eyebrow. "I only expect you to enjoy my latest creation."

"Naturally, Arrogant Chef..." I add with a shake of my head.

He grins wolfishly and corrals us into the kitchen of my duplex penthouse in The STEELE Tower.

My Baby Girl went to dinner with The Moms and Lola at La Goulue. So my siblings and I have the run of the kitchen—rather Lucien does.

The tantalizing aroma of spices captures our senses. My mouth waters.

"Have a seat at the banquette. I will serve tonight," Lucien says with a bow.

We chuckle at his drama, but hurry to the table, eager to eat. With his arm behind his back and the bottle of Jackson

Cabernet Sauvignon held at the bottom by his fingers à la a sommelier, Laurent pours a sample of the wine into my glass.

"My Lord CEO, does this vintage satisfy you?" He asks in his most upper crust accent.

I clear my throat as I sit straighter and reach for the stem. I hold the glass up to the white wall, then swirl the liquid to view the color and legs. My nose dips into the bowl for a sniff of the wine's flavor. A sip places it on my palette for me to savor the taste. I nod.

"Indeed. An excellent choice," I respond in a tone as posh as Laurent's version.

"Very good, My Lord CEO. My Lady COO, for you," he says with a bow of his tousled sable haired head.

Lydie laughs as he fills her glass. Then takes a sip as a proper woman of her station would if she so imbibed.

We laugh when Laurent swigs from the bottle before plopping onto the leather bench. He scoots next to Lydie at the top of the u-shaped seat.

"In all seriousness, I must say, I'm really proud of you guys. Dad is a stodgy blowhard and can't step outside of the last century," he says.

"I agree wholeheartedly," Lucien adds as he places our plates in front of us. "Based on your strengths and where one complements the other, it makes sense. When will you tell Dad? And what if he doesn't approve?"

Lydie looks to me to provide the answer.

I smile at her deferment.

"Lydie and I have a meeting with him in the morning.

As far as his approval, it is what it is. He wants me as CEO, and I want Lydie as COO. Period," I respond.

Lucien returns to the table with his plate and sits across from me.

"Good," he says. "Now, eat up and tell me your thoughts on my latest masterpiece!"

Our laughter morphs into groans of delight as we savor the food. The three of us guess the ingredients—much as we did when we were younger and Lucien cooked for us. Lydie comes the closest and scores an extra scoop of hand-churned pistachio ice cream for dessert.

As we hang out in the living sipping digestifs, my wife returns home. I jump to my feet to greet her with a back-bending kiss.

Lucien catcalls while Laurent wolf whistles and Lydie claps.

A flush-faced Haley curtsies when I lift her to my side.

"Wow! What a welcome!" She exclaims.

Lydie pats the sofa beside her, and my wife settles between us. She glances from my sister to me questioningly since she knows today was the talk. Lydie grins and stands.

"You're looking at the new COO of Jackson Corporation. The highest level a woman has achieved in the company's history!" She exclaims proudly.

My wife hops up and offers words of congratulations as she hugs my sister.

"We have to celebrate! Let's have a spa day on Saturday. Scrubs, massages, facials, manis/pedis, lunch, the works!

Then we can pick out some hot dresses and go dancing at this new salsa club Maribelle told me about yesterday—"

"Whoa there, little lass! Clubbing? In a hot dress? Ah, not without me," I interject with a scowl. Visions of suave wankers gawking at and flirting with my woman flash before my eyes. No fucking way!

"That sounds fantastic, Haley! You know what would be great? If we make it a night out for everyone. Chase is in town, and I'm sure Sebastian, Lola, and Harris would want to come too," Lydie says.

She distracts my wife from laying into me. But I still get the stink eye from her. She flips her hair over her shoulder as she turns back to Lydie.

"It's *your* celebration, *Lydie*. I'm down for whatever *you* want to do," my Naughty Girl replies.

Lydie maintains a neutral expression, even though her eyes dance with mirth.

"Perfect!" She responds and glances at her gold Rolex Ladies President. "Speaking of Chase, I need to get going."

She gives Haley a hug. Then as she hugs me, she whispers, "Bring it down a notch, caveman."

I grunt. Not happening.

Lucien and Laurent agree to Saturday's plans, then bid us good night and leave with Lydie.

My wife rounds on me the instant the private elevator doors close.

"Lachlan Jackson, you will not prevent me from going out. I mean it! I am a grown woman and know how to conduct myself. You caveman!" My Naughty Girl says as she glares at me with her arms folded across her tits. The position only makes her D-cups lift higher in her v-neck cashmere dress. The soft material clings to her luscious curves.

"Oh, how rich! Don't you dare ogle me up and down, Lachlan!" She snaps as she stomps her foot.

I smirk as her tits bounce.

She narrows her dove gray eyes to slits, curls her lower lip, and snarls at me in defiance.

My cock punches against the zipper of my jeans. The gleam in my eyes warns her because she pivots and races towards the stairs.

I throw my head back and howl.

Then take chase.

"No, no, no, no, no!" My curvy prey bleats.

Too late, she's set the beast loose. And there's no turning back now.

As she bounds up the stairs, her round ass shimmies like a flag before my hungry eyes. It spurs me on. I swipe at her calf. She yelps and hops up two stairs. I continue to toy with her until we reach the top. Then I throw my head back and howl again.

She glances over her shoulder and makes a run for our suite at the end of the hall.

I smirk and yank my cashmere sweater over my head, tossing it to the floor. My long strides catch her before she can close the double doors behind her. Hooded eyes filled with lust glance up at me as she backs into the sitting room.

When her butt hits the back of a chair, I growl and prowl towards her with my head low.

Her pants make her ample chest rise and fall enticingly.

I lick my lips.

She blinks and grips the sides of the chair.

"Tell me again how I will not prevent you from going out, Naughty Girl?" I growl as I tower over her.

She shudders and bites the corner of her mouth.

"Right," I smirk.

Then grab her by the hips and toss her over my shoulder. A succession of four smacks to her jiggling butt cheeks makes her squeal and pommel my ass with her fists ineffectively. She mutters a stream of obscenities as I carry her to our bedroom, kick the doors open, and sit on the edge of our bed. I shift her to my lap, lift the hem of her dress, and rip off her G-string.

"Don't you dare, Lachlan Jackson!"

I ignore her screech and smack a tattoo on her ass until it turns a rosy shade and warms beneath my palm. On a throaty moan, her legs part as I rub the heated flesh. A smack to her pussy coats my fingers with her juices. She mewls and lifts her hips wantonly.

I alternate spanking and finger fucking my Naughty Girl, bringing her to the edge of orgasms again and again. Her frustrated growls make me smirk. I lick her juices from my fingers and hand, then stand her before me on wobbly legs.

"Arms up," I command, and lift the dress over her head.

I nip a beaded bud through the silk of her front-closure bra.

"Lachlan," my Naughty Girl moans as she thrusts her tits in my face. "Please, My Lord."

With a shake of my head, I tsk at her. I make quick work of her bra and drop it to the floor with her dress and G-string. A lick to each nipple, and I lay her face down on the bed.

"Do not move," I command with a smack to each ass cheek.

She jolts but holds position.

I stride to the bathroom for the cooling gel. After I apply it to her ass, I flip her over.

Carnal want fills her face as her gaze trails over my naked body.

My hand strokes my erection.

She licks her lips.

I kneel on the bed and move forward between her parted thighs. My strokes increase in pace as I jerk my cock. My balls hang heavy, ready for release. On a roar, I cum. My jizz shoots out in a torrent to cover her stomach and tits. I don't stop fisting my cock until every bit of my seed creams her flesh.

She swipes some from her nipple and licks her pinky finger clean.

I growl and shoot some more. My thighs quiver, but I lean over to rub my seed into her skin like a true cream. Then I sit back on my haunches to admire my handiwork. Perfect.

"You are mine, Haley Jackson. Call me a caveman all you want. Only never forget. You. Are. MINE!"

She nods, then remembers herself and says, "Yes, My Lord."

"Good girl," I purr. "However, you will go unfulfilled and marked with my essence tonight."

I crawl over her and slant my mouth over hers for a toe-curling kiss. She whimpers and writhes beneath me. But I don't give in. Instead, I help her under the bedding and spoon her body with mine. Again she whimpers as my semi-erect cock presses against the crack of her ass. A low growl silences her unspoken demand.

Then I purr until she settles in my arms. Where she belongs.

"Okay Haley, sweetheart. Your guests confirmed. The menu is ready. The table setting will be impeccable with gorgeous floral arrangements. A perfect music playlist to enhance the atmosphere. The staff understands their responsibilities. I love your dress. How do *you* feel?"

Mom Lucie's warm hazel eyes scan my face as we sit in the tranquility room of her favorite spa in Aberdeen.

Over the past several weeks, she helped me to integrate into society throughout the UK. I've attended many lunches with heads of philanthropic organizations to decide which I will support as a patron. Other times, it was high tea with various nobles or members of the royal family. I spoke about STEM at a school in a lower income neighborhood to encourage the girls to pursue an education in science, technology, engineering, and math.

Not to mention studying Mom Lucie's primers of key

people to know that includes their names, titles, bios, tidbits, and photos plus another primer on historical to present-day Scotland. When she and Dad Connor became engaged, her mother-in-law gave her similar study guides. Mom Lucie continues the tradition with me. And I'm more than appreciative of her help.

As I am now.

I used her vendors to assist me with my first dinner party. Lachlan and I will host it at our penthouse. An intimate affair with four other couples. We want a mix of backgrounds since we're not only into nobility—Lachlan started going by his title because of me.

We have a pleasant mix of guests. Ewan and his wife, Anne. Sean McFarley and his wife Edith, who own popular pubs and a one Michelin star restaurant along with being on Lachlan's Jackson Tasters Circle. An English duke who has an American wife. A Scottish earl and countess who runs one of the philanthropic organizations that interests me. Our evening should go smoothly and pleasant for all.

I beam at Mom Lucie.

"Absolutely ah-mazing! I cannot wait for tonight. Lachlan teased me this morning, saying I was as excited as a lass on Christmas morning," I respond with a giggle. "And in a way, it is like a wonderful present. I appreciate all you do to help me navigate the ways of the titled."

Her eyes glisten with emotion.

I know from my mother stories of how some people treated Mom Lucie originally. Being from a family in New Orleans who didn't treat her well and not having money made her life different from the privileged. Then, add her being a bartender in a Jackson bar in New York City wasn't the background of a typical future marquess. But the bright side was her mother-in-law, who guided and protected her fiercely.

Although I come from an über-wealthy family and am accustomed to various social circles, the nobility and royalty have different rules and norms completely. And Mom Lucie will not allow me to flounder.

I rise from my chaise lounge and hug her close. We don't need words to express ourselves. Our love understands it all.

As we part, the spa manager enters the room with our aestheticians. We have a full day of the works, including makeup and hair for me. By the time we leave, we strut out of the spa feeling like a gazillion bucks!

"ALL SET FOR TONIGHT, sweetheart? Lucie told me you had a great day together. I'm so jealous!"

My mother's laughter tinkles over the FaceTime call. She's in Morocco with my father.

"Yes! Guests will arrive in thirty minutes," I respond. "And we had a wonderful day of pampering. But don't be jelly!"

More laughter, then my mother asks me to show her my dress since Mom Lucie raved about it. Happily, I oblige and place my mobile on the fireplace mantel, then step back so she can see me full length.

I want to stay true to myself and my love of mini dresses. So I opted for one of pink silk with a high neck, super billowy long sleeves, a teardrop cutout at the décolletage, and a flouncy pleated skirt. The special touches are dozens of laser-cut circular embellishments at the neck, cuffs, around the cutout and waist, and dripping from the skirt in diminishing sizes, all connected by tiny gold beads. My hair piled atop my head, minimal makeup, and straps of gold high-heel sandals wrap around my calf complete my look. My goal to convey a young, stylish, lighthearted woman who's also a countess.

Not to mention My Lord loves my legs!

"Oh, Haley! It's exquisite and so are you! Give a twirl, sweetheart," my mom gushes as she claps.

Again, I oblige with a giggle. The skirt rises and reveals the tops of my thighs. The light feel is delicate against my skin softened by scrubs and oils.

A wolf whistle pierces the air, and I pivot to find my husband. He's dashing in a deep navy blue suit. Subtle pinstripes hint of pink along with his silk tie and pocket square. His sable haired swept back highlights the smooth-shaven skin of his sculpted cheekbones and cleft chin. The emerald green in his eyes sparkle like the gemstones as they blaze a trail from my head to my red painted toenails and back to my dancing dove gray eyes.

"Look at you, bonny lass. Who are you all dressed up for?" He asks in his deep baritone voice laced with lust.

It only takes seconds for him to cross the living room and pull me into his arms for a mind-blowing kiss.

"Ahem."

He pulls back from devouring my mouth to glance over my shoulder at the mantel. He chuckles.

"Oh, hello there, Mom Shelley," my husband chuckles as his handsome face reddens. "I didn't realize you were on FaceTime."

She laughs and waves her hand.

"No worries, sweetheart. It's good to see you appreciate my daughter. Go and enjoy your dinner party. Haley, honey, tell me all about it tomorrow," my mother says and ends the call with a kiss.

Lachlan glances at me with his lower lip caught between his teeth. His eyes full of mirth.

I rise on my toes and nip his lip to suck it into my mouth with a moan.

He wraps his arms around me, and I meld against his solid body.

"I have something for you, Mrs. Jackson," he murmurs in my ear. His warm breath sends tingles skittering down my spine.

"Is that so, Mr. Jackson?" I purr.

He nods and steps back to remove a black velvet box from his suit pocket. He holds it in his palm for me to press the sapphire cabochon closure. On a bed of black silk, a pair of intricate pink diamond and platinum chandelier earrings and a matching hair clip sparkle in the light.

I gasp.

"Mom told me you chose a pink dress. These are the earrings and hair clip. The rest of the suite is upstairs since your dress covers your neck and wrists," he says. "I want to commemorate our first dinner party."

I throw my arms around his neck.

"Thank you, my love! You're so good to me," I gush.

"Pardon, My Lord and My Lady. Your guests arrive."

I kiss my husband's cheek, and switch from my diamond studs to my new earrings, then add the hair clip to the back of my head, giddy.

"Showtime, Countess of Aboyne," he murmurs as I finish and smooth my skirt.

I grin at him like the Cheshire Cat.

"Yes, My Lord," I respond as I take his proffered elbow.

* * *

"It's so good to see you, Haley! Thank you for inviting us! Or should I call you Countess? I've seen your photos online and in magazines so much—you and Lachlan."

Maribelle exclaims as we hug.

It's the night of the Jackson Foundation annual fundraiser at STEELE Aberdeen. My first as Lachlan's wife.

With fall kicking off the social calendar, we've attended countless engagements. Ultimately, our photos appear here and abroad. It's the story of two powerful billionaire families merging, plus the sudden popularity of nobility and royals makes us a hot topic. Ordinarily, the Steeles remain out of the public eye. But we can't help it. People love a fairytale as much as I do!

"I know it's crazy, isn't it!" I respond with equal enthusiasm.

"You're celebrities," Calvin says with a smile as he shakes Lachlan's hand. "Maribelle shows the pictures to me all the time."

Lachlan chuckles and shakes his head.

"Rarely did I use my title. Now, I hear it all the time, thanks to my wife and her love of fairytales and happily ever afters," he says as he pulls me into his side and kisses the top of my head.

We chat some more before Lachlan and I greet more guests.

As always, both of our families are present except for Malcolm and Starr, who are on their honeymoon. As Lachlan and I pass through the ballroom, we spot Lola with Baz speaking to a prince from Dubai, Lucien laughing with a Japanese chef, and Harris with an Australian apps genius. While the others mingle.

It was the same at the STEELE Foundation annual fundraiser in September. So the media speaks the truth about the merging of our families. Although we were always close, it's even more official with my marriage to Lachlan. And I couldn't be happier!

"Excuse me, Mr. Jackson. It's time for your interview with *The Wall Street Journal* columnist."

We glance around to find Isla—Lachlan's administrative assistant—behind us. He nods, and I tell him I'm going to the ladies' room.

As I make my way through the guests, I stop and speak

with some and nod at others in greeting. Over the months, I've become familiar with many of those in Aberdeen and the surrounding areas. Others I know previously.

After I leave the ladies' room, I come face-to-face with Princess Fiona the Fair. Fantastic.

She doesn't appear surprised like me. So I guess she was waiting to ambush me. Even better…

"Fiona," I say with a nod as I step around her.

She counters the move to block my path.

An inch taller than me, I glance up at her ethereal face—porcelain skin, violet eyes, and white-blonde hair. The fairies run through her blood definitely.

"Haley, may I have a word?" She asks and gestures down the corridor away from the other guests.

I arch an eyebrow and don't move.

"Only for a moment," she says. When I don't move, she adds, "Please."

I scan her face for any sign of guile. Finding none, I gesture for her to proceed before me. I follow her, and we stop out of earshot of the others. She turns to me and sighs.

"Haley, I am sure you would rather not hear this, but I want you to know anyway. I love Lachlan—"

I pivot and stride back towards the ballroom. Like hell, I'll listen to her!

A hand on my arm attempts to stop me. I yank away and glare at fucking Fiona.

"Stay away from my husband and from me, Fiona," I snarl.

She shakes her head. Her pale hair floats about her face.

"No, it's not what you think. Please give me a moment to explain, Haley," she says.

I narrow my eyes.

She rushes on.

"I thought he and I could have a wonderful life together. But he only ever wanted to be friends. But who can't fall in love with Lachlan Jackson?" She says with a sad smile.

Then she shakes her head as though to clear it of memories and continues.

"But I want you to know that Callum and I are happy together, and I wish to thank you. If your and Lachlan's love been breakable, Callum and I would never have come together. We truly mean it when we say we want to move beyond our past with the two of you. You and I may never be friends. But I hope we can have a cordial relationship. Okay?"

I stare at the woman who gave me nightmares when I thought of her with the only love of my life. Had our situation been different, Fiona and I could have been friends. But I don't trust her, no matter what she says to me. However, I will move forward since we're in the same circle and I'm confident in my marriage with Lachlan.

"Fine, Fiona. I wish Callum and you the best," I respond. With a nod, I turn on my heel and go to the man in my life —the man she will never ever have as her own.

When I see Lachlan across the ballroom, my heart swells with love. I hurry to him.

He must sense my need to be in his arms for his comforting embrace because he excuses himself from the couple he speaks with and strides towards me. He cocks his head to the side and scans my face as we near one another.

Opening his arms he asks, "What's wrong, Baby Girl? Did someone do something to you?"

He glances over my head behind me to search for whatever bothers me.

I shake my head and smile as I press my cheek to his shoulder.

"I just need some Lachlan," I respond.

He rubs my back with one hand as his other binds me to him. His lips brush the top of my head.

"Well, you got me, Baby Girl. All of me," he murmurs.

I say a silent prayer of thanks for our love. I will allow no one to break it.

"Hi… Hi… Hi!"

"Aaw, babe! Look at Slade! He's telling me hi and waving from the beach," I say without glancing up from my mobile's screen. "He's so bloody cute! I can't believe how big he's gotten each time Baz sends me videos or photos."

I play the video again, and Slade's laughter fills the air of my GulfStream G650 private jet. My Baby Girl and I are on our way to celebrate Thanksgiving at Baz and Lola's Bougainvillea Cay—their private island in the Bahamas.

More specifically, it's an island within the chain of the Exuma Cays known as the yachting, sailing, and fishing paradise of the Bahamas. The location offers an ideal spot for relaxation and fun activities.

The forty-million-dollar investment of Bougainvillea Cay lies in one of the most beautiful parts of the Bahamas. It features over five hundred acres of lush, tropical land with a network of paths and walkways. Surrounded by crystal clear turquoise waters, it boasts many white sandy beaches, three inner lakes, and different elevations for stunning views. An airstrip for us to fly in and out with ease makes it perfect for quick getaways. Another plus is its proximity to STEELE Exumas should we wish to use the recreational, spa, or dining facilities.

Two properties round out the island. A palatial two-story, ten-bedroom beachfront villa with saltwater pool, four guest cabanas, and a caretaker's house and an actual castle built by an Englishman in the 1930s.

Their parents and the rest of the siblings built villas along the coastline that features natural coves for privacy. With his STEELE division, Roger created a clubhouse on the largest beach for the family to gather. They added docks with lifts for sailboats, Jetskis, and other water toys.

Baz and Slade stand on the beach in front of the club-house waving. Lola and their twins—Sabrina and Stella—sit on oversized beach towels, laughing in the background. It's a beautiful sight of their little family's happiness and love.

I can't wait for the same with My Baby Girl, I muse. To see her belly swell from my seed and to watch her grow as my baby fills her womb. Feeding her weird shit like—I don't know—pickles and chocolate ice cream? Hear her curse me out like Baz and Roger said Lola and Leonie did to them during labor. And most important when for the first time, I hold my child in my arms and cradle its head to my chest with My Baby Girl smiling at us lovingly. Yeah! Call me Daddy Dom!

Then I realize she's silent next to me and not commenting on the video. I glance at her, and my chuckles stop immediately.

What the fuck?!

Creases form between her eyebrows while her cheeks brighten to a rosy hue. Soulful dove gray eyes shimmer with unshed tears. Her plump bottom lip trembles as she sucks in a ragged breath.

When her eyes lift from the mobile's screen and met mine, the tears slip down her cheeks. She jumps from her seat and rushes towards the back of the jet.

She's so quick and the move so unexpected, I sit dumbfounded stuck in my seat. A sob shakes me to act. Mobile forgotten, I hurry from my seat to follow her into the bedroom.

"Baby Girl, what's the matter?" I ask as I sit beside her on the bed and wrap my arm around her shoulders. As I envisioned my child, I cradle her head to my chest and coo to soothe her.

Even more sobs rack her body as she clings to my shirt.

My other hand strokes the back of her head while I try to figure out the cause of such immense heartache. We were talking about the activities we'd do. Then my mobile chimed with a text message from Baz, and I played the video.

Duh!

The video with babies.

Bloody hell…

Haley and I have been trying to get pregnant for months without success. Tests prove we're both perfectly healthy. But she's super stressed about it. Especially since her girls had their babies with ease. Damn!

"My love, please don't cry. Our time will come, and we'll have a whole polo team of babies. Hell, maybe a rugby team. Remember, I told you that before? And remember what Starr told you, all comes when it should. All right? Please don't cry, Baby Girl. I love you so much."

Her chest rises and falls with a deep inhalation. Undoubtedly, she's using another of Starr's yogic teachings: a deep cleansing breath to clear negativity and make way for the positive. Another breath, and My Baby Girl sits up and rests her head on my shoulder.

I tip her chin up with my forefinger to bring her eyes on a level with mine.

"Always remember I love you, Haley Jackson. Whether we have babies or we do not have babies, you will forever be the love of my life and the reason I awake each and every day. Do you understand?"

I enact my Alpha Dom to focus her sub.

She nods.

I arch my eyebrow.

A flicker of her innate submissive passes across her eyes, and she parts her lips on a breathy sigh.

"Yes, My Lord."

"Good girl."

．　．　．

WHEN WE'VE SETTLED in our beachfront villa, we drive our golf cart to Baz and Lola's villa, where the families gather. We're the last to arrive.

My parents, Lydie, Chase, and Laurent flew down from New York City on my parents' jet. While my in-laws and Harris flew in from the city on Dad Morgan's jet. The Paris contingent—Roger, Leonie, their babies, their nanny, her parents, and Lucien—flew in on Roger's jet. The West Coast crew—Malcolm, Starr, their twins, their nanny, and her parents—flew in on Malcolm's jet.

"Hey, hey! The gang's all here!" Harris exclaims when he spies My Baby Girl and me step onto the villa's deck.

Rounds of hugs and kisses greet us.

I surreptitiously watch my wife as she chats with Starr. She bounces Selina—Malcolm's baby—on her knee. No one would know my wife was in tears a few hours ago. I did my best to put a smile on her face—along with several orgasms.

But she still worries me.

My gaze seeks Lola and Leonie. I spot them sitting on chaise lounges and stride over. They shield their eyes from the sunlight as they glance up at me and smile.

"Hey, Lachlan!"

"*Ciao, chéri!*"

I smile and ask if I may speak with them. Lola scoots up, and I sit at the foot of her chaise lounge. I tell them how upset My Baby Girl is about not being pregnant yet. Then ask them—along with Starr—to speak with her sister to sister. They'll be able to give her a different level of comfort than I can since they're women and very close.

They agree wholeheartedly and give me hugs as they tell me not to worry, either.

Relief washes over me, and I thank them.

I'll do anything to make My Baby Girl happy. Her tears broke my heart. And she deserves nothing but joy in her life.

"Okay, fucker, what are you doing hugging my wife?"

We glance up to find Baz glaring at me.

When I open my mouth for a retort, he bursts out laughing.

"Like you'd be crazy enough to try anything!" He chortles.

I stand and punch him in his flank playfully.

"Watch your language around Slade, wanker!" I say as I take his son from his arms and coo at him.

"And *wanker* is okay?" He snorts.

I ignore Baz and bounce Slade on my hip. He's a mini Sebastian Steele, all gray eyes and ebony hair. I ruffle his soft locks, and he laughs.

The hairs on the back of my neck prickle. Slowly, I glance around and find My Baby Girl watching me. I smile at her and hope it doesn't sadden her to see me with Slade. When a beatific smile spreads across my wife's stunning face, I nearly weep myself.

She blows me a kiss, and I melt.

* * *

"YOU CHEATED, Malcolm! You're supposed to go around the *outside* of the buoy, and you know that, big cheater!"

Haley shouts as she storms towards her brother, already on the beach, having left his Jetski on the sand.

We've been on Bougainvillea Cay for a couple of fun-filled days. Lots of scuba diving, sailing, exploring the island, and hanging with our family. As a competitive bunch, we've had several races using all the toys. Today it's the Jetskis.

I watch Malcolm as he races towards Haley and lifts her off her feet before she can duck away. Spinning her in the air, he teases her about being his little sister and to respect her elders.

Haley huffs, but giggles when Malcolm tickles her silly.

He drapes his arm over her shoulders, and they walk back to where everyone gathers on the sand. His eyes meet mine. He arches his eyebrow at me in challenge with a look of *my little sister, fucker.*

Whatever, wanker, I muse and smirk over *my wife*'s head at Malcolm as she squirms from his embrace and hustles to me. He curls his lip in warning.

I pull her flush against my body and cover her mouth with mine for a searing kiss to put his panties in a bunch.

"Who's ready for some grilled lobster and shrimp?" Dad Morgan calls out from the pit we dug for cooking on the beach.

Sun Knight—Starr's mother—made her famous potato salad. Josy Beaulieu—Leonie's mother—baked her equally loved double-chocolate soufflés. Not to be outdone, Lola made delicious fried chicken. They teased Leonie was best left with tossing the green salad since she's famous for burning water.

"I'm starved!" Haley exclaims when I free her mouth.

I nip the sensitive juncture where her neck meets her shoulder and murmur, "So am I, Little Temptress."

Her cheeks pinken beautifully as she bites the corner of her mouth and blinks up at me.

We've made love so much, but I still can't get enough of my wife. She'll always be my sweet temptation.

"But you need your energy, so I guess food is in order," I say with a smirk.

She giggles and takes my hand to walk towards the tables laden with food.

"Malcolm did cheat you, Haley," Harris says. "But you should know that by now."

He chuckles and piles more potato salad onto his already overloaded plate. When he notices me eyeing the food, he pats his washboard abs.

"I'm a growing boy, Lach," he says with a wink.

I chuckle and hand a plate and fork to My Baby Girl. We get some of everything, then head over to the pit for Dad Morgan to add some seafood.

"The lobsters are succulent," he says as he places two tails on our plates. "Make sure you use the butter. Lucien seasoned it well."

We thank him and sit on an oversized beach blanket next to Lydie and Chase Wentworth—an Australian multi-billionaire apps developer. He and Haley talk about tech stuff while Lydie and I enjoy our food and chat about nothing in particular.

It's nice to relax beneath the warmth of the Caribbean sun, hearing the waves roll onto the white sandy shore mixed with the laughter and conversations of family. Rodolphe and Gaspard run around with their Bichon Frises and Slade's Siberian Huskies. When Gaspard stumbles to the sand, the dogs leap on him and lick his face. His twin throws himself down beside him and wraps his arms around a Husky as he buries his face in its gray fur. Their peals of laughter make me chuckle.

My Baby Girl glances at me and follows my line of sight to our nephews. She grins and turns to me.

"Let's get puppies!" She exclaims.

I blink in surprise, then shrug. Why the hell not? They'll help to keep her distracted from babies. So perfect.

"Good idea," I respond with a smile. "What breed do you want?"

"You know, everyone assumes Golden Retrievers are American. But they originated in the Scottish Highlands, actually. They're also like the two of you—American and Scottish," Lydie interjects.

I throw my head back and laugh.

"How do you know such a random fact?" I ask, chuckling.

She grins and shrugs.

"The things you find online when you can't sleep at night will amaze you!" She responds.

Chase snorts and eyes Lydie.

"Well, babe, there are much more interesting things to do *when you can't sleep at night*. Obviously I've been remiss, and that needs correction," he says.

Lydie blushes crimson from her hairline to her bikini top and bows her head.

I struggle to hold back a laugh at her unusual submissive behavior.

My Baby Girl jumps in with the save.

"Excellent idea, sis! I'll search for a breeder in Scotland. Go to the source as my dad says!"

Lydie shifts uncomfortably on the blanket and nods before she stands and walks to the table with her empty plate.

Chase watches her a moment. Then he turns back to us with a twinkle in his golden brown eyes and winks before he jumps up to follow.

My Baby Girl and I swivel our heads towards each other at the same time. She's bursting with suppressed laughter, as am I.

Lydie? A sub? Bloody hell!

"Bella… Bonnie… Come."

I call to my Christmas puppies Lachlan gave to me. The striking white blonde Golden Retrievers with honey-colored eyes bound towards me through the Alpine snow. They're eight-weeks old from a renown breeder in the Scottish Highlands known for show-winning litters.

When I opened the gigantic gold-foiled wrapped box with a big red velvet ribbon, they popped out with matching bows around their necks. I giggled as they licked my face. We named them for their exquisite beauty.

"I can't believe how quickly they learned their names!" Lachlan exclaims as they jump on us, feather tails wagging and tongues lolling. "What good girls! Yes, you are, Bella, Bonnie!"

I laugh behind my mobile as I hold it up to capture the moment on video. We want to keep track of their growth just as we would babies. We'll put the videos and photos into digital journals so we can look at them for years to come.

Snow falls and makes the scene even more picturesque. The snow-covered Swiss Alps rise in the background. They glitter like diamonds as the sunlight reflects off of the mountain slopes. Below us Verbier Village spreads out. The center festive with the Christmas market where stalls offer hand-knit scarves, hand-crafted wooden toys, and tasty treats with mulled wine and hot chocolate. The streets lined with wreaths, bells, and fairy lights that twinkle throughout the day and shine bright at night.

Roger and Leonie have their *Chalet de la Joie*—a magnificent five story, twelve bedroom residence where the Steeles stay for Christmas and New Year's—within STEELE Verbier Chalets. Dad Connor and Mom Lucie purchased an equally amazing chalet for the Jacksons' winter retreat last year, close to Roger and Leonie's.

Verbs, as the in-the-know jet-set calls it, is a town in the Swiss Alps. A part of the Valais canton in the southwest of Switzerland, France borders Verbier to the west with Italy to the south. It's the most exclusive ski destination in the world.

It's the winter version of Monaco, with the difference being people who go to Monaco want to watch or be watched. Whereas Verbier has an understated style where wealth is glamorous, stylish and tasteful. People are here for the reasons one goes to a ski resort—the superb skiing. Not to mention the phenomenal bars and restaurants; the après-ski is perfect for party lovers. Verbier is a glamorous winter playground.

The luxury chalets occupy the area south of the Médran lift. They're slightly away from town along Rue de Médran, where the extra space means they are rarely overlooked and have a private, exclusive vibe. The residential compound is opposite to the STEELE Verbier that's closer to the heart of the village square. The concept is for the STEELE Verbier Chalets to access the resort for its five-star amenities. The most important include the luxury thermal bath spa and the three Jackson Corporation restaurants headed by Lucien.

The location is a popular destination for our social circle. It's where Callum and I reconnected a few years ago. I've been nervous Lachlan and I would bump into him and Fiona during the holidays. So far, so good…

Besides, Lachlan keeps me occupied totally. Mornings snowboarding or ice skating; afternoons strolling through the Christmas market, where we find new goodies each time; evenings dining with family or cuddled up in our suite in front of the fireplace at Jackson Verbier Chalet.

He surprised me with a fully stocked wardrobe and all of my favorite toiletries, since I used to stay with Roger and Leonie. When I moved in with Lachlan, he told me he'd buy us a separate chalet if I preferred our own space. I told him no way since I love being around family, especially during the holidays. I could tell he was happy to hear my response, since his eyes glowed with love. He's as much a family man as I am a family woman.

Now, as I watch him play with Bella and Bonnie, he laughs at their shenanigans and rolls around in the snow with them. It makes my heart swell. He'll make a wonderful father. If only I can get pregnant and give him his heirs…

Lachlan must sense my change in mood because he sits up and cocks his head at me. Even though his mirrored Ray-Ban Aviators cover his eyes, I can tell he's concerned. I plaster a grin on my face to keep from ruining his fun. No need for both of us to suffer.

Although I expect caring for the puppies will distract me. They'll help with my mothering skills. If I can handle two rambunctious four-legged, furry wildlings, I can handle their human counterparts! The thought makes me smile, and Lachlan relax.

My mobile rings with a call from Starr. My smile widens.

She, Lola, and Leonie have been super attentive and helpful. Their support and words of encouragement help me tremendously. Part of my stress was not being as good as them in giving their husbands babies—like Starr pregnant with another set of twins. But as they say, just enjoy all the lovemaking sessions. And I do, trust!

"Hi, Starr!" I answer with a grin.

"Hey, Hal! Where are you guys? Malcolm and I are going to town for lunch. Do you and Lachlan want to join us?" She asks.

I ask Lachlan, and he nods vigorously. We've been out playing for over an hour and haven't eaten since breakfast.

I tell Starr we'll pick them up since we're higher up on the mountain.

Once the butler has Bella and Bonnie in hand, Lachlan and I hop into the Range Rover SVAutobiography. It's a brief ride to *Chalet de la Joie*, and Malcolm and Starr wait out front.

"Hey!" I say as I climb from the passenger seat to let Malcolm ride shotgun.

"Hey, yourself, little sis!" Malcolm responds as he busses my cheek, then helps Starr and me into the back seats. "And hello to you too, Little Lord Fauntleroy."

Lachlan rolls his eyes and shakes his head at Malcolm's running joke.

"Nice to see you, too, Malcolm," he replies, then grins. "Starr, as lovely as always."

She grins back at him and rubs his arm.

"Ignore, Malcolm. He'll get over you being married to Haley at some point," she says. Then, when Malcolm guffaws, she adds, "We can hope…"

Everyone laughs.

During the ride down to Verbier Village, we chat about going to the clubs tonight. We'll start at Farm Club Verbier and end at Public Verbier. I cannot wait to get my groove on in my new slinky, silver lamé mini dress!

Lachlan pulls in front of STEELE Verbier for the valet to park the truck. We stroll down Rue de Médran, scanning menus until we come across a restaurant that suits our tastebuds. Malcolm holds the door while we go in.

I have to suppress an eye roll when the hostesses gawk

at my brother and my husband. These women could not care less about the guys with Starr and me. They draw women's attention like moths to a flame. But if they don't stop drooling, I'm going to burn them.

As we settle into our banquette, I scan the room to check for Callum and Fiona. No sign of them, I think as I breathe a sigh of relief. I don't want another encounter like the last time I was in a restaurant, and Callum appeared unexpectedly.

Malcolm fusses over Starr to help her select her meal. He pulls his mobile from his pocket to check what she can and cannot eat while pregnant. She waves him off with a giggle. Then orders what she wants: a hearty dish of beef stew and vegetables. Malcolm approves.

I watch Lachlan from beneath my eyelashes to gauge his reaction to their interaction. He's oblivious as he reads the menu. A pang hits my chest as I wonder if he'll have the chance to worry about me. I glance down at my menu to hold back tears. Then glance up when Lachlan reaches up to rub my cheek with his thumb.

He smiles at me.

"And what will you have, babe?" He asks.

I have to bite my tongue for a bit of pain to stop the tears from falling. He's so attuned to me, it's shocking. After a deep, cleansing breath, I smile back at him.

"Do you want to share the cheese fondue with seared steak and frites?" I ask.

"Sounds delicious," he responds with a grin as his eyes fill with love.

My cheeks heat from the intensity. I love my man so much.

We place our orders, and the talk turns to an idea Harris has about a LEVELS here.

"Lucien tells me you're getting closer to LEVELS Verbier," Lachlan says to Malcolm.

He and Lucien founded the global, luxury, members-only BDSM/dance clubs after Lucien finished his hospitality and culinary training at Le Cordon Bleu in Paris. With locations in New York, Paris, London, and Beverly Hills, they're the places the crème de la crème of society goes to slake their sexual needs. Particularly since LEVELS requires every member and their guests to undergo in-depth background checks and to sign ironclad nondisclosure agreements. The clubs provide relative safety for consensual activities: dancing, dining, or sexual.

All the guys are Global All Access members and Lola, Leonie, and Starr. It wasn't until my relationship with Lachlan he bought me one, too. The Big Four would have lost their everlasting minds had I been a member. Even so, they gave Lachlan a hard time...

"We're awaiting approvals for a location atop the mountain for spectacular views to take the Mile High Club to another level," Malcolm replies with a wicked grin. "Not for you, Haley!"

I open my mouth for a retort. But he chuckles.

"Just make sure I am not present should you... take part," he says, shaking his head as his gaze flicks between Lachlan and me.

"We will be sure of that guaranteed," Lachlan replies with a smirk.

Starr and I turn to each other, and we burst out laughing. Alpha Doms… have got to love them.

For the rest of our lunch, we enjoy each other's company and the delicious food. Afterwards, we go to the Christmas market in search of more treasures.

Vendors fill their stalls with handcrafted music boxes and toys, knit sweaters, scarves, and gloves, and candles and ornaments. The cloves and spices of mulled wine mix with baked goods like bredele, semi-sweet cakes, pretzels, and macarons to scent the crisp air. Carolers dressed in costumes stroll through the aisles singing cheerfully and ringing bells.

Starr loops her arm through mine and points to a stall with stained glass ornaments.

"Ooh! Those remind me of your wedding at Jackson Chapel! Let's get some," she says as she pulls me along.

I laugh and hurry beside my sister.

It's such a festive atmosphere, I set aside all worries about babies.

"IF YOU DON'T STOP SHAKING your ass, I'm going to plug it with my cock. Right here. Right. Now."

Caught up in the hedonistic atmosphere, I throw my arms overhead and shimmy even more against my husband's thick length as we grind on the packed dance floor at Farm Club Verbier.

Since it opened in the early 1970s, it's become a world-famous dance and nightclub. Its popularity hasn't flagged for decades. Symbolized by its glamorous vibe and great reputation, people refer to it as the Studio 54 of Verbier.

A glance to my left reveals Harris wedged between two scantily clad, long-legged women. One of his hands disappears under the hem of the blonde's dress while his other one reaches back to grab the ass of the brunette behind him. The women grope him wherever their hands can touch. The trio might as well get a room! I laugh at my randy twin. When will he learn?

Chase has Lydie glued to his massive six-foot-five-inch frame as they rock to the beat. His sizable hands cup her ass to lock her to his groin. It's good to see her let loose for a change. Lachlan seems to like Chase. So it's all good.

Even though the club is jumping, I can still make out my brothers—Steele and Jackson—since they're amongst the tallest men here, being well over six feet. Everyone parties hardcore beneath the flashing disco lights.

A smack to my ass brings me back to my sexy AF Lord. I bite my lip to hold back a yelp as I rise to my toes in my strappy sandals. The thin metallic material of my mini dress offers no cushion from his well-placed spank.

"Last warning, Little Temptress."

I lower my arms and reach around to grab his firm ass, then squeeze. He growls in my ear. Warm breath skitters across my sweat-dampened skin. My nipples harden as I arch my back and moan wantonly.

My Lord presses kisses to the side of my neck in a trail

to my bare shoulder. His lips draw back as his teeth mark the skin. He sucks, then laves his mark. With a satisfied purr, he spins me around and covers my mouth with his.

His dominant possession makes my juices pool within my G-string. I rub my thighs together for some relief to the ache in my swollen clit. The sensuous bass of the music thrums through my body, mixing with his touch to drive me wild with desire. I can't wait any longer.

"Right here. Right. Now."

My Lord freezes and pulls back to stare down at me.

I meet his questioning expression with a lust-filled one. Then I raise up on my toes to cup the back of his head, drawing his mouth down to mine for a searing kiss. Our tongues duel for control. He wins with a guttural growl. I mewl in submission.

Before I can open my eyes, My Lord grabs my hand and pushes his way through the crowded dance floor. I quicken my pace to match his long, purposeful strides. I can't see beyond his broad back but trust him to guide me.

Moments later, we break free, and he leads me towards the restrooms. We don't stop at their doors, rather continue down the darkened hallway. At the end, he pulls me into an alcove and presses me against the wall.

My fingers caress his erection through his black leather pants. He swats my hand away, pops the button, and unzips the fly. I slip my G-string off and crumble the drenched scrap of silver silk in my hand.

He grips beneath my thighs to wrap my legs around his hips, then smacks his hands on either side of my head.

Using his powerful thighs, he holds me aloft and snaps his hips forward. In one thrust, he impales me on his ginormous dick.

We groan in unison.

The sounds of skin on skin slapping and the squelching of my soaked pussy surround us. As he pistons into my core, I bow my body and dig my fingernails into his shoulders. My mouth hangs slack with silent cries of carnal pleasure. He grunts.

When my pussy walls quiver from my impending climax, My Lord doubles his pace. I keen. He slams his mouth to mine, swallowing each of my throaty moans. My back slams against the wall over and over as he chases his release.

As his dick swells impossibly larger, he roars into my mouth and smacks the wall with his hands. His entire body quakes as copious ropes of his hot seed shoot out to coat my womb. Another orgasm rips through me in response. He groans as my pussy milks him dry.

My Lord buries his face in my neck, panting as his thrusts slow down to a lazy pace. I caress his back to soothe him.

"Fuck, Little Temptress. So good, baby... So good..." he says in a raspy voice.

I purr in the back of my throat, equally satisfied as my man with our erotic tango.

LACHLAN

The sun sparkles on the snow-capped peaks of the Swiss Alps, set against a topaz blue sky as we ride the Médran gondola to the top of the mountain. It's New Year's Eve, and we're out en masse for an early morning run. The Jackson and Steele clans, Chase, Knights, and Beaulieus plan to make our way from the top of the mountain piste to the base lodge. Once we make it to the bottom of the mountain, we'll have brunch on the lodge's deck.

The gondola's glass ceiling and windows frame the breathtaking panoramic views. But nothing compares to the beauty of my wife. Her dove gray eyes spark brighter than the sun as she laughs at a joke her twin made. Adorable dimples appear in her heart-shaped face. She's so at peace now. My heart swells with gratitude.

It does her good to be with family. The support her sisters give to her keeps my wife from fretting too much about babies. Even though I'm concerned and spoke with my doctor to re-confirm his findings, I don't worry her about it. It'll happen or not. Either way, we have each other and now our fur babies—Bella and Bonnie.

"Hey, bro, what's up?"

I turn at the sound of Baz's voice. Of course, my best friend would pick up on my state of mind.

"So grateful for my wife and our family," I say with a smile.

Baz glances over at Lola, then his eyes scan the rest as they stand around us, and he nods in agreement.

"We are a blessed bunch, huh?" He says with a satisfied smirk.

"I couldn't agree with you more, brother," I respond with a chuckle.

Soon, we pile out of the gondola and gather our gear.

"Get ready to eat my powder, Lachlan!" My Baby Girl says smugly as she bends over to check the bindings of her Rossignol skis.

I grin stupidly at the sight of her round ass looking like a full moon in an all-white Moncler Grenoble two-piece ski suit. I nearly throw my head back and howl lustily.

Then I wince when a ringing in my helmet follows a knock against it. I swing my head around to find Harris behind me. His ski pole drops back to his side.

"Quit ogling my twin's ass, Little Lord Fauntleroy, and get out of my way," he says as he pushes off and skis past me.

His partner in crime chuckles as he goes past.

"Bloody wanker!" I shout after Harris and Laurent. "Wait until we get to the bottom!"

I turn back around just in time to see my wife push off behind them.

"Bloody hell," I mutter out loud as I step into my binders to pursue them down the mountain.

"Out of the way! Coming through!"

My Baby Girl says to Malcolm and Starr, who still haven't stepped into their skis. He frowns, and My Baby Girl's tinkling laughter trails behind her as she zips ahead of me on the black diamond piste. Her fleeting figure a blur on her skis.

The sunlight glints off of her silver helmet with her eyes covered by matching gray Dragon googles. She zooms along as her long, toned legs help her carve through the fresh powder. She moves with ease and grace down the expert slope since she's skied from the time she could walk—as have we all.

My wife and I pulled a twin move wearing all white. I opted for a Moncler Grenoble hooded jacket with pale gray snowflakes on a white background and ski trousers. A Kask silver helmet with Anon mirrored googles and Hestra ski gloves complete my gear.

I salute Malcolm and wave to Starr as I schuss past them on Salomon skis.

It's a popular time to come out. So I bob and weave around other skiers to catch My Baby Girl. She laughs when I reach her and drops into a tuck. I growl. The chase is on!

. . .

MOMENTS LATER, we come to a stop in front of the base lodge. Our ski butlers help us remove our equipment and hand us our heated après-ski hats, sunglasses, and footwear.

"Ha! I beat you, Lachlan!" My wife gloats, her cheeks flushed from the race and the cold air.

I just smile since I let her win. Happy wife, happy life and all. I brush my lips across her forehead and place my hand on her lower back to guide her into the lodge. We walk through the great room on our way to the deck, kept warm by heat lamps.

We stop and chat with a few friends and acquaintances, also in Verbs for the holidays. Out of my periphery, a flash of pink catches my attention. I turn to see Graham and Fiona approaching. Instinctively, my hand slips around my wife's waist.

Mid-conversation with a friend, she glances up at me questioningly. Then stops speaking all together when she spies Graham and Fiona. With a final word to her friend, my wife turns into my side fully to face the couple.

"Happy New Year," Graham says with his hand extended to me.

I grip it and respond the same.

Fiona smiles at me then offers double kisses to my wife, who also responds in kind.

"We set the date for our wedding and want to let you know we'll send an invitation to you. It would be nice if you join us," Fiona says.

"Congratulations, and we wish you well," my wife

replies. Then looks at me and continues, "If our calendar allows, I'm sure we will attend your wedding."

"Yes, congratulations," I respond, and clap Graham on the shoulder. "Now, if you will excuse us. Our family awaits for brunch."

"Of course, enjoy," Graham says as his eyes flit to my wife.

I don't miss the brief expression of regret in his eyes before he turns to take Fiona's elbow and walks away.

Poor fellow. Haley Jackson is mine.

I take her hand, and we continue through to the deck.

We settle between Roger seated with Leonie and Lucien next to Harris at the table. The bounty of delicious food and steaming beverages perfect to make up for the energy spent on the challenging run. Once everyone arrives, we dig into the feast.

"So what's next on the agenda, Papa Griswold?" Leonie asks, referring to Roger as Clark Griswold from *National Lampoon's Christmas Vacation*.

Everyone laughs at the running joke, knowing Roger and his planned-down-to-the-minute activities for our time in Verbier.

"Hardy har har, Mama Griswold," he responds, not at all bothered by her teasing. "After this deluxe meal, time for a walk through town. And if you are good… we'll spend the afternoon soaking in the thermal baths at Lavey-les-Bains. *Bien?*"

"Ah, *oui, Mon Cœur!*" Leonie exclaims, clapping her hands and doing a shimmy in her chair.

"Spa Time!" Lydie laughs. "Now I can definitely get on board with that agenda item!"

The girls—including our mothers—chatter on about the benefits of the baths and the beauty products they prefer. The guys turn to talk about the sporting activities Roger has on the list. I agree to the snowmobiling and the off-piste run.

The sounds of shouts reach us from the front of the lodge. As the hullabaloo intensifies, people gather at the railings of the deck to get a better view. Whispers of a major crash and an intensive injury make Malcolm rise from his seat to get more information. Starr follows him. After a while, they return.

"What happened?"

"Is the person okay?"

We turn to listen as Malcolm fills us in. We agree it was good of him to offer the couple his doctor's information since the woman hit a tree and undoubtedly has a spinal injury. A look of concern for their brother passes between Baz and Roger. Malcolm smiles and inclines his head.

Roger nods in understanding. Then he claps his hands for everyone's attention.

"Time to move to the next item on our New Year's Day agenda, folks. Right this way!" Roger announces with a smirk as like a tour guide, he directs us to leave the lodge.

We laugh at his antics and head to the G-Wagens for a stop at the chalets before we go to the thermal baths.

It's the perfect time to relax in Lavey-led-Bains's idyllic setting surrounded by fragrant pine trees and the snow-capped Swiss Alps. We can all use a break after this roller-coaster year.

* * *

"WHAT DID you wish for at the stroke of midnight?"

My Baby Girl asks as her chin rests on my chest lying in our bed the next morning.

I run my fingers through her mussed ebony waves as I stare into her gorgeous grays so full of love. My hand drops to cup her cheek, and she tilts her head to kiss my palm. Then she brings her eyes back to mine.

"I wished we have the best year imaginable. For all of your dreams to come true," I respond.

Her eyes brighten as tears shimmer.

I shake my head.

"No more tears, Mrs. Jackson. We will release all negative thoughts and only focus on the positive as much as we can. Do you understand?" I say.

She presses her face to my chest and nods.

I chuckle and move her hair behind an ear. I won't allow her to hide behind the glossy curtain. We have to move behind the stress of babies. It makes no sense to dwell on it.

"Now, you know what I say when you do not verbalize your response, Naughty Girl," I chide. "I will ask again. Do you understand?"

As she sighs, her warm breath skitters across my skin.

I wait patiently for her response.

Finally, she lifts her head and gazes at me with narrowed eyes. A bit of her fire back in their depths.

"I understand, My Lord," she huffs. Then, as she sits up, she mumbles, "Not that I have to like it, *Sir*!"

Quick as a flash, I flip her onto her back and cover her with my body. My hands grip her wrists, pressed into the mattress on either side of her face. The tips of our noses touch as our eyes lock. We mingle breath during our face-off.

When she lowers her gaze, the thick fringe of her eyelashes dusts the tops of her pinkened cheeks. She wriggles in my grasp and bucks her hips up to lift me from her body.

Naughty Girl has some kick in her.

A wicked chuckle slips from my mouth, and I drag the tip of my nose along her cheek to her neck. I press a kiss to the tender skin at the base, then continue down to her tits. I kiss each peaked nipple. Then lift my gaze to her face. My tongue sweeps over my lips as I purr at her.

She trembles.

"I love you, Haley Jackson. Now, I will prove just how very much," I purr.

HALEY

"Lachlan, it's only food poisoning on top of a cold... I know... Yes, of course I'll call you after I speak with the doctor... I love you, too, My Lord. Now, get to your meeting already!"

I'd laugh at his overly protective behavior, but my stomach and head hurt too much. I thought the cold would go away by now since we've been back from Verbier for weeks. Also, I think I'm still getting used to the Scottish weather. February is rough!

"We arrived, My Lady."

Theodore rouses me from my musings and helps me from the back of the Rolls-Royce sedan.

I smile and thank him as another wave of nausea hits me. His grip tightens on my elbow when I misstep.

"Please be careful, My Lady," he urges as he guides me to the front door of my physician's office building.

"Thank you, Theodore. I'll send a text message when

I'm ready," I say with another smile. Ugh!

I don't have long to wait before the nurse escorts me to the examination room. After vitals and a urine sample, she leaves. As I sit on the exam table, I scroll through my work emails.

Harris has a new project he wants to discuss with me. It sounds pretty cool. I shoot him a quick response to talk later today. I Slack with my administrative assistant—Douglas Washington—to tell him to set time aside for my meeting with Harris. Once I leave the doctor, I'll head straight to the office for my team's weekly status meeting. Since the holidays passed, our workload ramped back up. It feels good to be busy again.

A knock at the door, and Dr. Lorna Breck enters with the nurse.

"Hello, Lady Aboyne, it's good to see you," Dr. Breck says. "My nurse tells me you think you have a cold and food poisoning. Well, I can confirm that differs from my diagnosis."

I frown, wondering how the heck she can diagnose me without an examination. As I open my mouth to say so, she smiles and stops in front of me.

"You really don't need to have an appointment with *me*. You need one with Dr. Ross," she says. Then continues at my look of confusion, "You're pregnant."

"—Lady Aboyne. Can you hear me?"

My eyes flutter open to the white ceiling above me. I tilt my head towards Dr. Breck's voice to find her staring down at me.

"You fainted. But we caught you. You're lying on the examination table. How do you feel?" She tells me.

I shake my head to clear it. My mind plays back what happened before I passed out.

"You're pregnant."

With a gasp, I jolt to a sitting position, then put my hand on the table to steady myself. I stare with wide eyes and my mouth agape at Dr. Breck.

She smiles and pats my hand.

"Yes, you're pregnant, Lady Aboyne. I apologize for startling you—"

"No, no!" I cut her off as I wave my hand. As tears fill my eyes, I ask, "How do you know?"

"The levels in your urine show pregnancy. I could do a check for a cold and food poisoning. But I think it's best you meet with your OB-GYN before I administer any medication," Dr. Breck responds with a smile. "Congratulations!"

I thank her and hurry to re-dress. My mind still processes me being pregnant. Pregnant! Holy shit! I cannot believe it! A bout of giggles overtakes me as I zip my Manolo Blahnik thigh-high boots. Laugher turns to more tears. Tears of pure happiness.

After a silent prayer of thanks, I call Dr. Astrid Ross and send another thanks since she has time for me in thirty minutes. A quick text to Theodore, and I rush from the office, waving at the receptionist as I zoom past her desk with my mobile to my ear.

"Excuse me, I have to take this call."

Rustling sounds, and Lachlan returns to the line.

"What—"

"WE'RE PREGNANT!!!"

A clatter as his mobile drops to the floor and a shout sound through my mobile's line.

I laugh out loud, ignoring the people around me as I rush through the lobby.

"*Taing do, Dhia!!!*"

"Yes! *Thank you, God*, my love!!!"

I slide into the back seat of the Rolls-Royce as I tell Theodore the address for Dr. Ross.

"Baby Girl, that's close to my office. I'll meet you there—"

"Oh! Then we can pick you up," I say, then tell Theodore about the change. "I'm so nervous, though. She didn't say how far along or—"

"Stop. We will only have positive thoughts, remember?" Lachlan interrupts.

I nod even though he can't see me, then respond, "Yes, yes, of course!"

We only end our call when Lachlan enters the elevator. By the time we reach Jackson Town House, I'm bouncing on the back seat, eager to get more news. I scoot over when I spot Lachlan pacing out front. He races to the sedan and waves Theodore off from exiting to get the door, telling him to go man, go!

My husband pulls me onto his lap and buries his face in my neck. I stroke his back when I feel his warm tears on my skin. Tears spill from my own eyes as he rocks me. Too overcome with emotion, we hold each other until Theodore announces we arrived.

I sit back and wipe my husband's handsome face clear of tears as he does the same for mine. We smile at each other, not needing words to express our joy and love.

We walk hand in hand to the townhouse's doorway. Lachlan holds it open as I enter, then takes my hand again with a lopsided grin. I giggle and reach up to kiss his lips.

The receptionist greets us, and we take a seat in the waiting room. Another couple sits on a sofa across from us. She's visibly pregnant with her hand resting on her belly. Her smile turns into a double take, as though she recognizes us. The husband nods. We smile and nod in return.

"Are you the Earl and Countess of Aboyne?" The wife asks as her eyes flit between Lachlan and me.

Her husband shakes his head and takes her hand to stop her from speaking.

She sits up and smiles.

"I only ask because I want to tell you, the work you're doing with underserved girls to increase their awareness of technology is phenomenal. It's nice to see those with titles actually doing actual work and not only cutting ribbons and smiling for the cameras before they disappear until the next photo-op," she says.

"Thank you so much. I appreciate your kind words. Technology is my passion, and the more girls can get involved in the industry, the better it will be," I respond humbly.

A nurse enters the waiting room and beckons for the

couple to follow her. We exchange good lucks as they leave.

"I told you you're making an impact, Baby Girl," Lachlan says softly. "You're going to make a wonderful mum."

Tears clog my throat, so I nod mutely at my husband.

"Lord and Lady Aboyne."

We glance up at the door and rise when a nurse beckons for us.

Lachlan squeezes my hand, and I smile up at him as I whisper, "And you will be an incredible father, my love."

He nods and bites his lower lip.

After I slip out of my pencil skirt and silk blouse, he chuckles, shaking his head.

"If it were another time, I would have you against the wall in a second flat. You're so sexy in your black lace lingerie and fuck-me boots," he says.

I unhook my bra and toss it at him with a smirk.

"Well, I certainly hope you don't intend to become a monk, Mr. Jackson. Because I don't intend to be a nun!" I retort as my thong lands on his lap.

He brings the wisp of lace to his nose and sniffs.

"Absolutely not, Mrs. Jackson!" He exclaims.

I nod and put a gown on. He helps me onto the examination table and kisses me softly.

A knock at the door makes us part.

"Hello, Lord and Lady Aboyne! I hear congratulations are in order!" Dr. Ross says as she enters with the nurse, who smiles.

"Yes!" We respond in unison, then laugh.

"Well, let's have a look, shall we?" She says with a grin.

After the exam, Dr. Ross places gel on my belly and tells Lachlan to join us. He jumps from the chair and rushes over, emerald eyes wide. She moves the ultrasound wand over my belly and works the machine. Lachlan and I stare at the screen, entranced.

Then she turns on the sound.

Multiple sets of rhythmic beats fill the room.

"Why does our baby's heart sound like that?" I cry.

Dr. Ross smiles and points at the screen.

"Look here… here, and… here," she says.

We peer closer and notice three distinct babies.

"THREE!" Lachlan and I shout at once. Then CRASH.

My head swings around to find Lachlan no longer by my side. The nurse gasps.

"Lachlan!!!" I cry as I struggle to sit up.

A groan floats up from the floor.

Dr. Ross and the nurse kneel quickly on either side of my husband, who's passed out flat on his back.

It proves too much for him.

More giggles burst from my mouth even as I try to cover it with both hands. Tears fill my eyes as laughter turns to snorts. What a story to tell our children, I muse.

He opens his eyes and sits up with the help of the doctor and the nurse, who appear to hold back their own laughter.

"Lord Aboyne, how do you feel? Any pain?" Dr. Ross asks with a twinkle in her honey brown eyes.

Color darkens Lachlan's cheeks as he shakes his head

and climbs to his feet.

Still giggling, I open my arms to him, and he leans over to bury his face in my neck.

"We'll give you a moment," Dr. Ross says.

"Oh, no, no. Kindly continue. Forgive me—"

"Nothing to forgive, My Lord! Trust me, you are not the first nor will you be the last man to pass out in this room!" Dr. Ross says with a warm smile.

She explains we're twelve-weeks pregnant with triplets and can learn their sex in four to six weeks. She advises I will need to have a prenatal visit once a month, then from weeks twenty-four through thirty-two every two weeks. With triplets, she expects me to give birth around week thirty-two.

As I re-dress, Lachlan stares at me in awe. I walk over to him and take his hand to place it on my only slightly pronounced lower belly.

"Your babies grow inside of me, Mr. Jackson," I whisper as I run my fingers through his slicked back hair, now not so neat from him tugging the strands. "You did it during Thanksgiving based on the timing, my love."

He wraps his arms around my hips and presses three kisses to my belly.

"Daddy loves you so very much, little ones, and can't wait to hold you close to my heart," he murmurs.

I swipe tears from my cheeks. My heart is so full of love and joy.

After a moment, he rises and cups my face.

"And I love you, Mummy, so very… very… much…" he

says between kisses.

"We love you, too, Daddy," I respond. "Now let's meet with the doctor so we can hurry and tell everyone!"

Lachlan smirks and grabs my hand.

After we meet with Dr. Ross and schedule my appointments, we settle onto the back seat of the sedan. Lachlan grins at me, and I grin at him. We're in a daze.

"My Lady, Douglas called the car. He said you had a meeting," Theodore says once he's behind the wheel. "Shall we return to your office? And you, My Lord?"

I smack my hand to my forehead. Damn! I completely forgot!

"Baby Girl, I'm canceling the rest of my day. You should do the same. In fact, I have an idea," Lachlan says.

I shift in my seat to look at him. He's grinning wider than the Cheshire Cat. Emerald eyes blaze green fire.

"You want to tell everyone. Well, let's fly to New York City now and tell them in person," he says triumphantly. "There's nothing more important than family and this is a stupendous occasion!"

Now, my smile beats his as I wrap my arms around his neck and squeal.

"WELL, Hal, while we're all so very glad you want to make dinner for us, tell us why you had to fly over to do so, unexpectedly…"

Harris says drolly.

A few things worked in favor for Lachlan and me.

1. A five-hour time difference makes it dinnertime.

2. Malcolm and Starr stopped by New York on their way from business in Europe before they continued home to Beverly Hills.

3. Roger and Leonie flew from their home base of Paris for business in the city.

4. Lucien is in town for a conference instead of being in Paris, his principal residence.

I bite my lower lip, unable to contain myself any longer, and glance up at Lachlan.

He grins down at me and nods.

"WE'RE PREGNANT!!!"

The living room in our duplex penthouse at The STEELE Tower explodes in a cacophony of shouts, screams, and gasps followed by wolf whistles and words of congratulations.

I'm swept from Lachlan's side as The Moms pull me into their embrace. I'm wedged between them, then my sisters.

Dad Connor sings in Scottish Gaelic while hugging Lachlan, who's then pulled into a hug by my father and given slaps on the back by our brothers.

It's a total lovefest!

"Oh, shit! Do you smell smoke?!"

Everyone screeches to a halt at Roger's observation. He rushes from the living room to the kitchen. We scramble after him. Smoke tendrils curl from the Wolf wall oven.

"Damn! The bread!" I yell and rush forward.

Lachlan yanks me back while Lucien races past us.

"Keep the door shut and step back!" He yells as he turns the oven off. "The fire will go out on its own from lack of oxygen."

Everyone sighs in relief.

Then Harris, shaking his head in mock disappointment, says, "The bread? Damn. Well, so much for the cooking lessons you've been taking, Hal…"

I throw the dish towel I was going to use on the fire at him. He catches it and chuckles.

"Now, I'm not the only one known for being a terror in the kitchen! *Non?*" Leonie giggles as she wraps an arm around my shoulders. "Do not worry, *chérie*. That's what a chef is for! Right Lucien?"

Everyone laughs.

"Exactly!" Lucien says, chuckling as he eyes the wall oven. The smoke already abates with the heat gone. "No offense, sis. How about we go to my steakhouse instead? A preggie lady needs her protein!"

Another raucous uproar, and we troop out of the kitchen to the entry foyer for our family's private elevator. The guys make calls to our drivers. While Lucien calls the general manager of his restaurant to claim the private room for our impromptu dinner party.

"You see, Haley, the universe has a way of making everything right. It may not happen when you want. But it will happen when it should." Starr whispers as she loops her arm through mine.

I smile at my sister with tears shining in my eyes.

"How right you are, sis. How right you are."

LACHLAN

"Oh… My… God… Lachlan… Fuuuck!!!"

My wife's scream of carnal pleasure is erotic music to my ears.

Her slick pussy meets my forceful thrusts as each arc of the sex swing impales her on my rigid ten inches. The dove gray of her irises disappears as they roll back to reveal the whites of the eyes. Tendrils of ebony hair stick to the sides of her sweaty, flushed face as she thrashes her head from side to side.

It's the only part of her body she can move since I have her harnessed into the sex swing, wrists and ankles bound to the cords. She's spread wide open for my carnal pleasure.

A pleasure so intense, my thighs quiver and my knees wobble as I throw my head back and punch the musky sex scented air with a mighty roar. From my crown to the tips of my toes, erotic energy zings down and up to zap my heavy balls. Another roar reverberates around the play-room in our Aberdeen penthouse.

"FUUUCK!!! YES! YES! YES!!!"

I grip her hips to lock her in place as I bow my body rising to the balls of my feet as thick ropes of jizz explode from my cock. My hold so tight my fingers are bound to leave marks on her skin. A combination of her juices and my cream leaks from her pussy and drips to the hardwood floor.

Lightning flashes behind my eyes squeezed shut as the aftershocks of a massive release roll through me. I pant as my heartbeat races from the carnal exhilaration. My entire body thrums.

Compressions on my cock make me groan and open my eyes.

My wife stares up at me lasciviously. Eyes narrowed as the tip of her little pink tongue darts out to swipe across her lower lip before she pulls the plump flesh between her teeth. She purrs and squeezes my cock with the inner walls of her pussy—grown stronger by her regular Kegel exercises, as advised by her sisters.

And damn, don't the stainless-steel balls work.

"I want some more," she purrs.

I blink and shake my head.

A fourth round???

Fuck. Me.

My horny Hot Mama blames her urges on the hormones: *Two boys, Lachlan? And a girl? All swirled up with my hormones!*

Yeah, we found out we're expecting two boys and a girl a few days ago. And since—well, truth be told, even before—my Hot Mama can't get enough of her Daddy Dom.

I run my fingers through my sweat-soaked hair and shake my head at my wife, who winks at me. Little Temptress.

"Woman, you will be the death of me yet..." I grouse.

But damned if my cock doesn't twitch from more flutters of her pussy along my length. I slip out, drawing a groan of loss from both of us. I need to free her from the sex swing and tend to her with some almost-aftercare before the next round.

She pouts as I loosen her ankles and rub them. I press a kiss to each one, then reach up for her wrists. She sighs as I massage her arms from her wrists to her shoulders. As I unbuckle the harness straps, she leans forward and drapes her arms over my shoulders.

"You're the sexiest Daddy Dom I've ever seen," she whispers in my ear, then licks the delicate shell.

A shiver skitters down my spine, reawakening my semi-erect cock.

"I am the *only* Daddy Dom you have ever seen, Naughty Girl," I growl.

She yelps from a smack on her ass.

I carry her to the king-size bed in the center of the playroom. Gently, I lay her down, then press a kiss to her belly full of my babies. Her fingers thread through my hair as she sighs.

"Why do you have to waste time cleaning me when you're only going to make me messy again?"

I glance up at her pouty face and chuckle. But ignore her as I rise and stride to the en suite bathroom.

"I love being sticky from you!" She shouts after me.

When I return with a clean cock and a warm damp cloth, my wife is curled onto one side with her head on her forearm. The other hand rests on her babies bump. Soft snores fill the air.

I snort and smile at the sight.

She may be a horny Hot Mama. But she tires easily.

Without disturbing her too much, I wipe her face, neck, and thighs. She's too exhausted to notice.

I pull the emerald green silk and velvet cover from one side of the bed, curl my body around hers, and settle the cover over us. Even in her sleep, she reaches for me and places my hand on her belly. I kiss the back of her head as I whisper words of love for my wife and my babies. Then we sleep peacefully.

"Oh, yes, it's extremely important to get everything in order now. You don't want to wait until the last few weeks—"

"Especially carrying triplets! *Mon Dieu!*"

"Right! You have even less time to get ready. And you're halfway there now!"

"Oh, hi, Lachlan!"

"Ciao, Papa!"

I chuckle and wave at my sisters-in-law.

They're on a video conference with My Baby Girl to help her plan for our babies' arrival. I couldn't help but to listen from the door and come in to say hi. It's great how much they support her.

"It's good you're here. We have some questions for you, Lachlan," Starr says. "Do you have time?"

I grin and respond, "For my wife and you lovely ladies, but of course!"

They giggle and launch into a list of questions.

We spend the next forty minutes going over details until we have a well-laid-out plan. I actually feel a lot better not having realized the extent of logistics, space, and timing. I thank the trio and leave the room for them to chat some more with My Baby Girl.

I call Baz to get his side of things as I head to my home office.

"Hey, Lach. What's up, bro?" He asks after the first ring.

I chuckle, sure he was awaiting my call thanks to Lola.

"Hey, I just left Haley with Lola, Leonie, and Starr on video conference. They are a wealth of knowledge for us. Now, I want to pick your brain," I respond.

"You know I got your back, bro!" Baz chuckles. "So shoot."

"Cool, thanks! I suggest you get a snifter of your Jackson Special Blend Scotch. I sure as hell am because we'll need it for this convo!" With a laugh, I close the door to my office and head for the bar cart.

"On it!" Baz replies.

I get comfortable on the leather tufted sofa and launch my own list of questions for my best friend's advice. After a half an hour of baby prep talk, babymoon and push present —push present???—suggestions, diaper changing hits or misses, and post-natal intimacy, we shoot the shit.

My Baby Girl pokes her head in the office, and I tell Baz I have to go. We make plans for squash and dinner when I fly to New York City for business next week, then end our call.

"We had quite a day of learning, huh?" I ask as I hold my arms out for my wife to lie on the sofa with me. "How do you feel?"

She scoots her back closer to my front and rests her hand on top of mine as it draws circles on her babies bump. The jewels in her engagement ring and eternity wedding band glint in the lamplight.

"Superb. I made a spreadsheet of all the tasks and will create an app to track everything. It'll make things easier for us," she responds, then tilts her head to look at me. "What about you? Was Baz helpful, too?"

I nod and tell her about our conversation—except for the baby moon and push present since I'll surprise her with those items. She giggles about the intimacy questions, knowing how touchy the subject of our sex life is with her brother. But he was surprisingly cool about it and pretty candid. So I appreciate our bro talk.

My Baby Girl's stomach grumbles from hunger, and we laugh.

"There goes the dinner bell!" I tease her as we sit up.

I stand her between my legs and lean my forehead against her babies bump. She curls her fingers in my hair, and I hum a Scottish lullaby. We stay caught in the moment until her stomach protests again.

"Time to feed my wife and My Trips," I announce as I stand and sweep her off of her feet.

I stride with her in a bridal carry to the office door and out to the kitchen.

After the burnt bread disaster, Lucien has one of his restaurants send food over for our dinner whenever we call. And neither My Baby Girl nor I have any complaints about it!

I set her on a high chair at the marble island and go to the refrigerator. You must love my brother. Every item neatly labeled with the name, ingredients—carefully selected not to harm her pregnancy—and warming instructions. He's Mr. Perfectionist, and his restaurant staff and Jackson Corporation team better follow suit, or the *Sexy Chef* turns into a caustic dictator.

"Tonight, My Lady, you have the option of Chicken Paillard over a bed of fresh mixed greens with EVOO and balsamic vinaigrette or Dover Sole Meunière with balsamic parmesan roasted asparagus and tomatoes. Kindly tell me your preference," I say, mimicking a server at any of Lucien's eateries.

She giggles and sits straighter in her chair.

"If you would be so kind, My Lord, the Dover Sole

Meunière," she responds in a Northeastern United States lockjaw accent.

I bow, then burst out in laughter when she giggles again.

After I prepare the dishes to the exact specifications of the *Sexy Chef*'s instructions, we sit at the banquette. I join my preggie wife with a glass of iced lemon ginger tea—her new favorite drink.

"So, I spoke with Anita, and she agreed to be my doula! I'm so excited! She helped Leonie when Starr helped Lola, then Anita helped Starr. She and Norman are fine with staying at Jackson Castle or renting a property nearby—"

"We'll have none of that! They'll reside in the guest wing of the castle or in one of the houses on the property. Norman liked the lodge my brothers and I use as a getaway. So they may prefer to stay there. But they're like family, and we don't leave family to rent some stranger's house," I interrupt.

My Baby Girl grins and thanks me with kisses.

"I can't wait to see the renditions Leonie will come up with for the nurseries. She's working on ones for The STEELE Tower, Southampton, London, and the castle in addition to here and at my parents' residences. Do you think Dad Connor and Mom Lucie will want one too?" She asks.

I grin and nod.

"Oh, absolutely! Why don't we call them after dinner and ask?" I suggest.

She claps her hands and digs in to her food.

A comfortable silence descends as we enjoy the savory meals Lucien had prepared. Later, we do a FaceTime call with my parents, and they agree wholeheartedly. When we fill them in on our plan to move to the castle after Haley gives birth, my mother shrieks with happiness.

She declares she will return to Banff permanently to be close to her grandbabies—and to us, of course, she adds with a laugh. My father adds we should explore the storage facility with Leonie for Jackson family heirlooms to use in the nurseries. We maintain generations of furniture, prams, clothes, and accessories, among other items, under temperature-controlled conditions—a treasure trove.

I wrap my arm around My Baby Girl's shoulders as tears slip down her cheeks. She's so elated everyone wants the very best for our little family.

Later that night, as we lie in bed, tears fill my eyes at the magnitude of the situation. I'm about to be a father to three innocents. My responsibilities to them and to their mother are of the utmost importance to me and not taken lightly in any way.

I slide closer behind my wife and bury my face in her fragrant hair. A peace falls over me. My heart so full of pure love. I fall asleep with a satisfied smile on my face.

HALEY

"*L*ook at your babies bump, *chérie*! And I thought mine was big at twenty weeks! Ha!"

"Aaw, don't tease her! She's adorable!"

"Oh, my baby girl is going to be a mommy! I can't believe it, sweetheart!"

"I remember when I held you in my arms, honey!"

I stick my tongue out at Leonie, smile at Anita, and hug The Moms.

They just arrived from the airport along with their children, Roger, Norman, and The Dads. After a round of hugs, the guys went to Lachlan's study while we settled in the living room. The nannies took the kids to play in the park with Bella and Bonnie and The Twins' Bichon Frises.

It's so good to see everyone. In only eight weeks, I've changed so much including a fuller babies bump! And to Lachlan's delight, bigger boobs…

We take pictures and a video each week for our babies

diary. He's taking after Baz and bought a snazzy camera outfit so he can take the *best photos of his babies' growth*. It's too cute to watch him position me, take my measurements, and jot it all down in the book. Then I sit on his lap while we go through the diary from the first entry to the current one. It's become our weekly ritual we look forward to each Sunday morning before brunch.

The nightly showers during which Lachlan bathes me, then lays me on the massage table and rubs fragrant warm oils all over me. He concentrates on my feet, calves, and belly. A scalp massage tops off the entire relaxing treat.

He read about it in a book Roger recommended to him. My brother lavished Leonie with daily full-body rubs throughout both of her pregnancies. He told Lachlan he scored major cool points with her—and BJs. TMI...

I, in turn, ride My Lord every single chance I get. Even to the point *he* begs *me* for no more! Between the bouts of marathon sex and the out-of-the-blue water works of tears, my hormones continue to rage. Starr tells me they're well worth a wrecked pussy by a master lover. Again TMI...

But as always, I appreciate the love and support our families and friends give to Lachlan and me. And their trips here are no exception.

We're in full-on prep mode. The next two days we'll work on the nurseries, my hospital bag, and clothes shopping for The Trips and for my growing bump in Aberdeen. Then spend the weekend at Jackson Castle. Anita and Norman will choose where they'll stay. We'll go to the storage facility for the nurseries. Plus get the suite Lachlan and I use ready for our postnatal move. After the weekend, we'll go to London for the nursery and more shopping.

As far as STEELE Technology and Cyber Security, I intend to work as close to my due date as possible. Harris told me to take it easy and he would step in. But I love my work and don't want to skip out on my responsibilities to my clients and for my half of our subsidiary. However, I have a backup plan for my team to handle our tasks and for Harris to run my side, just in case. Better to be prepared now than to flail around later, as my Dad says.

Even though Lachlan agrees with Harris stating a triplet pregnancy can be taxing on me, my husband gave in when I promised I wouldn't overexert myself. I've seen photos of women as the weeks get closer to delivery. So I'll work from my home office when my babies bump morphs into two giant watermelons stacked on top of one another and my waddle won't let me get very far.

For now, it's action time!

"Did you come all the way here to make fun of me or to help me, Leonie?" I chide with my head cocked to the side and my arms crossed over my boobs in mock anger.

She jumps up from the sofa and wraps her arms around me while she smothers me with kisses. I giggle and duck. But she's relentless.

"*Mais non, chérie!* I am here to help you!" She insists between kisses.

"Okay, ladies. Then it's time to get to work!"

Sergeant Shelley returns in full force, ready for Project The Trips.

With one last buss to my cheek, Leonie sits on the sofa. I giggle, then sit up straight when my mother gives me the eye. Ooh… She is serious!

"Let's begin with the nursery here. Leonie, gather what you need for your design. Haley, show us the rooms you have in mind," Sergeant Shelley commands.

Like well-trained troops, we follow her orders.

Originally, Lachlan and I thought to convert the guest suite closest to our rooms into a nursery. But that was with one baby in mind. With three, we may need to use two suites. We want a spacious lounge, a room for the cribs, a closet, and an en suite bathroom. A pram room will require a reconfiguration of the penthouse's entry.

Once The Trips reach the stage they need their own rooms, we'll need to move to another flat. But that's for another day…

"*Chérie*, here's my recommendation based on the previous schematics and your wants. The original guest suite plus the one beside it will combine into one large nursery. The cribs room will be closest to your bedroom suite with the lounge between the en suite bathroom and the walk-in closet with dressing area," Leonie says as she walks us through the rooms and her drawings. "We'll cut a door through the wall that separates your salon from the nursery. That way you won't have to go out of your suite into the hallway to reach theirs."

After she's finished, I throw my arms around her.

"I love it! Just what Lachlan and I had in mind!" I exclaim. "The varying shades of green with dove gray accents is the perfect color scheme for our boys and our girl. Jackson and Steele merged!"

"And the mural of the Scottish Highlands brings the beauty of nature into their space," Anita adds. "Very tranquil and grounding."

"Yes, Leonie, you did a wonderful job, honey!" Mom Lucie agrees with a smile. "I can't wait to see which pieces you'll select from the family heirlooms."

"Ah, yes! And some from the Steeles' collection, too," my mother adds. "You'll have more than enough for each of the residences."

We move back to the entry foyer.

Leonie pulls up the drawings for the pram closet and shows us the changes she recommends. The existing coat closet will bump out into the private elevator foyer and extend further inside of the penthouse flat. With a pram for three, strollers, and other accessories, we'll need the extra space. Fortunately, the way Leonie designed it, the closet won't detract from the penthouse's overall layout.

"How's it going?"

We turn around to find Lachlan behind us.

"I know I said to have at it, but couldn't resist a peek," he says with a grin.

I clap and bounce on the balls of my feet.

"Come, Leonie can show the plans to you!" I respond happily.

Lachlan strides over and wraps his arms around my

waist, resting his hands on my babies bump from behind as he stares at Leonie's iPad over my shoulder. When she finishes, he kisses my cheek.

"Do you like it?" He asks.

I nod and tilt my head to gaze at him.

"Absolutely! Do you?"

He grins and nods.

"I love it! Leonie, well done, thank you!"

"Yes, my wife is a wiz!"

Roger appears and tucks Leonie into his side as he kisses her cheek. He smiles with pride at his wife. She blushes and leans her head against his shoulder.

"How about we go to lunch, then you lasses shop while we go to the club," Dad Connor suggests.

Everyone agrees readily, and we gather our handbags while Lachlan calls Theodore for the Mercedes-Benz Sprinters. Once we're downstairs, we pile into the tricked-out vans for a quick ride to a nearby chippy. I have a taste for some good ole crispy fish and chips with lots of chippy sauce. Yum!

"It's good to see you have a hearty appetite, daughter," Dad Connor says with a broad smile. "You're eating for the future Jacksons. The first—of many—grandchildren."

I grin as I take another bite of my haddock. The fish is so flaky it melts in my mouth, and I close my eyes as I groan in pleasure.

He chuckles and raises his pint of stout in salute.

Lachlan leans over and kisses my temple.

"That's My Baby Girl," he murmurs in my ear. "Keep my babies well fed."

After lunch, we part.

The guys go to the gentleman's club—The Royal Northern & University Club Aberdeen. The Jackson forefathers were founding members. They'll do whatever *gentlemen* do at the club while we head to Union Street—the primary shopping spot in Aberdeen.

I googled the best baby boutiques, so we go from one to the next until we have enough items to fill our own boutique. Tomorrow, I'll shop for some new clothes before we fly up to Banff.

Hours later, we're back at the penthouse flat. Lachlan gets a kick out of the matching sailor outfits. He exclaims The Trips will wear them on their maiden voyage aboard *Gorm Domhainn*—his full-rigged sailing yacht in the North Sea.

When I fail to hide a yawn behind my hand, my husband declares it's time for me to take a nap. The Steeles and the Greens go to STEELE Aberdeen while Dad Connor and Mom Lucie head to their penthouse. We'll meet up for dinner later in the evening at Lucien's restaurant at the hotel.

Once they're on the elevator, Lachlan scoops me in his arms and carries me to our bedroom. Before he lays me on the bed, I'm fast asleep.

* * *

"I THOUGHT we had incredible pieces at Beaulieu Enterprises SAS' warehouses and in our family's private storage. But this is extraordinary, too!"

Leonie spins in a circle inside of the vast multi-level facility the Jacksons built on the castle's grounds generations ago.

Dad Connor grins. He knows the luxuries and priceless pieces Leonie's family accumulated over the centuries as a prominent Parisian family of merchants who dates back to the Merchant Court of the eighteenth-century.

"We take pride in our family's treasures," he says. "Come, let me show you."

He leads us to the area for children, and we set to exploring.

By the time we finish, tags—colored according to the nursery residence—hang from a number of pieces. The facility's manager will coordinate the shipments with Leonie's team at STEELE International.

Meanwhile, Lachlan, Roger, and Norman went to the lodge. Norman sent Anita a video of it, and she agreed the property would make a lovely place for them to stay. They'll convert one room into a yoga studio so she can teach her clients via Skype and film her programs. The castle's steward will ensure they complete the project to her specifications, the lodge well stocked with their food preferences, and arrange for a driver, chef and maids dedicated to their family's needs.

Norman decided to open an Aberdeen location for his eponymous Elite Training Facility. A call to Malcolm, and he contacted his commercial real estate UK lead to find an appropriate location. I'm excited about it since I can train there. The London location and my trainer are fantastic. But one in Aberdeen is better since I'll spend less time in London.

We gather for dinner back at the castle. After a long day of tromping through the storage facility and reviewing Leonie's recommendations for the suite Lachlan and I use, I'm exhausted. My husband insists everyone enjoy the rest of the evening with billiards or movies. But he bundles me up in the Range Rover and drives us to our enchanted Watchtower.

As we lie in bed after he made slow, sweet love to me, I feel such a sense of peace. Everything is on track for the birth of The Trips. I entwine my fingers with his as our hands rest on my babies bump. Lachlan nuzzles my neck and whispers words of love in a voice raspy from his carnal cries of passion.

"We love you, too, My Lord," I whisper. Then sigh contentedly as my eyelids drift shut.

HALEY

"You love to blindfold me. Don't you, Mr. Jackson?"

I giggle as Lachlan ties a white silk mask over my eyes.

We flew from Aberdeen nine hours ago on his Gulfstream G650. Which means we could be anywhere in the world in a five-thousand mile radius roughly. I can't get a clue from my clothes since Lachlan packed my luggage.

So once again—as he did for our honeymoon—my husband keeps me in the dark, literally.

I reach to scratch my forehead, and he swats my hand away with a warning growl. Of course, my traitorous body responds immediately with pebbled nipples and a quiver in my pussy. I sigh and rest my head on his shoulder until the private jet lands.

"Up you go, Mrs. Jackson. Now, I'm going to hold your waist, so you don't stumble. Trust me?"

An unexpected shudder sneaks through me as my husband's warm breath skitters over the delicate shell of my ear. His wicked chuckle—knowing his erotic effect on my horny hormones—blows tendrils of my hair across my upturned face. I nod and moan at the same time.

My husband guides me from the seat and places me in front of him. His hands grip my flanks. No more waist for me at twenty-four weeks pregnant with three babies! Slowly, we make our way to the door of the jet.

Warm air kisses my face. I lift it towards the sun and inhale deeply. The fragrant scents of bougainvillea and hibiscus mingle with the distinct smell of salty air waft through my nostrils. A breeze ruffles my loose ebony waves.

"The Caribbean!" I exclaim, guessing from the flight time, tropical heat, and the smells.

The blindfold slips from my eyes.

I blink from the brightness of the sun. When my vision adjusts, I swivel my head around for another clue as to the exact island. I spy the blue ensign with the British flag and a coat of arms with three dolphins waving in the breeze.

"Anguilla!" I shout triumphantly, as I tilt my head back to face Lachlan.

He grins and nods.

"Yes, Mrs. Jackson, you guessed correctly. Welcome to your babymoon! Sugary white sand and crystal-clear azure waters await you at our beachfront private villa on Barnes Bay!"

I reach up and press my palm to his face.

"You mean *our* babymoon, my love. These are our babies," I say with a grin as I pat his hand still on my side. "You have more than a nickel in this dime, as my Dad says!"

Lachlan throws his head back and laughs.

"Indeed, I do!" He chuckles. "Well, then, let's be on our way. *Our* babymoon starts officially now."

He holds my hand as he helps me down the stairs and to the Mercedes-Benz G-Wagen with an open panoramic sunroof. I gaze up at the clear blue sky, delighted to have our babymoon after hearing about my sisters' fun during their trips. A smile spreads across my face as the sun and breeze fill the truck.

Lachlan keeps his hand on my right thigh—squeezing it at times—as we drive along to the West End of the island. I reach over and cup the back of his head. His sable locks soft as silk against my fingers. He flashes his movie-star smile at me, and I melt.

Damn, my man is gorgeous!

Twenty minutes later, we turn off the road to wrought-iron gates in a white stone wall. A security guard sits inside of a little white stone house. He waves and the gates open. As we drive along the road for the gated community, I catch glimpses of luxurious villas, also white.

At the end, we pull up to a secluded, massive, two-story white villa with matching surrounding walls on either side lined with palm trees. Sand colored travertine pavers lead to the entry with an area of grass and a palm tree in the center. Lachlan pulls in front of the two-car garage and hops out as the villa's staff approach.

"Welcome My Lord and My Lady to *The Beach Villa!*"

The butler greets us and introduces himself and the others as the chef offers us refreshing glasses of fruit punch.

We thank them and follow him for a tour while the maids take care of our luggage. It's 18,000 square feet of contemporary and sumptuous living space with eight bedroom suites, water features, floor-to-ceiling windows and sliding doors that lead to a huge terrace facing the Caribbean Sea. It's a marvelous villa with every amenity imaginable from an infinity pool and jacuzzi to a tennis court to an alfresco dining area with built-in barbecue and landscaped gardens.

Mesmerized by the panoramic view of the azure waters, we step out onto the glass-walled terrace off of the primary bedroom suite. Beyond the all-white twin sofas and chaise lounges, the powdery sand beach beckons to us.

Lachlan slides his arms around me from behind and leans his chin on top of my head.

"What would you like to do first, Mrs. Jackson?" He murmurs.

I point to the water.

"Swim like a mermaid, Mr. Jackson," I respond.

"Your wish shall be granted," he says with a chuckle. "And what a sexy mermaid you are, Hot Mama."

I smile, knowing he said it to make me feel better since I've complained of feeling like a giant beachball. I'm super grateful for our babies, but good grief!

We walk back inside, and the maids follow the butler

from the suite. They and the chef won't return until we call for them. So we have the villa all to ourselves.

Curious to see what Lachlan packed for me, I head to my walk-in closet. Colorful dresses from flowy and long to short and fitted hang from the rods. Bikinis in white, black, and vibrant hues and gauzy sarongs nestle in the drawers. I notice no panties, only Lola's Coterie bras for my heavy breasts. Not even a negligee to be found. Only two white silk floor-length kimonos.

I shake my head. It's obvious my husband packed for me. No matter what stage it's in, he loves my body.

He wolf whistles when I come out dressed in a fuchsia pink bikini with a bandeau top and tiny string bottoms. I grin since he's pleased and do a twirl.

He claps and holds his arms open.

"Come here, Hot Mama!"

I rush into them and wrap my arms around his neck, getting as close to him as our babies bump allows.

"Thank you, Daddy Dom. This is going to be ah-mazing!" I declare. "The best babymoon ever!"

AFTER A SUNSET DINNER, the sky glows violet, cream, and gold. Soft music plays over the outdoor surround sound speakers and blends with the splashing of the waves as they roll onto the beach. The candlelight flickers inside of the glass hurricane holders. It dances across my husband's handsome face as he tells me about plans for tomorrow.

I'm more mesmerized by him than I was of the beach

earlier. He's making it his mission to keep me happy during our trip. And it's working.

I reach over and take his hand, bringing the knuckles to my lips.

His emerald green eyes dilate to obsidian as he senses my change in mood. He cocks his head and scans my face. Without a word, he rises and lifts me from my chair. He carries me to the sunken bed of oversized pillows that overlooks the darkening sea.

He kneels and sets me in the middle. One tug and the silk kimono slips open to frame my full breasts and belly. With a groan, he lowers his head to suckle a peaked nipple through the silk bra while his hand kneads my other breast. Warm air blows across the dampened material and makes my nipple tighten even more. A flick of his wrist, and my bra falls open.

I shrug out of it and cradle his head to my other breast. A low moan slips from my mouth as my head falls back. The wet sound of his suckling matches the waves below us. And my pussy floods.

My hands push at his emerald green silk kimono, eager to touch his bare skin, feel it against mine.

Lachlan sits back on his haunches and unties his robe, then tosses it with mine aside. His heated gaze leaves a trail of goosebumps over my body as he takes me in from my head to my parted thighs. He purrs when he spies the glistening wetness of my pussy lips.

"On your side, woman, knees bent one in front of the other."

I hurry to comply as more of my juices flow in response to his command.

The giant pillows cradle my babies bump as I lower myself amongst them. But I don't move fast enough for my impatient husband.

He guides me to my side and lifts my top leg over his forearm as he leans down. The tip of his tongue laves me from my puckered hole, past my wet lips, to my engorged clit. He rolls it with his tongue and sucks it into his mouth.

We groan in unison as my hips jerk.

Despite a delicious dinner, he makes a meal of my pussy as it gushes again and again from his tongue, teeth, and fingers. His feral grunts and growls turn me on even more.

The first orgasm builds within my core. When he nips my clit, my toes curl, and I keen towards the stars-filled sky. Waves of erotic pleasure roll through me as my juices splash across his face.

But he doesn't stop.

My husband feasts until I cum several more times and beg for him to fuck me.

"As you wish, My Lady," he purrs as he envelops me from behind and the bulbous head of his massive cock kisses my pussy lips.

He snaps his hips.

Again we groan as one as his girth stretches my little pussy and bottoms out. His heavy balls smack the lower curve of my ass cheeks.

As he braces himself on one elbow, My Lord wraps his fingers around my throat with that hand and the other clamps onto my thigh. Held in place, he pistons in and out of my throbbing, soaked pussy.

I meet each of his thrusts with the bucking of my hips.

Our skin slaps together in an erotic rhythm. Cries of passion create the high notes. And our synchronized climaxes the crescendo. A carnal symphony.

My Lord collapses behind me and presses a kiss to the back of my neck. We lie connected as one until my sweat-damped skin makes me shiver. He rises and carries me to our bedroom suite, where he cleans me in the shower.

We end the first night of our babymoon wrapped in each other's arms. Lulled to sleep by the sounds of the waves and the scent of hibiscus from the gardens below.

THE LAST DAY of our babymoon coincides with the one-year anniversary of our vow renewal wedding. I originally thought our trip was to mark the occasion. So I brought my gift for Lachlan hidden in my handbag.

When he comes out of the shower with a towel slung low around his narrow hips and his treasure trail dipping beneath it, I nearly forget my thought. His chuckle as he dries his hair with another towel brings my focus back from the outline of his big dick beneath the terrycloth.

I blink, and he laughs some more as he drops the towels to the white tile floor.

"See something you crave, My Lady?" He asks as his dick bobs with each step towards me.

Mutely I nod. Then squeak when he pounces onto the bed. He lands on his hands and knees on either side of my legs, with his face inches from mine. He rubs his nose to mine and purrs.

"Tell me your wish, My Lady," he demands.

I palm the sides of his face and whisper, "Forever and a day with you, My Lord."

His eyes shine before he slants his mouth over mine. The kiss is deep and full of emotion. When he passes for a breath, I press my finger to his lips.

He cocks his eyebrow.

I smile as I reach behind my pillow and lift the gift-wrapped box between us.

"What's this?" He asks as he takes the box and sits beside me.

I grin wider and respond, "Happy vow renewal wedding anniversary, My Lord!"

He drops his head back with a groan.

"I was so focused on your—I mean our babymoon, today's date slipped past me. Do you forgive me?"

I pretend to pout but can't hold back my giggles.

"Of course! Don't be silly," I answer. "Now, open your present."

My husband pulls the green and blue ribbon and ties it in a bow around my neck. Then he kisses me and tells me I'm the only present he'll ever want before he winks and tears through the metallic green paper.

He pauses when the green box for Rolex watches appears.

"Go on!" I urge.

He nods and presses the closure. Then gapes.

"It's the 1971 Cosmograph Daytona Reference 6265, also known as 'The Unicorn.' Do you know why I choose it for you?" I ask, so excited I grin like a loon.

He shakes his head.

"It's the only known white gold, manual-winding Daytona ever crafted by Rolex. So it's extremely rare. Just like you, and our love that withstood years of us being apart only for us to be together forever. Not only are you the hero in my childhood fantasies. But you are the unicorn in my real life. I love you, Lachlan Jackson," I say.

My words end on a sob. But it's not from the hormones. I truly love my man with all of my heart.

Tears in his eyes match mine as he pulls me onto his lap and buries his face in my neck. His shoulders shake as he cries softly against my skin. Instinctively, I stroke his back and hum the Scottish lullaby he taught to me. It soothes him when, moments later, he sits back and cups my face.

"You, Haley Jackson, are my life and my soul. The mother of my children. I honor you and I love you for all of eternity," he says gruffly.

Through my tears, I repeat his words, changing them for his name and father.

We spend the rest of the morning in bed, honoring and loving one another.

And as I expected, we have the most ah-mazing baby-moon ever!

"I hear your line will continue. How marvelous. So, I guess congratulations are in order, Jackson."

Bram Stewart's snide comments irk the bloody hell out of me. As always.

I have the unfortunate luck to bump into him on my way to the dining room for lunch with my father at The Royal Northern & University Club Aberdeen.

He and his older brother Chester, aka Chet, are vice presidents of Stewart Scotch while their father Magnus retains the titles of CEO and Chairman of the Board. However, it's well known the brothers vie for the lead positions. Their father encourages the competition and will only announce his successor when they "prove their worth."

Not only is Stewart Scotch Jackson Corporation's top competitor, but the bad blood also goes back for centuries.

The bitter feud resulted from the Stewarts' jealousy King James VI favored the Jacksons. The title of Marquess of Huntly proved too much for the Stewarts as the King snubbed them. Each successive generation sets out to outmaneuver us as individuals and their ultimate goal— Jackson Corporation.

I didn't score any high marks with Bram when I beat him to acquire Ainsley Scotch almost two years ago. Unlike the brothers, I made a sound business decision, not a vendetta. But as I learned through the grapevine, it cost Bram a leg up on Chet. Their father raged within their offices at the loss. And the younger brother does not appreciate it.

Obviously, Bram isn't over it.

Oh, bloody well.

I school my face and nod at him.

"If you offer congratulations, I accept," I say and pause.

He blusters at being called out for his half-ass compliments. Then extends his hand.

My gaze flicks to his hand and back to his piggy eyes before I grasp it firmly.

"Yes, congratulations and all," Bram says with a smirk.

"Thank you," I respond, then tilt my head towards the dining room's arched entry. "Now, if you will excuse me."

He glances over his shoulder in an attempt to see with whom I'm lunching. The sneer on his face proves he spots my father. Magnus and Connor don't share any love no more than my siblings and I do with the sons.

"Ah, well, enjoy your meal with the *Marquess of Huntly*,"

Bram says, curling his lip at the coveted title. "Do give him my regards."

"I will do so. Good day, Stewart," I say as I stride past him without a backwards glance.

As I move around the tables, several members greet me, and the servers bow their heads respectfully. I acknowledge them all and stop to chat briefly with some.

When I reach my father at our family's reserved table placed prominently in the center of the room, he stands and embraces me with a smile.

"You know how to work a room, lad!" He says with a clap on my shoulder. When we sit, he leans forward and continues. "I saw that Stewart boy. What did he have to say?"

"Ah, yes. A pseudo-congratulations for… How did he phrase it? Continuation of the Jackson line," I respond with a snort. "Oh, and to give *the Marquess of Huntly* his regards."

My father sits back and laughs.

"Bah! They'll never let it go. Will they?" He says with a shake of his head. "Speaking of which, how's Haley and your babies? Well, I presume?"

I grin as I reach into my suit jacket for my mobile. I unlock the screen and show my latest photos of my twenty-eight-weeks-pregnant wife. We're in the park with Bella and Bonnie for a walk.

He remarks how very well she looks, nice and radiant.

Then I pull up the latest ultrasound where their eyes are open. One boy even has his tongue sticking out. My father comments he's like Laurent—a prankster. We reminisce about some of my youngest brother's antics. Then my father reminds me of some of mine. It's an easygoing conversation. One of the best I've ever had with him.

As we share a Porterhouse Steak with Chopped Herb Sauce, I bring him up to speed on the latest with Jackson Corporation. He may have retired for over a year now. But he likes to stay abreast of major happenings. My mother says it keeps him out of her hair. So I oblige him as much for his advice as for her sake.

Once we finish our meal, we move to the smoking lounge for Jackson Cigars and Scotch digestifs. Several members come over to speak with my father. Since he spends most of his time in New York City, it's not often he visits the club.

Some of the younger crowd stop by to talk me up, too. Not so much since they don't see me. Rather business opportunities or invitations to events they want to share. As much as I thought Lydie could be CEO, she would have missed a great deal of business discussed at the men-only club. Many members of Scotland's oldest families and most influential tycoons converge here.

My mobile vibrates in my pocket. I smile when I see it's a text message from My Baby Girl.

Hi! We're all ready to go when you get here. Tell Dad Connor hello! Love you much! :)

I chuckle and respond.

Perfect, Baby Girl. We'll be there in an hour. Love you more. xoxo

"Haley?"

I glance up to find my father smiling at me. He inclines his head towards my mobile.

"Yes. She says hi. They're ready to go when we get to the penthouse flat. I told her we'll be there in an hour—"

"An hour? Since she's ready, let's go, lad! No keeping your expecting wife waiting. Remember that," he says with an arched eyebrow as he rises from his leather wing chair and buttons his suit jacket. He nods at the member he was speaking with and gestures for me to go.

I chuckle.

Who knew a baby shower would hype up Connor Jackson? But then, he said he wanted heirs like yesterday.

My Baby Girl is due to give birth to my babies in a month. Her sisters said it's the perfect time to have her baby shower. They flew to Jackson Castle yesterday to prep the garden for the party. We decided to make it unisex as her sisters did for their showers. Which is a good thing since I would have shown up, anyway.

My protective instinct has grown stronger over the last few weeks. The sharp, shooting pain and tingling in her buttocks down the back of her legs that knocks her breathless and the bouts of dizziness make me want to stay by her side all day and night long.

Add in My Baby Girl's babies bump growing exponentially. It went from a small beach ball to a giant one in what seems like overnight. At her last prenatal checkup, Dr. Ross told us it's natural now that My Baby Girl is in her third trimester.

It reminds me my babies will enter the world soon, and

I have to keep them safe. Not to mention their mother's safety.

I swear, I'll have gray hair prematurely with this level of stress. Bloody hell!

How do Baz, Malcolm, and Roger it? I don't know.

My mobile vibrates as my father and I step out of the club.

Speak of the devil!

"Hey, bro. What's up?" I ask my best friend.

"Pulling Daddy duty while Lola helps with the baby shower. When are you getting up here? Haley says you're leaving the club in an hour?" He asks as Slade talks to his sisters—baby Sabrina and Stella—in the background.

That'll be me soon, I think with a smile.

"Actually, my dad and I just left the club for the penthouse. We'll pick up Haley, Mom Shelley, and Anita. Then we'll go to the helipad at STEELE Aberdeen. So we'll be there soon," I respond.

"Sounds good. See you then," Baz says, then calls to Slade. "Look, bro, I have to go. Slade's getting into something. Slade!"

Baz ends the call before I can ask what claimed Slade's attention.

I chuckle and call My Baby Girl to tell her we're on our way. She's so excited she drops her mobile and groans when she can't reach it. Mom Shelley picks it up for her.

Yeah, I can feel the brown fading to gray already...

* * *

"How do you like your new penthouse flat?"

Dad Morgan and I stroll around the park-like grounds of Jackson Castle for a bonding session after breakfast. He and Mom Shelley bought a property close to Union Street where My Baby Girl and I live. Like my parents, they want to be near to The Trips with a true residence and not the President's Suite at STEELE Aberdeen. For babysitting, they say.

They spent months in each city after their other grandchildren were born. So we expected the same treatment. Not that we mind it at all. It's good to have family close.

"Aberdeen is a beautiful city. We were fortunate to get the top floor in one of the historic buildings. The penthouse flat required little work. The redesign took less time than we thought," Dad Morgan responds. "I'm surprised Shelley and I didn't buy a residence here sooner considering the amount of time we spend for her to visit Lucie."

He stops and turns to me and continues.

"It's different when your child has children—especially your youngest and a girl. The President's Suite at the hotel wouldn't do. Becoming a husband is one step in a man's life. But children are on a different level. Tell me, how do you feel?"

I pause to consider my sentiments. They're as I thought on my way up to Banff. Children are a major responsibility from the moment they're conceived. Even as adults, my children will always be my top priority. The fruit of my loins.

I tell Dad Morgan as much, and he agrees.

For the rest of our walk, he gives me advice on fatherhood and as a husband. The most poignant being to allow my children to make mistakes so they can grow. But be there to help them through the aftereffects. He also ends with the same thing Baz stands by: happy wife, happy life. A lesson I apply daily!

As we re-enter the castle, the sounds of female laughter drifts from the floral salon. Thinking as one, Dad Morgan and I head towards my mother's entertaining room. We find her along with the rest of the women. They glance up when we step into the room.

My Baby Girl beams at me.

She's so stunningly beautiful, all aglow with impending motherhood. Her ebony waves cascade past her butt since she refuses to trim her hair before she gives birth—some old wives' tale. Bright dove gray eyes flick between me and Dad Morgan. Her enhanced greatest assets sit up high beneath her Diane von Furstenberg silk wrap dress—my favorite style on her. I simply can't get enough of her tits. She laughs they'll go back down after she stops breastfeeding, and I retort no need to stop ever!

She raises her arms and beckons to me.

"Hi! How was your walk?" She asks as I squat in front of her for a hug.

"Great. Dad Morgan handed down his expert advice. It's a man's thing. So no questions," I respond as I wink at him over my shoulder.

"Exactly!" He adds as he kisses the top of Mom Shelley's head.

My Baby Girl pretends to pout, and I buss her cheek. She giggles and shoos me away.

"Well, fine! Don't share. But we're having a women's talk. So skedaddle!" She retorts.

One more buss, and I stand. A salute to the women, and I follow Dad Morgan from the room. The butler tells us the guys are playing tennis, out for a ride, or in the gym. Dad Morgan goes to the office to catch up with my father while I head to the gym.

As I come out of the locker room changed into a t-shirt, shorts, and sneakers, I see the two world champs—Norman and Borya—sparring on the mat. Ewan acts as referee while Malcolm, Anton, and Calvin watch. I greet them and step onto the treadmill for a warm-up.

"Good talk?"

I glance over to find Baz starting the treadmill next to mine.

"Yeah. Noble words of wisdom," I respond and increase my speed. "I can't wait for Haley to give birth. I want to hold my babies already."

Baz chuckles.

"Yeah, I know the feeling very well. It's awesome to hold your creation in your hands. Damn. Words can't even describe it," he says with a faraway expression on his face. He smiles to himself and hits the speed.

The reformed Alpha Dom playboy. I chuckle to myself at the change in my best friend.

We jog, then run in silence for the next thirty minutes. Afterwards, we hit the weights and stretch. As we sit in the steam room, Baz gives me more dad pointers. I tell him we should do a blog called *Dad Encounters*. He laughs and agrees it would be a hit.

Later that afternoon, everyone gathers for our baby shower in the south garden. They decorated it in shades of blue, pink, and gold. Cream leather sofas, oversized chairs, and side tables form seating areas. Two comfy chairs—one pink and one blue—adorned with flowers and ribbons sit in the middle. Stations set up for games and a photo booth add to the festivities. A cream canopy flutters above tables with silver chafing dishes and beverages behind which servers stand. Another canopy covered table holds tons of beautifully wrapped presents. The transformation of the garden is spectacular.

I glance down at my wife and squeeze her hand.

She smiles up at me and bites the corner of her mouth to hold back the tears shining in her eyes.

I lean over and kiss her lips, sucking the bottom one into my mouth.

"No lip biting, or we will have to postpone the party until after I fuck you," I murmur in her ear. Then chuckle wickedly at her shocked gasp. I knew a bit of raunch would straighten her out. "Come, Little Temptress. Let us enjoy our special day."

"**D**AMN YOU, LACHLAN JACKSON!!!"

My Baby Girl yells after an obviously painful contraction. Her dove gray eyes shoot platinum daggers at me as she white-knuckle grips the side rails of the hospital bed. Sweat glistens on her crimson face as she bares her fangs at me with a snarl.

"LOOK AT WHAT YOU DID TO ME!!! AARGH!!!"

Her eyes roll back as another contraction takes hold of her.

Had she not nearly broken my hand a moment ago from her Herculean grip, I would hold her hand now to soothe her.

Yeah, right, soothe her. Not if I want to keep my face intact.

She swung on me when I told her how well she was doing. Had I not ducked, I would have a bloody nose. Fuck. Me.

Anita struggles to hold back a giggle and wipes a cool cloth over My Baby Girl's brow.

"Breathe, Haley. It may seem crazy now, but it will help. Okay?" Anita says softly.

"Yes, Lady Aboyne, your first baby is crowning. You can do this," Dr. Ross adds with an encouraging smile.

I open my mouth to agree. But snap it closed when I receive another death glare.

Moments later, our baby girl's cries fill the delivery room in the suite of rooms at the hospital. After I cut her umbilical cord, I follow close behind Dr. Kirk Wallace—their pediatrician—as he carries my baby to the side to clean her and for a checkup. I breathe a sigh of relief when he confirms she's in excellent health, as he places her swaddled little form in my arms.

Then I choke up with emotion as I stare into her tiny pink face. The old wives' tale must have worked because she has a head covered in sable brown hair. She makes suckling motions with her mouth. I stand mesmerized by her.

My first baby. In my arms at last. Mine to protect. Mine!

"Is she okay?"

Roused by my wife's plaintive cry, I pivot and stride to her as I cradle my baby girl to my chest.

"She's a miracle," I respond, still in awe.

I lift her for my wife to see for herself and she smiles wanly. A cry alerts us to her hunger. I glance down into her emerald green eyes before my wife takes my baby girl to her breast. Tears fill my eyes at the sight. My wife and my first baby.

However, her brothers grow impatient, and contractions begin again. Dr. Wallace places my baby girl in an incubator, and I return my attention to my wife. Her sweet smile of a moment ago vanishes.

Here we go…

With as much cursing and threats as the first round, my second child and first son makes his appearance. His loud wails resound around the room. Once again, I cut the umbilical cord and follow behind Dr. Wallace possessively, only relaxed when my healthy son rests in my arms.

He opens his eyes and emerald green meets emerald green. And I swear he smiles at me. I grin like a loon back at him. My son. Mine!

"How is he?"

This time, I stride over to show my wife my handsome boy. Unlike before, she only has a few minutes to breastfeed him before their younger brother demands his debut. Just as his siblings before, Dr. Wallace declares him healthy, and I cradle him to my chest for our first father-son bonding.

Like his identical twin brother and fraternal sister, he's healthy and has emerald green eyes and sable brown hair—the Jackson family traits. My heart swells with joy. I give a silent prayer of thanks as I return to my wife's bedside.

Our eyes meet and the most beatific smiles spreads across her face. My heart nearly bursts with love.

"Thank you, my love," I murmur, too choked with emotion to speak louder. "I love you so much."

Tears spill down her cheeks as she reaches up and cups my face.

"I love you more," she whispers.

Our baby boy voices his hunger, and she takes him to her breast. I stare at them, content. When he has his fill, Dr. Wallace places him in another incubator. The nurses tend to my wife while Anita and I stand by the sleeping Trips.

"Congratulations, Lachlan," she says with a warm smile. "Your babies are strong and healthy. Not to mention adorable."

I wrap my arm around her shoulder and thank her for all of her help from the month prior to now. She's been at my wife's side to offer her comfort and support daily. Anita is an incredible doula and, just as importantly, a wonderful friend to both of us.

With a last squeeze, she leaves the room with the medical team and an attendant who wheels the bed used for the delivery from the suite.

Alone at last, I stand beside my wife and clasp her hand between both of mine. I bring it to my lips and kiss it softly.

"How do you feel, Hot Mama?" I ask, knowing she needs a boost.

As expected, she grins at me—a bit lopsided, but brilliant, nonetheless. She pats the double-size bed for me to sit next to her.

I grin back and gently lower myself to the edge so as not to jostle her.

"Closer. I want to rest my head on your shoulder," she says.

"As you wish, My Lady," I respond to make her giggle.

I get into position and put my arm around her shoulders.

She snuggles into me with a soft sigh and entwines our fingers.

A pang hits my chest from her bare left ring finger. Towards the end of her pregnancy, her fingers swelled. So she couldn't wear her wedding jewelry or her collar. Who knew being pregnant increased the size of a woman's neck??

I kiss the top of her head to dissipate those thoughts. I have a lot to be thankful for.

"So, how do you feel, Hot Mama?" I ask again as I caress her arm. My hand glides along the silk of her robe.

Leonie put together a whole pre-and postnatal trousseau from her collection for Lola's Coterie, including some custom pieces I requested. A bra with cutouts for the nipples with matching crotchless panties proves mighty handy...

My wife stifles a yawn. After sixteen plus hours of pre-labor and labor delivery for triplets, she's exhausted. It triggers one in me, and we laugh.

"Better than I expected," she starts, then peeks up at me from beneath her eyelashes. "You don't hold the things I said against me. Do you?"

I grin wolfishly and respond, "The only thing I want to hold against you is my body."

She pulls away and pushes against my chest as she groans.

"That's what got us here in the first place, Lachlan Jackson! Ugh!" She responds with a frown.

I chuckle, getting the reaction I wanted from her. Then pull her back into my arms and bury my face in her freshly washed hair. I take a deep inhalation and sigh.

"Only teasing you, the Original My Baby Girl," I say.

She glances up at me with a questioning look.

"Well, now I have my baby girl. So, I'll need to distinguish the two of you," I answer.

She giggles and yawns.

My mobile vibrates in my pocket. I smile when I see my father's name on the screen.

"Time to introduce the heirs," I say to my wife. "Are you up to it?"

She nods and sits up. I fluff the pillows behind her back as I answer my mobile.

"Hi, Dad. Come on in to meet your grandchildren," I say happily.

He doesn't even answer, just ends the call as I hear him telling everyone it's time. I chuckle.

Once our family and friends crowd into the bedroom of the suite. Expectant faces stare at my wife and me. We glance at each other, eager to reveal The Trips' names. She nods for me to deliver the news since she delivered the babies.

I move closer to their cribs and carry one after the other to their mother. She holds my boys against her silk-covered breasts while I hold my baby girl.

Proudly, I turn her to face them and announce, "Meet Lady Lilias Jackson, born first. Leith Jackson, The Right Honorable Viscount of Melgum, our second born and first son. The Honorable Lewis Jackson, our third born and second son."

Everyone claps softly, and I continue.

"As you know, my name means land of lakes, and my favorite pastime is sailing. Lilias is the Scottish name for lily or water lily. Leith is a river in Edinburgh and Scottish Gaelic for life. Lewis—along with Harris—forms the primary island of the Outer Hebrides off the west coast of Scotland."

"Naturally, I get recognition from my twin!" Harris—the man—snickers.

"Yes," my wife says with a smile.

He bows.

"Spot on! You did well," my father exclaims. "We're very proud of you both!"

"Indeed! Congratulations!" Dad Morgan says. "New Steele grandbabies and the first Jacksons!"

Then the others step forward to get closer looks at my babies. They hug the Original My Baby Girl and me. But when she yawns, The Moms shoo everyone out and tell us they'll be back in the morning. Anita goes to her suite across the hall while the others head to STEELE Aberdeen or to their residences.

I place Lilias in her crib, then turn to my wife.

"Time for bed and no hanky-panky, Hot Mama. You had a big day, my love," I say as I cup her chin to stare into her sleepy eyes.

She smiles and nods.

I lean over and kiss her lips before I take first one and then my other son from her arms. Without a fuss, they settle in their cribs. I watch them a moment as I say another prayer of thanks for them and for their mother.

"Time for you to come to bed, Daddy Dom."

I grin and stride over to the dresser where I switch into black silk pajamas bottoms. Then I head to the bathroom to prepare for bed. When I come out, the Original My Baby Girl sleeps on her side. Soft snores prove just how worn out she is from birthing three babies.

Trying not to disturb her, I slip in the bed and slide my front to her back with my hand resting between her thighs possessively. She murmurs my name, and I nuzzle the side of her neck as I whisper how much I love her and my babies.

For a while, I watch over my wife as she sleeps in my arms and my babies in their cribs over her shoulder beside the bed. Peace settles around us.

At that moment, I vow to love my little family and to protect them with my life.

* * *

"I REMEMBER when you were newborn, honey. My second baby and first son. My heart was and still is so full of love for you, Lachlan. Now, you're a father. I am so very proud of you. I love you so very much."

Tears fill my mother's hazel eyes as she smiles up at me.

The next morning, we're standing by the cribs watching Lilias, Leith, and Lewis sleep. Their mother rests after breastfeeding them. So my mother and I have a moment to share.

I smile at her with tears swimming in my eyes. Too choked up to speak, I nod my head and pull her into an embrace. Her signature patchouli perfume—a scent of deep amber and woody mixed with warm vanilla and praline notes I can remember as far back as a toddler—fills my nostrils. I inhale of the soothing scent deeply to quiet my emotions.

My mother rubs my back.

"It's a beautiful thing to have your own family. Trust me. Having your father, you, and your siblings changed my life. I am so grateful for you and know you will come to feel the same for your little family," she whispers.

A hint of her New Orleans accent appears as it does when her emotions overwhelm her. She doesn't speak much about the family she left behind decades ago. But we know there's no love lost on her part. And we have no interest in connecting with people who hurt our mother.

I squeeze her tightly and rub her back to soothe her, too.

After a moment, we part with smiles of understanding.

She pats my cheek and turns back to face my babies. A broad smile replaces her tears as she touches each of their backs, as though claiming them as her own. More family to bring her endless joy.

I put my arm around my mother's shoulders, and she leans into me as we continue to watch over my babies before us and my wife asleep at our side.

My world is right.

HALEY

"Hello, my loves. Did you miss your Mummy? I missed you. Daddy is still asleep since you kept him up. All. Night. Long. Oooh! Guess what today is? Your one-month birthday! Yay You! After your checkup with Dr. Wallace, we'll have a party. Sounds good, Lilias, Leith, Lewis?"

I can't believe an entire month passed. A month of adjustments, learning, and tears of joy and frustration. Three newborn babies at once? Oooh wee, chile!

Thank goodness for our support system.

My siblings arrived a couple of days before my due date and stayed for two weeks after. They and Leonie worked from STEELE London, commuting to and from Banff each day after I gave birth. Lola worked from my home office in Aberdeen, then at the castle. Starr taught yoga and Pilates classes at Norman's newly opened training facility in

Aberdeen, then did Skype with her private clients from the castle's yoga studio.

It was fantastic having Starr and Anita here to get me moving again. They created a wellness program for me to follow—from meals to fitness and meditation. Even after they returned to Beverly Hills and Paris, respectively, we do our sessions via Skype. Norman even had me boxing for cardio. To be in the ring with the Champ was awesome. Time to get my body snatched again. Yaaasss, honey!

Lydie and Laurent worked out of their offices in Jackson Town House while Lucien bounced between his offices there and his restaurants. He even did some filming for his shows. After The Trips were born, they commuted between Aberdeen and Banff. They only returned to New York City and Paris a few days ago.

While Lachlan and I take baby leave for two months, our siblings divide our responsibilities. Harris will split his time between New York City and London. Lydie will step into the CEO's role and bring critical decisions to Lachlan before she makes the call. The rest of them will help where they can. We're ever so thankful to have this bonding time with our babies and as a family.

Our parents were on baby duty from day one! They came to the hospital every day, then flew up with us to the castle when we the doctors discharged us. At any time of the day or night, they're willing to help us. Or rather help their grandbabies, I tease them.

A key addition to our support team is our live-in nanny, Gail McClintock. When Leonie was pregnant with The

Twins, Roger's assistant found the global agency the über-wealthy and celebrities use to source their nannies, nurses, and governesses. Their training is top notch in everything from changing a diaper to language lessons to disarming a would-be kidnapper.

After Lachlan and I conducted several interviews and The Moms met with the last two candidates, Nanny Gail proved the most suitable for the position. Then our fathers ran separate extensive background checks on her. Fortunately, she satisfied everyone.

Of course, she's well trained and highly skilled. As a bonus, she comes from a long line of Scottish nannies and governesses who worked for nobles and royalty. Equally important, Nanny Gail has the stamina to handle three newborn babies.

However, Lachlan and I intend to be hands-on parents. No passing our babies off to the nanny. So although she lives with us, we only ask for her help when one of us isn't around. Here, she stays in her room upstairs with the other staff. In Aberdeen, we purchased a one-bedroom flat in our building for her residence, and in our penthouse, she has a room near the service entrance.

Now, it's my turn to care for our little babies.

I continue to talk to them as I change their diapers and wash their faces. That clean up will do for now. When Lachlan wakes, we'll bathe them together.

Since Leith is the lease demanding of The Trips, I set him in his bassinet while I sit in the glider to breastfeed his siblings. Sometimes I joke three breasts would be great.

Naturally, Lachlan grins and nods lasciviously. I shake my head now as I did then.

By the time I finish with their feeding, Lachlan appears in the doorway leading to our bedroom.

Even disheveled with mussed hair and three-day stubble, my man is sexy as sin. He likes to care for The Trips bare chested so they can feel his body heat and recognize his natural scent easily. I think he does it to make me jump in bed with him before I'm ready. All drool worthy in his low-slung black silk pajamas bottoms with his pecs and abs on full blast. He runs his fingers through his hair, and his biceps bulge.

Damn.

"Hi, babe," he says huskily from sleep.

I lick the drool from the corners of my mouth before I respond.

"Hi. Did you get some rest?" I ask.

He nods and yawns. Then chuckles as he stretches his arms overhead. More muscles flex.

Good gotdamn.

"See something you like, Hot Mama?"

His words draw my eyes from his feathery happy trail.

My cheeks heat with a blush. I glance away and busy myself with Lilias' onesie as I lean over her crib.

"Ready to bathe them?" I counter.

Suddenly, Lachlan's hands rest on the curve of my hips. I jolt upright. The warmth of his chest seeps through my thin silk tank top. My lower back bumps into his groin. His groin where his sizable morning erection presses against me. An uncontrollable mewl slips from between my lips.

"You didn't answer my question," Lachlan murmurs against the shell of my ear.

I shiver as his breath skitters across the delicate skin.

"Chilly?" He asks. The deep rumble in his chest vibrates through my back, straight to my clit.

I whine and try to step sideways from his hold—not only on my physical, but on my mental. As much as I want my husband to pound into me and can't keep lustful thoughts out of my mind, my body just isn't quite ready yet.

He chuckles and steps back.

"Just checking to see if I still got it or not," he says, waggling his eyebrows teasingly. "Judging by your reaction, I haven't lost my touch. At. All."

I throw Leith's burp cloth at my husband.

"Rude!" I snip.

He chuckles some more as he lifts Lewis and Leith from their cribs and strides to the en suite bathroom talking to his sons.

I take a deep cleansing breath à la Starr before I gather Lilias into my arms.

"Your Daddy is such a tease, my little love," I tell her.

"I heard that!" Lachlan shouts from the bathroom, above the sound of running water.

I giggle.

After we bathe and dress The Trips, we call Nanny Gail to watch them while we get ready for the day.

Lachlan heads into the shower, and I dawdle at my vanity. Once his back turns to me, I step into the oversized shower behind him.

The sight of water sluicing down the taut muscles of his shoulders, back, and thighs makes me drool. Again.

But two can play at the teasing game.

The cool breeze as the glass door opens alerts him to my presence. He glances over his shoulder, then does a double take.

Held aloft, cream-colored body wash drips from the bottle to the tops of my triple D-cups. It cascades down over the tops of my mounds to the tips of my distended nipples. Droplets drip from them to the marble tile below.

I stretch one arm up to place the bottle on the alcove shelf while I cup one breast. My fingers massage the body wash into my wet skin. My nipple plays hide and seek with the suds. I cry out softly when my palm brushes over the sensitive tip. Then bite my lower lip as I stare at Lachlan wide-eyed, pretending to be in shock from the unexpected sensation.

His jaw tenses.

My hands slide over my belly, down to the juncture at the apex of my thighs. Bending over slightly so my breasts jiggle, I slip my hands between my thighs and down. Standing, I balance on one leg—thank goodness for my tree asana—while I bend the other to rub my hands over it. I straighten the leg and hold my big toe—yup, Starr and Anita would be proud—as I pretend to rinse the soap off.

Before I can begin my other leg, Lachlan slams me into

the wall. His big body presses against me as he bends his knees to bring our gazes on level.

Green fire rages in his eyes.

"Tempting me, Naughty Girl?" He asks through clenched teeth as he grinds his ginormous cock into my mons.

I narrow my eyes and curl my lip.

"Tempting *me*, Naughty Boy?" I snarl.

We have a face-off.

I refuse to break first and flare my nostrils.

His eyes narrow. When he nods his head and chuckles wickedly, I know I'm in trouble. As he lowers his head to trail the flat of his tongue from my neck down my breast to the pebbled nipple, I drop my head back and close my eyes. The stubble on his face tickles my skin.

My guttural groan mingles with the steam surrounding us.

He laves the tip, then suckles. Hard.

Milk fills his mouth, and I shudder.

Lachlan takes his pleasure in feeding from me.

And I writhe and moan the entire time.

The sensation is so intense, my clit throbs, and I rub it against Lachlan's muscular thigh wedged between my legs. He stiffens his leg to let me have at it. Then he pulls his leg away. I growl in frustration.

My nipple pops from his mouth.

"Only I can give you your release, Naughty Girl," he growls back at me.

"You started this, Lachlan Jackson!" I growl.

He slams his mouth over mine for a dominate, toe-curling kiss. He nips at my lips until I part them with a moan. His tongue tangles with mine as he tastes every corner of my mouth. When his finger slips between our melded bodies to press my swollen clit, then pinch it, I go off like a firecracker.

My hips buck as I ride his palm through the waves of my climax. Then I sag against his powerful frame as he supports my limp body. My chest heaves as I catch my breath.

"You're welcome," he snickers cockily against my ear.

His chuckles stop as he watches me lower to my knees before him. Our eyes lock.

"Your turn," I purr.

His emerald eyes darken to obsidian when I lick the bead of pre-cum from his mushroom head. His engorged cock bobs in response.

My mouth widens as I use my tongue to lap his length inside. It swirls around his girth like a lollipop until his tip reaches the back of my throat.

I gag.

He groans.

Lachlan's fingers dive into my hair to tilt my head, then hold it at an optimal position for him to fuck my face. His groans increase as I open my throat for his carnal pleasure. My hums of delight make him rise to his toes as the vibrations enhance the sensation of him deep throating me.

"Fuuuck!!! Aaaahhh… Yeesss…"

My hand slips between my thighs to tug at my aching

clit. I hum some more from my own pleasure, and it elicits more groans from Lachlan.

His cock thickens and throbs.

He snaps his hips as he holds the sides of my head.

With a roar that reverberates off of the shower's marble walls, he explodes deep down my throat to fill my belly with ropes of his seed. Tears fill my eyes as my breathing cuts short while he thrusts again and again. My nose kisses his groin on the last pulse from his dick.

When he releases my head, my butt hits the backs of my calves as tears slip down my face. He groans and reaches down to swipe his thumb over my swollen lips.

"You're welcome," I repeat against his digit.

Lachlan chuckles and nods.

"Touché."

"You have some very healthy and happy babies, Lord Aboyne and Lady Aboyne. They're right on track in their development. I don't see any reason they cannot travel aboard your private jet to New York City. Do you have any questions for me?"

I turn to Lachlan, and he shakes his head.

We thank Dr. Wallace, and Lachlan sees him to the nursery's door where Nanny Gail waits to escort him to the castle's entry. He'll fly back to Aberdeen on our Sikorsky S-92 Executive Helicopter.

"Well, that's great news!" Lachlan says, as he kisses my lips. "Good work, Hot Mama."

I grin and shake my head.

"We did this together, Daddy Dom," I correct him. "And I'm glad he approved them flying internationally. I've never missed the STEELE Foundation annual fundraiser."

Lachlan picks Lilias up as she fusses and coos to her.

He holds her to his chest over his heart—so she can feel the calming rhythmic beats, he says—and rocks her. After a while, her fussy whimpers end. But he continues to rock and hum to his baby girl. His gaze moves to Leith and Lewis who sleep in their cribs.

When he turns to face me, I smile at my sexy as sin husband-cum Daddy Dom. He grins in return and winks at me.

After months of stress and disappointment, I still can't believe we have our little family finally. And all in one go! So worth the achy back, swollen ankles, and labor pains. I would do it all over again without the least bit of hesitation. Especially seeing the expression of pure joy on my husband's face.

"See something you like, Hot Mama?"

I grin like the Cheshire Cat and bite the corner of my mouth as I nod.

"Oh, absolutely, Daddy Dom. Absolutely!"

LACHLAN

"And this is where I proposed to your Mum. I couldn't take another day without her being my wife. Mine. All. Mine. I vowed to give your Mum her happily ever after. She married me and became my wife that day, and two years later, the mother of my children. I love you Lilias, Leith, Lewis, and your Mum very, very much."

My eyes meet hers over my Tom Ford aviators as I finish my declaration.

She bites the corner of her lush mouth to hold back tears that fill her eyes.

"It's so true. Two years ago, the love of my life asked me to be his wife and the mother of his children. And here we are, My Lord," she says as she places her palm on my cheek. Rising to her toes, she presses her mouth to mine.

I wrap one arm around her waist to meld her to my body while the other holds The Trips' pram. The

Piazza Francesco Saverio Gargiulo in Sorrento, Italy fades. Only we exist as she pours her love into the kiss.

When she lowers to her feet and rests her forehead against my chest, the sounds of the bustling piazza return. Her arms wound around my waist as we're lost in our thoughts.

It was a simple choice to select Sorrento to celebrate our two-year anniversary and to mark the end of our baby leave. I want to bring her back to Chiostro di San Francesco—the town's famous church, monastery, and cloisters—where we wed in an en masse marriage ceremony. Even though The Trips are only two-months old, I want them in the place where the path to our little family started.

Surprisingly, the villa we rented the last time and booked for this trip is for sale. It's a magnificent stone mansion with a pool set in a beautiful garden high above the bay on the Sorrentine Peninsula. Sweeping views of the Amalfi Coast and the islands of Ischia and Procida add to the villa's majesty.

I take its availability as a sign we should make it our residence. Then we can turn the trip into an annual tradition. It'll hold wonderful memories of each year. I make a mental note to call the property agent when we leave the church.

I give my wife a squeeze, and she tilts her head back to gaze at me. I lean over and kiss her lips softly.

"Let's go inside of the church," I tell her.

She nods and loops her hand around my arm as I push The Trips' pram up the hill.

We glance around us at the picture-perfect gem of a town on the Italian coast. Perched atop a cliff facing the Bay of Naples, Sorrento boasts panoramic views over the coast and its marina at the base. Built along the cliff, the town stacks to give it a distinct look: glittering water with bobbing boats topped by rows of colorful buildings. The charm of the old town continues with its warren of tiny streets and alleys lined with pretty historic properties, like the one leading to Chiostro di San Francesco.

We walk through its Arabic portico with interlaced arches interwoven with fragrant flowers, plants, and ornamental trees. The pleasant sound of birds and the murmurs of other visitors fill the charming space and replaces the piazza's hustle and bustle.

"It's as beautiful as I remember. We had the best wedding ever. Not even our fairytale castle vow renewal can compare to the day you made me your bride. Oh, Lachlan, this was a fantastic idea," my wife says as her gaze flits around, absorbing our surroundings.

A pale yellow butterfly flutters about Lilias' face as she lays in the front pushchair. Her laugher rings out when it lands on her nose. Startled, it floats up and over the hood of her pushchair to flutter above the two her brothers rest in behind her. They ah-goo as it dances in the air.

We laugh, and others turn towards us. Then join in when they notice The Trips and the butterfly.

Quickly, I lift my camera for some shots. I carry it

everywhere to capture my babies and their growth. After I take a few still shots, I switch to video.

My Baby Girl holds her index finger out, and the butterfly lands on it as though needing to take a rest after playing with my babies. A brilliant smile spreads across her face. Not wanting to disturb the butterfly, she stands still.

It allows me to get some shots of my wife with my babies beside her. Their laughter and ah-goos continue as they watch their Mum and the gently flapping wings of the butterfly.

After a moment's rest, it lifts off and flutters over them once more before it zigzags away to a flower. I follow its movement with the camera's lens. It's the perfect ending for the video.

When I lower the camera, I find My Baby Girl smiling at me with an expression of pure love on her gorgeous face. I wrap my arm around her waist and pull her close as I lower my head.

She sighs in my embrace once more caught up in a passionate kiss.

"I love you, My Lord," she whispers.

"I love you more, My Lady," I respond as I brush my lips over hers, not in a hurry to part from her.

She smiles against my mouth and nips my lower lip.

"I know," she purrs as she shimmies her hips.

My cock twitches.

I shake my head at My Little Temptress. So naughty knowing she's not giving it up to me. I groan with an ache to bury myself deep in her tight pussy. But I have to satisfy myself with her warm, wet mouth.

I lean further to press my lips to her ear.

"Oh, Naughty Girl. You tempt me in church with your wanton ways? What shall be your punishment?" I rumble deep in my chest.

She shudders, and a puff of her warm breath ruffles my hair.

I chuckle wickedly and stand to my full six feet, four inches to tower over her in a show of dominance.

She glances up at me from beneath the thick ebony fringe of her eyelashes. Her teeth worry her lower lip as she shuffles on her feet. Undoubtedly, she's as turned on as I am and attempting to assuage her ache.

Well, it's her idea for us to wait another six weeks…

I step back with a smirk.

"Come, Little Temptress, before the walls of Chiostro di San Francesco tumble down," I say, crooking my finger at her as I push The Trips' pram.

She giggles and rushes to catch up to us.

Along the way to the exit, we spot the priest who performed the marriage ceremony. We wait until he finishes speaking with a couple before we approach. Once we tell him he married us two years ago during the en masse service, he greets us warmly and congratulates us on The Trips.

"I think we should become patrons to give back for the happiness it brought us. What do you think?" My Baby Girl asks as we stroll out to the piazza.

I nod at her and move my little family to the side, out of the way of others around us.

"That's a great idea. And I have another. We should purchase the villa and make this an annual trip—along with any other time you want to come—to celebrate our anniversary. What do *you* think?" I respond with a grin.

She claps her hands and bounces on the balls of her feet. The Trips join in with laughter, sensing their Mum's excitement. I grin wider.

"I take that's a yes. Let's call the property agent now," I say.

We make a multimillion-dollar cash offer, and the agent agrees to have an answer within a few minutes.

My Baby Girl bites the corner of her lip again, and I free it with my thumb then slip it over her mouth.

"No worries. It's ours. Let's find a restaurant and have lunch alfresco," I tell her.

"Okay," she responds and holds my arm.

Just as we settle at a table of a nearby trattoria, my mobile vibrates in my pants pocket. I wink at My Baby Girl when I recognize the agent's number on the screen. She sits forward, eager to hear, so I put it on speaker.

"*Congratulazioni*, Lord Aboyne! The owners accept your offer. My office will draw up the paperwork. Shall we send it to your personal assistant?" He says.

"Excellent! Yes, along with the wire details. I want to close before my family and I leave," I respond.

He assures me all will go as I request, and we end the call.

"Yippee!!!" My Baby Girl squeals as she jumps up from her chair and throws her arms around my neck.

I push my chair back and pull her onto my lap.

"Not thrilled, huh?" I tease.

She grins and cups my face.

"Beyond happy, My Lord. Thank you!" She exclaims before she kisses me soundly.

Over a lunch of fresh pasta and roasted vegetables, we talk about the changes she wants to make to the villa and plan our next trip. The ten-acre estate has the villa with ten bedrooms and twelve bathrooms plus a two-bedroom, three-bathroom guest house and a caretaker's house. Of course, we'll ask Leonie to help us with the changes since she did such fantastic jobs with our other residences. We'll come back when she's available to spend time here.

"What should we name it?" I ask as I sip a glass of limoncello.

My Baby Girl sits back and taps her chin with her fore-finger as she thinks. A smile spreads across her face. She leans forward and reaches for my hand.

"How do you say wishes in Italian?" She asks since I'm fluent in Italian among other languages.

"*Desideri*," I respond, matching her smile since I know where she's going.

She squeezes my hand.

"You make all of my wishes come true with the biggest of them all right here. So, how's *Villa dei Desideri*?" She asks.

I return the squeeze and grin as I nod enthusiastically.

"I love it! *Villa of Wishes*. How apropos," I respond, then continue softly. "As I vowed to make you happy, any desire you have is for me to grant, my love."

My wife bows her head. The ebony curtain of her hair drops over her face.

I raise my other hand to sweep the glossy tresses behind her ear and grasp her chin between my thumb and forefinger. With our eyes on a level, I hold her gaze.

"No tears, Baby Girl. I only want to see you smile," I say.

She nods, then catches herself and adds, "Yes, My Lord."

My cock twitches again, and I shift in my seat.

She notices my discomfort and giggles.

I roll my eyes to the sky as I shake my head.

"*Aiutami dalla mia Piccola Tentatrice, per favore,*" I groan beseechingly.

She giggles some more at my request for help to save me from My Little Temptress.

"Come on, let's go back to *Villa dei Desideri* so I can show you just how thrilled I am..." she purrs, full of promise.

I make haste to get the attention of the server to pay while she checks on my babies.

We make our way to the marina where I parked the Alfa Romeo Stelvio Quadrifoglio. The beauty of Sorrento distracts us momentarily. But once we buckle The Trips into the backseat of the luxury SUV, I hold the back of My Little Temptress' head and kiss her until she moans into my mouth breathlessly. I sit back and give her a look full of so much lust her swollen lips part on a gasp and her plump nipples pebble beneath her shirtdress. I smirk and start the engine. It purrs to life like My Little Temptress.

When we return to *Villa dei Desideri*, we leave The Trips with Nanny Gail in the guest house. Then make a beeline for the primary suite in the villa. I chase My Little Temptress up the stairs and straight through the suite's lounge to the bedroom.

In a flash, I grab her by the hips and toss her onto the bed. She lands on all fours and flips her waist-length hair over a shoulder to look at me. Then shakes her round ass.

"I suppose my little bottom hole isn't quite the same as my pussy, My Lord. Shall I thank you for your gracious gift with access to my most naughty place?" She purrs seductively with a hooded gaze.

Forget a twitch. My cock damn near cums in my pants.

I growl and pounce.

She yelps.

Like a starved man before a gourmet buffet, I pull the hem of her shirtdress up and over her head and roll the delicate pink silk panties over her hips and down her legs. While I toss them to the floor, she unbuttons her dress and slings it aside.

My gaze zooms to her pussy and puckered hole bared to me. One glistens and the other clenches with her arousal. I don't notice she removed her bra until she breathes a sigh. Her heavy breasts tipped with nipples tinged dark pink jiggle as she resumes the position—head low, ass high.

A groan rumbles from the depths of my chest at the erotic sight.

I fall forward with my nose against her flesh and inhale rapturously of her fragrant arousal. The tip of my tongue darts out to lap at her juices. One taste, and a veil of carnal need drops before my eyes.

I feast.

She undulates her hips with throaty moans.

My fingers dig into her grip-worthy hips to still her as my tongue probes her innermost core. The rough texture of her G-spot greets me. I toy with it as she whimpers. Deeper, I dive as my tongue seeks every inch of her pussy.

She gushes, and her juices explode across my palate.

We groan in unison.

I nip her clit, and she explodes with a scream.

My balls tighten in their sac, eager for release.

My cock throbs.

But she must give me one more orgasm before I claim her ass.

I double my ministrations and grip her tighter when she attempts to crawl away from my demanding mouth. She stills when I growl into her pussy. It quivers. I latch onto her clit and hollow out my cheeks as I suck. Hard.

On the cusp of a fourth orgasm, My Little Temptress's entire body tightens. She sucks in a breath, then expels it on an unending wail.

I gulp down every sweet bit of her pussy juices as I purr with contentment.

Her head and torso collapse to the bed. Her body only held aloft by my unceasing grip on her hips.

Needing my release, I set her down and tear at the button and zipper of my pants. I stand and kick free of them and my boxer briefs as I yank my sweater over my head.

I fist my cock and stroke it to lessen the ache before I go all caveman. Two pillows beneath her hips raise her to the optimum position as she returns to her forearms. When she glances at me with pupils blown from carnal lust and wiggles her ass again, I don't hesitate to press my mushroom head to her puckered hole.

She tenses. But I reach around her hip to caress her engorged clit. As the sensations overtake her, she loosens her ass muscles, and I slip inside. The ring of muscles reactivates to force me from her forbidden hole.

I groan and tug at her clit as I round over her back.

Her moans signal me to press in further. I don't stop until I bottom out—groin to her ass and heavy balls to her clit. Both hands lock onto her hips, and I move with purpose. To cum.

After so many weeks without being inside of My Little Temptress makes the vise-like grip of her ass on my turgid length even more decadent. I relish in the sensation of it pulling me in and drawing me back as I thrust in and out.

It feels so bloody good my eyes squeeze shut as my head lolls back and my toes dig into the soft white duvet beneath us. The sounds of our skin slapping together as she meets each of my thrusts, her pants, and my grunts float all around us in harmony. An erotic symphony for a starved man as he sates his needs.

The base of my spine tingles as my release rushes forward. My grip tightens as I squat behind her to change the angle and thrust down into her tight ass, pinning her into the mattress.

She squeals and bucks. Her muscles flex on my cock.

I hiss and drive harder.

When my balls draw up, I reach around and cover a tit with my sizable hand as I squeeze the nipple between my fingers. She mewls as her milk coats them, and I bring my hand to my mouth to slake my thirst. My hips never stop pistoning.

"Oh, My Lord!! Please… please…" My Little Temptress cries out as she thrashes and bows her back.

I hiss as she tightens around my girth. My roar punches the air, bringing the erotic symphony to a carnal crescendo. I nearly pass out as my cock grows thicker and pumps my seed deep within her ass.

Instead, I band my arms around her waist and lower us —still intimately connected—onto our sides. I bury my face in her damp hair and groan. She sighs and scoots back against me as my pelvis cradles her ass.

"Did I show you just how thrilled I am, My Lord?" The vixen purrs.

I chuckle wickedly and lean back to rub her bottom— the touch soothing, possessive, and provocative. Then I smack that ass for her cheekiness.

She yelps from the unexpected sting.

"Yes, you did, My Little Temptress. And I thanked you immensely. Did I not?" I purr as I flex my cock still buried inside of her proffered hole.

She moans and arches her back as she glances over her shoulder at me.

"Absolutely, My Lord. Absolutely," she purrs in response.

I chuckle and pull her back into my embrace.

Villa dei Desideri satisfies my wishes, too.

HALEY

"This is a special place and time for us. We want to include all of our little ones, as Starr and I claim our love as a family forever. I'm grateful everyone is here. Yes, even you, Little Lord Fauntleroy."

Malcolm ends with a smirk as his platinum gray gaze flicks to Lachlan beside me.

We arrived yesterday evening along with the rest of our family. Malcolm and Starr, their babies, and Nanny Patience were on their private Laucala Island in Fiji for a week prior. The happy couple will have their vow renewal on the beach with us and their friends present.

My rebel brother may be *The Enforcer* of the Steeles. But he's a lovestruck puppy for his wife. Like the rest of the men in our family, he will do anything to keep a smile on her face. Just as she is now sitting next to him at the table for breakfast.

"Oh, Malcolm, don't you start in on Lachlan! You know

you're cool with him and Haley being married," Starr chides her husband as she cups his stubbled cheek. "And yes, we're so very grateful to celebrate our love with *all* of you!"

"Thank you, Starr. You're too gracious for this bloke!" Lachlan laughs as he raises his Mimosa in salute to her.

She grins and lifts her glass.

Everyone follows suit, even a reluctant Malcolm.

"Well, it's great to be in your company. However, I look forward to visiting the other side of your island for some action at LEVELS!" Laurent chimes in and raises his crystal flute higher. "Thank you, Starr, for an excellent idea!"

During their honeymoon on Laucala Island, Malcolm presented it to her as a wedding gift. Since her history with the luxury tropical paradise goes back years to when she hosted her first international retreat here and met Lola, then their surprise wedding, it makes the perfect gift.

Starr had the idea for Malcolm and Lucien to convert the original resort into LEVELS Laucala Island. BDSM on the Beach she dubbed it. For the first exclusive members-only BDSM resort.

While completing his hospitality and culinary training at the prestigious Le Cordon Bleu in Paris, Lucien thought of a BDSM/dance club. He figured the club would fill the void for safe, uninhibited sexual activities amongst the world's wealthiest and most influential people. He told Malcolm—his partner in crime—about it, and they convinced Sebastian a global, luxury, members-only entertainment venue focused on hedonism would add to

STEELE's bottom line. Baz, the net-net guy, saw the potential and gave them the green light.

Their venture with a high profit margin proved it's bigger than "a titty bar" as Baz originally called LEVELS New York, the flagship location. Malcolm and Lucien opened additional clubs in Paris, London, Beverly Hills, and most recently, here. An idea Lucien *The Sexy Chef* literally cooked up is worth millions.

We're all Global All Access Members. Although it took me being with Lachlan to gain entry since The Big Four forbid me from membership. And boy, do I love it!

"Well, I want to go to Starr's spa for that incredible massage with the warm frangipani oil," Lydie says.

"Oh, you'll need it after LEVELS," Chase murmurs.

I giggle since I'm seated next to him and hear his scandalous comment.

He turns and winks at me while Lydie flushes scarlet and sips her Mimosa to hide her gasp.

"Of course! I have a full day planned for tomorrow with classes, lunch, and spa treatments. After the long flight, everyone needs to unwind," Starr says.

Always the yogi to think of others' wellbeing, she also suggested she open Starr Light Fitness & Wellness Laucala Island to keep LEVELS LI members limber. It's one of many properties she's opened over the years through her partnership with STEELE International and Malcolm's Entertainment Properties Division in particular.

And keeping the family in mind, she kept the other side of the island private for us with the original six villas. Since then, they built six more as our family grows. I surprised Lachlan with one for us. Each has amazing views of the Pacific Ocean or sits directly on the beach.

We're on the terrace of Malcolm and Starr's sumptuous beachfront villa. It's so tranquil—just like Starr—in soothing tones of cream, white, and brown with turquoise accents. It blends in with the surrounding landscape seamlessly.

The children gather on blankets in the grass with the dogs and the nannies. Their laughter and barks blend with the sound of the waves rolling onto the shore.

"Shall we make the trip over to LEVELS later, My Little Temptress?"

Lachlan's warm breath against my ear jolts me from my musings, and he chuckles wickedly.

I turn to him and lean over as I rub my breasts against his arm surreptitiously. My hand ghosts up his thigh to squeeze his bountiful package.

He grunts and thumps my palm.

"Tonight's your lucky night, *Sir*," I croon in his ear.

His head spins so fast, he almost bumps my nose with his cheek. He gapes at me, surprised since I told him more time than I needed. My goal to make love here on this stunningly romantic island.

I wink at him and bite a carrot stick. The snap makes *him* jolt. I giggle and turn back to hear what Anita is saying at the other end of the table. But I don't get to hear much.

Lachlan rises and takes my elbow, lifting me to my feet with him.

"Excuse us a moment," he says to the table.

I have to hustle to keep up with his long strides as we round the corner of the villa. Then bump into his side when he stops just out of sight of the others.

He narrows his eyes as he towers over me.

"You said six weeks only three weeks ago, Haley Jackson. Did you lie to me?" He asks.

I bite the corner of my mouth as my gaze darts from his emerald fire to the azure waters of the Pacific.

"Well?" He demands.

I giggle nervously and slip my hand up the bridge of my nose as I did when I wore glasses.

He inhales sharply, recognizing my tell.

My back hits the wall as he slaps his hands on either side of my head. He cages me with his body. Flashes spark from his eyes.

"Why, you Naughty, Naughty, Naughty Girl... How I will punish you for your transgressions tonight. The Big Four cannot help you. Not. One. Bit."

He drives the last words home with snaps of his hips. His ginormous erection pokes my mons, drawing a gasp from my parted lips.

I grind back against him, and he growls like a feral caveman.

Oh dear, am I in for it now...

He stands to his full height, flares his nostrils, and points for me to walk back to the table.

As I pass between him and the wall, I dance to the tips of my toes as his massive hand spanks the sensitive juncture where my ass meets the tops of my thighs. One of my hands instinctively covers my butt while the other slaps over my mouth to hold back the yelp.

I glance over my shoulder at him, and he raises his eyebrow.

"That was only a taste of what's in store for you, Naughty, Naughty, Naughty Girl," he smirks.

I swallow and hurry further from his reach around the corner.

His wicked chuckles spur me on.

"Do you see that brunette woman hanging there bound by Shibari ropes? Her Domme flogging her upended pussy. What about the blindfolded man with the cock and ball cage cuffed to the St. Andrew's Cross and his Dom holding a cane? Over there, the crying woman astride the Sybian? Her Master watching her break for him as he sits in the leather chair."

In the Cellar, I swivel my head to find each person My Lord indicates and reply with a yes, My Lord dutifully.

Thirty minutes ago, we arrived at the club for LEVELS Laucala Island—the five-star beachfront resort spans across several buildings around the club. The Head of Membership took Lachlan and me on a tour of the seven levels. Instead of being like the other clubs in one building, each level exists in different Fijian bures. Or rather Malcolm and Lucien's luxurious versions of the traditional Fijian men's houses. As always, they play on the local area when they design a club. Paris is within the former home of a courtesan to a French king set behind double doors with an interior courtyard and a view of the Eiffel Tower.

Here, the Sky Lounge in the 7th bure sits on the beach with stunning views of the sunset over the Pacific Ocean and a bar, restaurant by day, dance club by night, with a coverable pool to extend the dance floor. The bure for the 6th and 5th levels that comprise the multilevel dance club with two bars and a lounge for food and drinks sits to one side of the Sky Lounge. On the other side, the 4th level bure has the Level 4 Restaurant and bar open for breakfast, lunch, and dinner. Rising above the dance club and built into the cliffside is the 3rd level with a two-story bure for twelve private bedrooms where members can continue their pleasure apart from the BDSM levels. Next to it above the Sky Lounge is the bure for the 2nd Level Peepshow for BDSM with seating alcoves, main stage, performance rooms, and a bar that serves non-alcoholic mocktails. A bure serves as the entrance where the 1st level Cellar BDSM dungeon with mocktails bar built directly into the cliff as a giant cave as opposed to being below ground. Covered paths lead from one bure to the other for an interconnecting city of consensual sin.

Overall, the guys did an amazing job recreating LEVELS to match the tropical island vibe while maintaining its core purpose. BDSM on the Beach!

My pussy clenches as my juices slip down my inner thighs at the carnal sights and sounds of the Cellar. Made even more otherworldly as the cries and moans of members echo off of the cave's natural rock walls and floor. Lights that resemble flickering torches in brackets on the walls and in metal stands scattered around the cave, an assortment of what looks like medieval torture devices placed in clusters. Hooks on adjustable chains swing alongside the wrought-iron chandeliers as they hang from the ceiling that soars high above us.

The sensual rhythm of music emanating from hidden speakers mix with the erotic smack of flesh and groans to make my nipples pebble tighter beneath my Lola's Coterie diaphanous chemise. Sex and pheromones fill the air. I close my eyes and inhale deeply of the aroma.

"Enjoying the moment, Naughty, Naughty, Naughty Girl?"

My Lord's warm breath skitters above my diamond collar before he nips where my neck and shoulder meet.

I tremble perched on my six-inch platform mules.

"Y—Y—Yes, My Lord, thank you," I stutter.

His wicked chuckle blows loose tendrils from my upswept bun.

"Now, come with me. You did not think I forgot your punishment. Did you?" He asks in a low rumble as he pats the underside of my ass. His fingertips skim below the hem of the super short lingerie.

I gasp and shake my head. Then squeak when he smacks my bottom.

"Words, Naughty, Naughty, Naughty Girl. I will have your words," he demands.

"Yes, My Lord, Sir," I whine as much from the pain as from my impatience for the pleasure to come.

"Very good. Come," he says as he lifts his hand to the small of my back and guides me further into the cave.

I can't help but to glimpse at the other members in various throes of fucking or watching as we pass more stages and alcoves. The entire scene exudes erotic hedonism. I worry my bottom lip, eager to partake.

We stop before an alcove with vamp red crystal beads held back by wrought-iron stays. As we step inside, I note the vamp red leather spanking horse in the center. I swallow. My gaze moves to the side where a hutch displays a variety of implements and toys on its shelves. Across from it, an oversized vamp red leather bench stretches out.

A tinkling sound behind me makes me pivot.

My Lord loosened the beads. They come together to form a semi-transparent curtain that separates us from the main room of the Cellar. He stands before the beaded backdrop as his eyes scan my body from head to toe and back to my eyes.

I blink and shift on my feet.

He taps his long index finger against his full lips as he surveys the hutch. With a satisfied nod, he strides forward. His muscular thighs flex beneath his black leather pants. He picks up a crop and flicks his wrist. The crop snaps in the air.

I flinch.

Oh, my damn.

"Thirty lashes should suffice," My Lord states matter-of-factly to himself.

Then turns to me as he rolls back the sleeves of his black silk lace-up shirt.

Our eyes meet—wide dove gray to sparkling emerald green. It's as though he's lit from within, ready to light a fire under me.

I drop my eyes submissively.

"Oh, no, Naughty, Naughty, Naughty Girl. Too late for your redemption," he purrs as he stands before me. "Off."

He snaps the crop at the hem of my chemise to indicate its removal.

I jump and comply immediately. The soft fabric drifts to the stone floor on a whisper.

Goosebumps raise on the surface of my skin as his fiery gaze travels over my body once again. My nipples ache from being so taut. His heat reaches into my lower belly to make my ovaries explode. An uncontrollable moan slips from my lips. My cheeks flush crimson.

"So beautiful you are, Naughty, Naughty, Naughty Girl," he purrs as the leather tongue of the crop licks along my inner thighs. He taps it against my pussy seam and lifts the crop in the flickering light.

A sheen gleams.

I mewl, embarrassed by the sight of my undeniable arousal on the leather tongue.

My Lord chuckles as he brings the tongue to my mouth. He taps it against my upper lips.

I part them, and my tongue darts out to lick the leather

tongue clean. An unbidden moan fills the air between us. Unsure whether it's from me or My Lord, I glance up into his hooded eyes.

"On the spanking bench. Now," he commands.

I scuttle forward and drape my body over the buttery soft leather already broken in from prior use. I fidget with my eagerness, then sigh and sink into the softness of the leather when My Lord secures the velvet-lined leather cuffs to my wrists and ankles.

The gentle sweep of the crop over my buttocks and up my spine draws a mewl from me. My Lord repeats the erotic caress until I'm lulled into a false sense of ease.

"Why will I punish you, Naughty, Naughty, Naughty Girl?" He asks as he drapes his torso over mine. The enormous bulge at his crotch kisses the seam of my ass.

I shift as much as my bonds allow to press back against him.

Abruptly, he stands.

The whistle of the crop as it slashes through the air alerts me to his displeasure.

I yelp when the leather tongue bites at my bottom.

"Do not move unless I tell you to do so, Naughty, Naughty, Naughty Girl!" He chastises me. "Now, answer my question."

I gulp in air to even my tone and answer.

"You will punish me because I lied to you about when we can make love again. Penetrative love by your dick in my pussy, My Lord."

He drops to his heels beside my head.

I turn in his direction.

"Exactly," he says. "You will count each lash. If you miss, we will start anew. At any time, you may use your safeword —mercy. Do you understand, Naughty, Naughty, Naughty Girl?"

"Yes, My Lord!" I respond.

My heartbeat increases when he stands and strides behind me. I clench my fists and toes as I brace myself.

The whistle pierces the air, and I flinch. But only a soft tap lands on my hand.

"Do you trust me?" He asks, and I nod. "Then relax, Naughty, Naughty, Naughty Girl."

Once my shoulders drop and my thighs ease against the leather, he begins with my punishment.

I don't miss one count or use my safeword. As soon as thirty falls from my lips on a relieved sigh, I hear the crop clatter to the stone floor. My Lord removes the cuffs from my ankles and wrists, rubbing each one. I'm lifted into the air and held to his chest closely as he murmurs words of love in my hair.

He settles on the leather bench with my legs straddling his hips and my arms draped over his wide shoulders. The emerald fire simmers in his smoky eyes as he gazes at me lovingly.

I lean forward and press my lips to his lush mouth. I start the kiss, but he takes control. Our tongues dance until I roll my hips to bring my dripping core to his bulge that threatens to punch a hole through the soft leather of his pants.

He groans into my mouth and squeezes my ass.

A strangled cry from the erotic pain on my punished bottom gets swallowed up by My Lord as he deepens our passionate kiss. He squeezes my ass again, and I moan as the pain morphs to pleasure. My hips roll once more.

I reach between us and hesitate to unfasten his pants without his permission.

He thrusts up and groans into my mouth.

I moan and free his turgid length eagerly.

My Lord pulls back from our kiss for our eyes to meet.

"I do not want to overwhelm you with my size after such a long time. You ride me and take what you need at your pace," he says.

I brush my lips against his mouth and respond, "Yes, My Lord, thank you."

Then I rise to my knees and fist his dick to align it with my pussy. My gaze never waivers from his as I impale myself on his thick, long velvet-coated steel. I feel every ridge, every vein, and every inch of him until his dick reaches the very end of my core to possess me fully. I cry out from the burn of the stretch as my pussy walls acclimate to his size.

My Lord grasps my ass in his hands to hold me steady. His fingernails graze the welts, and I whimper. He lowers his head and laps at my peaked nipple. Then brings his lips to lick at my mouth voraciously.

"I want you. I crave you," he murmurs in a hoarse voice I strain to hear above the erotic din of the Cellar.

His need spurs me into action.

I lift slowly, and we groan as one. Then grunt when I slam back down. My sore ass kisses his groin. But I don't stop riding My Lord. I clench and release his dick with each move.

He takes a nipple into his mouth as my tits bounce before his face. My milk flows into his mouth readily, and he gobbles it down with groans.

My toes curl as my orgasm races closer. I throw my head back and scream. At last, my cries of sheer euphoria rise to the roof of the Cellar's cave with those from others around us. We're as one with them in our pursuit of carnal bliss.

"Baby Girl, I can't hold back anymore," my lover says past his clenched jaw tight with the exertion to hold back.

"Don't," I pant and squeeze his dick with my inner walls grown stronger through relentless rounds of Kegels.

He grunts and grips my ass to the point of pain as he locks me in place. He thrusts up.

I wail.

He stills, and with a panicked expression, searches my face.

"Again!" I demand and squeeze.

His eyes roll back, and he jackhammers into me. He's so powerful I fear we'll break the bench beneath us. But it stays strong through his release. Copious amounts of his thick milky seed scorch my womb. It triggers another orgasm from me. He rides it out with slow thrusts.

Sated, we collapse back against the wall.

After our heartbeats return to normal, Lachlan lays me

on the bench and goes to the hutch. He tends to my sore bottom and cleans our combined essence from my thighs. Then retrieves my chemise and places it over my head to fall to my upper thighs. I step into my mules.

In silence, we leave the club and walk to the resort where we reserved a suite facing the Pacific Ocean. We take a luxurious soak in the outdoor sunken tub with the stars and moon shining above us.

I lean back against Lachlan's firm chest, and he wraps his arms beneath my breasts.

"Well, if that's the punishment I receive for lying to you, I should do it more often," I say.

He growls and tweaks both nipples at once.

I squeal and bring my hands up to protect my sensitive tips.

"Never again!" I cry out.

"Lesson learned, Naughty, Naughty, Naughty Girl?" He asks gruffly.

"Yes, My Lord, thank you," I whisper.

"Good, girl," he murmurs as he kisses my neck.

His dick thumps against my back.

I mewl, knowing our night only begun.

LACHLAN

"Thank you. Your team is having an impressive quarter. At this pace, you will end the year above the prior. If you do, you can look forward to sizable bonuses."

"Thank you, Mr. Jackson. We appreciate your recognition. I will relay your message to the entire team today, sir."

I nod at my Head of Production.

She smiles before she gathers her laptop and exits the conference room with her second in command.

When the double doors close behind them, I shift in my chair to face Lydie. She flew in last night from New York City for the week.

We had the first round of team reviews before the year ends next month. Over the next few days, we'll complete them. Then finish with the executive team meetings and a group dinner. I like to let my staff know where they stand before the quarter ends so they can push to catch up to or exceed projections. Lydie agrees.

"Tell me your thoughts on their presentation," I say.

She nods as she sits back in her chair and re-crosses her long legs. She picks up her Montblanc, gold, fountain pen and twirls it between her fingers deftly.

"They're spot-on with their numbers and have been consistent throughout the year. The new head had a lot to do with their growth. She's one to watch should a more senior position open," Lydie responds.

We continue to discuss the reviews we had earlier before we break for lunch with the CEO of a potential distributor. He wanted to take us to a well-known restaurant across town. But I prefer for distributors to sample Jackson's brands while we dine. So, we'll meet him downstairs in the bar of the Jackson Restaurant. Then eat lunch.

Lucien used his magic touch to turn the original restaurant of Jackson Town House into a three Michelin star eatery his first year as chef. His versions of traditional Scottish fare combined with skills he learned at Le Cordon Bleu earned him the recognition.

Besides business purposes, the restaurant is one of my regular eateries in all of Aberdeen. My Baby Girl enjoys its menu, too. Especially since it's near our penthouse flat, and she's still not the best cook despite her best efforts...

"Oh, I meant to tell you earlier, but we've been so busy with the meetings," Lydie says as she scrolls through her email. She closes her laptop and leans forward. "I saw Chet Stewart while at the business conference in Tokyo. Never the most pleasant fellow. This time his demeanor was quite smug, as though Stewart Scotch had a one up on Jackson Corporation. He made comments that hinted at something big happening on several occasions, and always when I was near enough to overhear. Have you caught wind of any news on their front?"

I sit back and frown as I rack my brain for a clue.

"Other than a brief encounter with Bram at the club five months ago, nothing comes to mind," I respond. "Then seeing the brothers and their parents at social functions. No instances that stand out."

Lydie purses her lips and shakes her head.

"How did Bram act? Did he say anything untoward?" She asks.

I shake my head and respond, "The usual snide comments. This time a fake congratulations for the continuation of the Jackson line and a hello to the Marquess of Huntly. But if Chet's behavior bothers you, I'll ask my guy if he's heard about anything happening at Stewart."

"Good, because we can never be too careful with those snakes!" Lydie exclaims. "And to think I let Chet kiss me when we were kids. Ewww!"

I throw my head back and laugh at the memory.

"Oh, you mean when you—"

"Don't you dare remind me of the details, Lachlan Jackson!" Lydie cuts in as she points her Montblanc at me threateningly. "You have your own mistakes in the romance department, you know!"

My laughter stops abruptly, and my cheeks heat.

That's the thing with siblings who are close. We know way too much about each other…

"Fine. No Memory Lane visits for either of us. Come on, let's go to the restaurant. I could use a taste to clear the vision of you and Chet—Ow!"

I rub my flank and glance around at Lydie.

She's glaring at me with her pen held out like an épée. Her emerald green eyes flash.

Did I say she's a shark in the boardroom, or what?

I hold my hands up, palms out in surrender. But I can't help a chuckle at her fierceness. Chet is a thorn in her side. Or rather, mine. Ouch.

"Don't say I didn't warn you, Lachlan," Lydie smirks as she slips the fountain-pen-cum-weapon into her Chanel portfolio.

I grin and hold out my arm as I respond, "You certainly did."

She links arms with me, and we stride out of the conference room.

As we pass through the executive floor, our staff greets us, and we stop to chat with a few. Our father taught all of us the value of being in touch with the people who work with you, including knowing something personal about them. It makes their connection to us and to Jackson Corporation stronger.

When we arrive at Jackson Restaurant, the distributor sits at the bar talking to a woman. As Lydie and I near him, he raises his head and smiles. The woman spins around on the stool and smiles, too.

I guess she's here for the meeting.

"Hello, Lachlan," Klaus says as he extends his hand. "Thank you for meeting with me."

I shake his hand as I respond, "Hello, Klaus. Of course. Your offer intrigues us."

His smile broadens, and he glances at Lydie. His icy blue eyes trail over her, from topknot to sky-high stilettos. An appreciative expression dawns on his face.

"I see you brought your secretary with you, as did I. This is Petra," he says without glancing away from Lydie. "And who might this delightful *fräulein* be?"

Did I say great white shark or bull shark? Maybe the tiger shark. The three most feared apex predators of them all.

A slow smile spreads across Lydie's face as her eyes gleam and narrow on Klaus. She arches an elegant eyebrow.

"Who might *I* be?" She repeats his question. Then she leans in when his eyes widen at her reaction. "Your worse bloody nightmare, *Klaus.* A beautiful woman with a brain and a pussy who could use both to fuck you so well she leaves you broken, if she so chose. That's who Lydie Jackson is to minor men like you."

Klaus' mouth hits the floor as his face reddens.

Petra gasps and clutches her pearls.

Lydie needs zero help from me. So, I bite my tongue between my teeth to hold back uproarious laughter.

"Now that we completed the introductions. Either put out what you can do for Jackson Corporation's bottom line. Or get the fuck out of my house—Jackson Town House—Klaus," Lydie finishes. The mighty shark circles back around for the death bite.

Klaus bows his head, stripped of his balls dangling from *The Shark*'s mouth.

"My sincere apologies, Ms. Jackson. I did not know. Please forgive my inexcusable behavior," he says. "If it pleases you, I would appreciate the opportunity to discuss business with you and Mr. Jackson."

Lydie eyes him until he lowers his submissively. Only then does she answer.

"Carry on," she says and sweeps past him with her head held high towards the restaurant's maître d'. Her heels click on the hardwood floor.

I gesture for Petra, then Klaus, to follow in her wake.

He babbles more apologies as he passes me.

"Not a good beginning, Klaus. You better hope your offer is worth our time," I tell him.

He nods repeatedly and walks ahead of me.

"Damn, Lydie, you devoured that sexist sack of shit! The bloody kicker is you had him eating out of the palm of your hand. Then he added more to the deal than he originally mentioned."

I chortle, reliving the moment.

We're back in the conference room for the afternoon round of team review meetings. We have ten minutes before the first one starts. So, we can have a good laugh at the lunch.

Lydie smirks.

"Oh, you know me, take no prisoners," she says, jabbing her Montblanc in the air for emphasis.

We crack up some more before deciding to proceed with the deal. Sure, Klaus is a bloody wanker. But he learned a solid lesson this day. And as our father taught us, business is business, and you don't have to like everyone. But they sure as hell better respect you and make you money in the process.

In Klaus' case, he'll do both thanks to *The Shark*!

The rest of the day goes by in a blur of back-to-back meetings. It's satisfying to see the results of each team. Even the ones that need more attention since their improvement will reflect how in tune we are with our staff and helping them to perform at their best.

I send My Baby Girl a text message to let her know Lydie and I are on our way home. She's coming over for dinner and to spend time with her niece and nephews. We picked up some dishes from Jackson Restaurant before we left the office. Since My Baby Girl still breastfeeds, she won't partake of the new blend of Scotch. Lydie and I will savor it for her.

"How was your day?" My Baby Girl asks when Lydie and I enter the lounge at the penthouse flat.

Lilias—with a red toy in her hand—sits on her mother's lap. Meanwhile, Leith lies on his tummy raised on his arms, watching them, and Lewis stands as Nanny Gail holds his hands. She greets us with a warm smile.

At four-months old, The Trips can do so much more. Every day brings something new. This morning it was Lewis saying ba-ba-ba-ba. I thought it was Dada and spilled coffee on my shirt in surprise. Naturally, My Baby Girl laughed.

Lydie rushes over and lowers to a cross-legged position gracefully, and scoops Leith into her arms. He laughs and swings his chubby arms in the air.

"Hello, sweeties! Your Auntie missed you so much! Look how big you are now," she exclaims as she tickles Lilias' tummy and strokes Lewis' cheek.

I pull out my mobile to snap some candid shots. Then call their names to wave—another favorite of The Trips.

"We had a productive day," I answer My Baby Girl as I drop down beside her and reach for Lewis. "Thank you, Nanny Gail. You may take the rest of the night."

She thanks me and leaves for her flat downstairs.

"Oh, and we had a shark feeding, too," I add, with a straight face. "What a bloody mess that was, huh, Lydie?"

She snorts, and My Baby Girl frowns as she glances between my sister and me.

"What do you mean?" She asks.

I recount Lydie's pre-lunch appetizer, and My Baby Girl high fives her.

"Who Runs the World?!" My Baby Girl shouts.

Lydie throws her head back and responds, "Girls!"

They continue to sing while The Trips laugh and ga-ga-ga-ga right along with them.

I shake my head at their rendition of Beyoncé's girl-power song. But I can't disagree.

Hands down, Lydie damn sure proved it today!

"See something you like, Mrs. Jackson?"

Lachlan asks with a smirk as he saunters out of the en suite bathroom in our Paris penthouse, bare-chested with a towel slung around his narrow hips. His biceps and pecs bulge as he dries his hair with a towel. The outline of his mouth-watering dick as it hangs along his thigh presses against the terry cloth. The glint of his platinum wedding band catches my eye, and I smile.

My man is a living and breathing, sexy AF Adonis.

I roll over onto my belly amongst the sheets strewn across the bed, sated from our morning romp. Purposefully, I push my ample triple D-cups together as I sit up on my elbows. I glide the tip of my tongue along my upper lip as I narrow my hooded gaze at my man.

"Hmmm… Maybe," I purr.

"Oh no, My Little Temptress. You've already delayed me once with your wanton ways. Not all of us can decide to take another month off from work, you know," he says as he drops his towel and marches into his walk-in closet.

I wolf whistle at the sight of his tight ass and the backs of his muscular legs as they flex with each step. Then drag myself from the comfort of our bed to follow him. I wobble on still-jellified legs as I stand. My pussy throbs from the aftershocks of his pounding. I sigh and grin with contentment.

"Don't hate, Mr. CEO," I say as I fold my arms under my breasts and lean buck naked against the doorjamb. "I can run the world from home. Boop."

I give Lachlan the drop-the-mic mime and stroll over to stand before him.

"And I can still take care of my man," I add as I swat his hands away from his shirt and slip the buttons through the holes for him.

Then I go over to the rack of ties to select one to match his bespoke three-piece pinstripe suit. Turning with one that has a navy background and miniatures of Hermès' iconic *Chaîne d'ancre* links in green and light blue. The perfect complement to the navy suit and white shirt.

Lachlan watches me as I complete the Full Windsor Knot and slip the matching pocket square into his jacket, hanging on the wooden valet.

He grips my hips and pulls me flush against his hard body.

"Merci beaucoup, Madame Jackson," my lover says.

I shudder at the deep resonance of his baritone voice as he thanks me very much. Aside from English and Scottish

Gaelic, my man's fluency extends to French, Italian, and German.

He chuckles and kisses the tip of my nose.

I continue to watch him as he slips into his A. Testoni Oxfords and slides into his suit jacket. When he's fully dressed, I put on my kimono to walk him to our private elevator.

"Have fun with your sisters," Lachlan says as he presses the call button. "We'll see you for dinner later tonight. But first…"

He slips his hand inside of my kimono to cup my breast. The silk whispers across my skin and makes my nipples pucker. He dips his head to draw a plump nub between his lips. The deliberate suckling makes my milk flow into his eager mouth. He swallows it down on a groan as I arc my back.

The elevator doors ping open.

Lachlan stands and swipes a stray droplet from the corner of his mouth and sucks on the digit. With a wink, he backs into the elevator, and the doors close.

I melt on the spot.

"Yes, Mom, we're flying out of Milan. Lachlan has some business in Italy before we meet everyone in Verbier… I know! It'll be their first Christmas… Oh, please don't go overboard with presents… Yes, it is your right as a grand-mother… Tell Dad hi and I love you guys. We just pulled up to the gates… Will do… Yes… Bye… Bye!"

I giggle as I sit back and glance out the window as my Mercedes-Benz G-Wagen passes through the gates at *Le Beaulieu Manoir*.

It's the ancestral home of Leonie's family on the westernmost part of the outskirts of Paris in Neuilly-Auteuil-Passy. The majestic property features manicured park-like grounds, stables, tennis court, swimming pool and cabana, and a palatial French Rococo mansion. A part of the 16th arrondissement, it's in the wealthiest neighborhood.

They built the hamlet between the thirteenth and seventeenth centuries. Later, during the reign of Louis XV, it became a fashionable country retreat for French elites. The Beaulieu's twenty acres of land border Bois de Boulogne with parts of the acreage awarded to their ancestors by the monarch.

With weddings, births, the busyness of life, we haven't had a Girls' Getaway in a while. As it happens, Sebastian and Malcolm have STEELE business in Paris at the same time as Lachlan for Jackson Corporation. So my sisters and I decided to hang out for a Girls' Day. Lola and Starr flew over with my brothers, and Leonie and Anita are already here. Since her parents were traveling, Leonie offered her childhood home as the location for our impromptu get together.

Anita has a morning yoga and meditation class to kick the day off with some movement and centering. After lunch, Starr will take us through a Pilates and barre session. We'll end the day being pampered by Leonie's favorite spa's aestheticians, treating us to facials and massages. Then her hair and makeup glam squad will prep us for a night out with our men at LEVELS Paris for dinner, dancing, and the dungeon.

The nannies will watch our children and their dogs while we reconnect. It's wonderful how well they get along. Today is as much of a respite for them as it is for us!

The SUV pulls up to the large, ornate, hand-carved door of the mansion. The guard at the gate must have told Leonie we arrived since she and Nanny Grace open the doors and rush out to greet us.

"*Chérie*! So good to see you!" Leonie exclaims as she hugs me close. "Let's get you and The Trips inside. It's freezing out here!"

Nanny Gail steps out of the passenger front seat and helps the three of us while my driver opens the other back door. Each of us takes one of The Trips and our bags inside the residence.

Whenever I enter *Le Beaulieu Manoir*, I can't help but to look around.

The interior decor is just as impressive as the outside. The furniture, paintings, and sculpture mimic the light elements with curves and natural patterns to form the delicacy and playfulness influenced by Rococo designs.

The proof of the Beaulieus being centuries-long, wealthy merchants who traveled the world for the most luxurious items is clear. The mixture of Asian, North African, and Russian influences appears in the tapestries, wall panels, and fabrics. The modern era shows through in accessories, other artwork, and air-conditioning and heating systems. It's an incredible treasure trove that forever changes as Josy swaps old finds with new ones.

"We'll take The Trips to the playroom where the other children and the dogs are with Nanny Janice and Nanny Patience. Then you can change before we meet the girls in the solarium. *Bien, chérie?*" Leonie says.

"*Oui bien,*" I respond, being fluent in French.

Leonie's amber eyes glitter as she loops arms with me, and we stride along to the playroom. Once we settle The Trips and I hug my nieces and nephews, Leonie shows me to a bathroom. I change, and we walk past beautifully appointed salons to the all-glass solarium that in the warmer months overlooks the rear rose garden. Now it's a winter wonderland of snow-covered lawns, bushes, and trees. The large windows and glass ceiling bring the outdoors inside for a lovely spot to practice yoga.

"Hey, Haley!"

"Hi! Where are my babies?"

"I love your leggings!"

My girls surround me for hugs before we take to our mats.

"Take a comfortable seat. Use a block, bolster, or your folded blanket. Whichever allows your body to sit without tension. Place your hands on your thighs, easy at the elbows. We will begin with pranayama to bring us into the space and to clear our minds for our practice," Anita says as she sits before us on her mat.

I take a lotus position and slide my blanket under my sits bones to align my spine, then place my hands on my thighs. My eyes close as Anita begins our breathing practice. With each inhalation and exhalation, the everyday stresses of life seep from my body. Thoughts clear as I find myself enchanted by her soft words as she guides us.

"You may remain seated as you are or switch to another comfortable seated position with your eyes open or closed as you listen to my dharma talk. Today, let us focus on our wellbeing, peace, fulfillment, and auspiciousness…"

Afterwards, Anita's vigorous vinyasa flow builds to a forearm hollow back asana—a challenging pose that requires absolute concentration and breathing. As I hold the asana, its therapeutic benefits of relieving stress and lifting your mood make a smile spread across my face. I feel light, fierce, and free!

Once we've recovered during savasana, Anita announces it's time for our japa practice. She rises elegantly from her hero's pose and removes pouches from a bag under a window. She turns and smiles at us.

"For our meditation practice, I have gifts of malas made from selenite for you. We know selenite for its cleansing properties—including clearing blocked energy—and promotes peace and calm," Anita says as she hands a pouch to each of us. Then she settles back on her mat to lead us in a mantra while she uses a singing bowl. It ends our practice with deep relaxation.

"Oh, Anita, that was a phenomenal session. Thank you so much!" Lola exclaims.

Starr bows her head with hands at her heart and adds,

"The theme from start to finish was wonderful, much gratitude."

"I agree. This was just what I needed," I say.

Leonie takes us to the guest wing, where the maids put our bags in rooms. We shower and meet up back in the solarium.

The staff switched out the mats for a table and chairs for our lunch and a sideboard arranged for a buffet-style service. The chef created a bounty of mouth-watering dishes with herb-crusted salmon, roasted chicken, root vegetables, and green salads. A tantalizing aroma of savory dishes fills the air.

My stomach growls after the workout, and I cannot wait to fill my plate.

"Haley, you're the newest mother. How do you feel with The Trips five-months old?" Leonie asks, the first of us to give birth.

I take a moment to reflect on her question and glance out of the windows as snow falls. It's been an incredible time. More than I expected or ever dreamed my fairytale life would be.

Motherhood puts so much into perspective for me. My work at STEELE Technology and Cyber Security still ranks high. But my babies come first, which is why I took another month off. Although Harris and my team can contact me if necessary. After the struggle Lachlan and I had to conceive, I want to cherish every moment with Lilias, Leith, and Lewis. At some point, I'll return full-time to work.

I share my thoughts with my sisters, and they nod in agreement.

"I know what you mean. It took me time to want to have children for preferring to keep Lola's Coterie—my first baby—first. But when I had Slade—even while pregnant—I knew my life would shift," Lola says. "And I *do not* regret it at all. Especially with the birth of Sabrina and Stella. My munchkins take top priority. Well, along with their father, of course!"

Starr and Leonie express how they love their babies. But still work. Just not the long hours they did before. Anita agrees and tells us how, as her daughters reached pre-school, she was ready to go back to her regular hours. But it helps since she too runs her own company and can set her schedule with ease.

We move to one of the salons to chat some more and hang out before our afternoon Pilates and barre session. Once we finish, our excitement increases as the time nears for the glam squad to arrive and get us ready for a night out at LEVELS Paris.

By the time our men meet us in the entry hall of *Le Beaulieu Manoir*, we can hardly contain our eagerness to party and indulge in whatever tickles our fancy.

"Don't you look appetizing, My Little Temptress," Lachlan murmurs in my ear when he sees me. "How was your day with your sisters?"

I give him a twirl to show off my vintage Versace platinum chain mail mini slip dress. Lace trims the cups and the hem, making it the perfect choice to carry me from dinner to dancing to the dungeon—or wherever My Lord wants.

My hand loops around his elbow as I complete my spin, and I pull him down to whisper in his ear.

"Fun. But not as much pleasure as I hope you will give me, *My Lord.*"

He smirks and nods.

"Oh, of that you can be certain, My Little Temptress," he rejoins with a promise-filled chuckle.

HALEY

"Ugh… This is the worse… Sorry. Oh!"

It's Saturday morning, and I'm hugging the toilet bowl in the en suite of our Aberdeen penthouse flat. Lachlan holds my hair back from my face—bless him—as I empty the contents of my stomach. At this point, it's dry heaving. Nausea roils my stomach, giving me a headache.

"Never sorry, My Baby Girl. Just take it easy and breathe," Lachlan says calmly as he wipes my neck with a cool cloth. "Do you want some tea?"

If I weren't so violently ill, I'd giggle at his go-to suggestion for all ailments—Scottish Breakfast tea. But the thought of anything in my mouth makes me hurl. I clench the porcelain bowl tighter.

A moan slips from my mouth as tears of frustration stain my flushed cheeks.

It's been this way off and on for weeks—it could be in the morning or whenever I smell something unappealing.

Unfortunately, this past week it's gotten worse. Much worse. Yuck.

My first thought was I'm pregnant. But I haven't missed a month of my period, so I ruled pregnancy out. Then once again, we just returned from Verbier. Maybe I caught a bug. It hurts my head too much to try and figure it out now, though.

Another wave hits me, and I slump to the floor, exhausted.

"Come here, lass," Lachlan says as he lifts me onto his lap. "You know what I think?"

I grunt a no as I burrow my face into his neck. His delicious scent envelops me, and I sigh at ease.

"You're pregnant," he states matter-of-factly.

My heart rate speeds up as I shift to read his face.

He shrugs.

"When you're steady, I'm going to the pharmacy for some tests. If they're not positive, I'm calling your physician for a home visit," Lachlan responds to my unasked question.

I nod and take a breath to try and get myself together.

After a while, he carries me into the shower and bathes me. Then leans his butt against my vanity as I brush my teeth. And gargle repeatedly. He settles me back in bed after fluffing the pillows. A kiss to my forehead, and he leaves.

The whole time he's gone, I worry. It took us forever to conceive before The Trips. Sure, I'm not on any birth control, so it's highly plausible I'm preggie again. And The

Trips are only six-months old! Is Lachlan ready for another baby so soon? Am I?

My stomach knots, and I groan as I drag myself back to the bathroom.

By the time Lachlan returns, I'm back in bed speaking with Nanny Gail to thank her for working on the weekend. I end the call when he appears in our bedroom's doorway.

He lifts a bag bulging with more than one pregnancy test.

I can't help a nervous giggle.

Lachlan shrugs.

Scooping me up from the bed, he carries me and the bag into the bathroom and deposits me on my vanity.

"Okay, laugh all you want, Mrs. Jackson. But I want to be sure," he says as he rummages through the bag and sets each test beside me.

I lift a box up and scan the directions. Then a different brand. And another. Good grief. My husband bought six tests!

Opting for the least complicated one, I open the packaging, then slip off of the vanity. As I walk to the toilet, I hear Lachlan behind me.

"What are you doing?" I ask over my shoulder.

"I want to see, obviously," he responds with an indignant scowl.

I frown back and put my hands on my hips.

"Ah, no. No way are you watching me pee on a stick, Lachlan Jackson!" I snap.

He mimics my stance and cocks an eyebrow.

"Well, it's my baby, too, Haley Jackson!" He retorts.

My gaze softens, and my arms drop to my sides. He's right. It must be my hormones. My eyes widen as I realize I do think I'm pregnant.

"Sorry, my love. You're absolutely right," I say with a soft smile. I take a deep, mind-cleansing breath. "Well, let's do this!"

As it turns out, Lachlan is a great assistant. He opens the rest of the tests and passes one at a time to me. After the fourth, I whine about how I have no more pee left! He offers to get me some water. Then grumbles when I glare at him. He nods and turns back to the vanity, where he placed the used tests in a row.

Anxiously, we hover over them as we wait for a sign. One after the other displays a plus sign, two lines, or the words *You're Pregnant*.

I gasp.

Lachlan inhales sharply.

Then he wraps his arms around me and lifts me from the floor as he whoops. He spins in a circle, and my stomach clenches. I cover my mouth with one hand and push his shoulder with the other. His eyes widen, and he places me in front of the vanity. Now the sink welcomes me.

After I gargle for the millionth time, he wipes my face with another damp cloth as he levels his gaze with mine.

"Okay, My Baby Girl?" He asks softly.

I nod and offer a half smile to ease the concern in his emerald green orbs. He grins back, and they dance with his happiness. He places his hand on my lower belly, then drops to kneel before me as he presses his lips to my belly.

"Thank you, my love," he murmurs.

So, I guess he is ready for another baby so soon after The Trips.

I cup the back of his tousled head and smile.

And I'm ready, too!

"ARE you sure you don't want me to have Dr. Astrid come over today? It's only Saturday, so we'll have to wait two more days if you go when her office opens. I'll pay her well for her time, Haley."

Lachlan frowns as he stares at me from where he sits on the floor with Lewis and Lilias. He's serious when he calls me by my given name. Oh, boy.

I watch him as I rest on the sofa with Leith in the sitting room of our bedroom suite.

Now that I feel better and know the cause of my ailment, we told Nanny Gail she doesn't need to watch The Trips. But we'll stay close to the bed... and to the bathroom.

Also, since the tests proved positive, I factor in the tenderness of my breasts and my sleepiness. Without a doubt, I'm pregnant. The one concern is me still having my period. So I understand Lachlan's sense of urgency.

I glance at him again, and he has a scowl on his gorgeous face as he plays with his babies.

"Fine," I say. When he grins, I hold up my hand and add, "But *you* call her. Not me. Deal?"

"Hell, yeah!" He exclaims as he reaches for his mobile on the coffee table.

He saves all of my doctors' office and personal phone numbers and email addresses in his contacts app—my obsessive caveman.

Dr. Ross agrees to come over in an hour, he tells me triumphantly after he ends the call.

I giggle and shake my head.

Already dressed in a Lola's Coterie cashmere maxi lounge dress, I don't need to change. I breastfeed The Trips before Dr. Ross arrives so they can sleep while the doctor examines me. She can tend to me in one of the guest suites.

Right on time, the doorman announces her arrival. Lachlan and I wait for her at the private elevator, then we go to the suite.

I'm impressed Dr. Ross has a portable ultrasound. She explains it's for times like these, and she smiles at Lachlan. I should have known since her patients are the wealthiest in Aberdeen, and the husbands are as demanding as mine. No is not in their vocabulary.

I easily swap my lounge dress for the gown she hands to me and lie down on the bed. After an examination, she sets up the ultrasound machine. I glance at Lachlan, who has an expression of concern in the depths of his emerald eyes. He notices me watching him and the corners of his mouth lift slightly to ease my worry.

Relief washes over both of our faces as soon as the

rhythmic heartbeat fills the room. Then frown when a separate beat sounds. We gawk at the monitor.

"Congratulations, Lord and Lady Aboyne! You're pregnant with twins!" Dr. Ross announces.

The bed dips and the ultrasound probe slips from my belly.

Dr. Ross and I whip our heads around to find Lachlan slumped on the edge of the bed with his hand over his eyes. As before, he passed out at the news of us having multiples. Dr. Ross and I laugh heartily.

He lifts his gaze to the monitor, then to me, and smiles sheepishly. His cheeks flush crimson.

I pat his hand and grin.

"Sure you're ready, My Lord?" I ask.

He sits up tall and squares his shoulders.

"Absolutely, My Lady!" He affirms.

"Well, you have twenty-four weeks to prepare. You're twelve weeks, Lady Aboyne. Twins come at thirty-six weeks. So, you have more time than you did with your triplets," Dr. Ross tells us.

Lachlan and I exchange glances.

Holy mackerel!

"My secretary will call you on Monday to schedule your appointments. You will follow the same instructions as before. But just in case, here's a packet for you, including vitamins. My secretary will contact your pharmacy for the full prescription, too. Do you have any questions?" Dr. Ross continues.

I shake my head and look at Lachlan, who does the same.

She smiles and hands a towel to me to remove the ultrasound gel.

We thank her as she packs up. Lachlan sees her to the elevator while I re-dress.

I stand in front of the mirror with my hands on my lower belly, turning to see different angles. How will my body appear with only two babies growing inside? I remember how Leonie, Starr, and Lola looked. You could only tell they were pregnant from the front and the sides with their sets of twins. Not that I mind. My babies' health is more important to me than my waist size!

A sound behind me makes me glance up.

Lachlan stands in the doorway watching me with eyes so full of awe and love, it takes my breath away. They shine with a hint of tears before he blinks and strides forward. He puts his arms around me from behind and places his hands on top of mine. His chin rests on my shoulder as he stares at our reflection.

We stay holding one another for a moment as we absorb the news of our latest blessings.

"Six months. The countdown begins," I say with a smile.

Lachlan grins back and brushes his thumbs over my belly as he responds.

"Indeed, Mrs. Jackson. Indeed."

LACHLAN

"One day, one of you will sit here, Lilias, Leith, and Lewis. Right in your Daddy's seat. The next generation to run Jackson Corporation. That is, if you want to work in our family's business. No pressure whatsoever. I will support whatever you wish to do. Do you understand?"

I say to my babies as they sit with me in my office at Jackson Town House. It's almost the end of the day. My Baby Girl brought them with her since we're meeting our parents for an early dinner before they fly to Bali to cruise aboard *Temptation* for the month. They want to see their grandbabies before they leave. We want to tell them about our news in person.

I still can't believe we're expecting a baby, let alone twins to boot! I grin at the thought.

My smile widens when Lilias is the first to speak up, clapping her pudgy hands and smiling with one tooth showing as she laughs. Her brothers take notice and follow suit. Leith bounces on my lap as he laughs. While Lewis investigates the top of my desk.

Too fucking adorable for words.

"Okay, Dad Connor," My Baby Girl says with an arched eyebrow as she stares down at me. "We will not have our children vying for leadership. No. Way."

"Is that what I said? Uh, no. At this point, they're the only Jackson grandchildren, so one of them may want to take the lead role. When my siblings have children, we'll see who makes the best fit based on experience, regardless of age or gender. I'm not like my father in that sense. Thank you very much," I respond with a snort.

She bends over and cups my cheek to turn my face back to hers. A frown mars her beautiful face as she shakes her head.

"I know you're not like Dad Connor *in that sense*. I just want them to make their own way. Look at Harris and me. We created a subsidiary based on our love of tech," My Baby Girl says. Then she adds saucily, "Do *you* understand, Mr. Jackson?"

I balance Lilias and Leith on my lap and reach my hand around her hip to give her ass a resounding smack. She yelps and stands up straight as she covers her butt with both of her hands. Her mouth a perfect O—perfect to fit my cock inside.

"Watch your tone, Naughty Girl," I growl.

She lowers her eyes as her cheeks pinken. My sub bows to her Dom.

Too fucking sexy for words.

"Mr. Jackson? Are you ready to meet with us?"

Isla's voice carries over the intercom and stops any wayward thoughts of mine.

I clear my throat and press the button to respond positively.

My Baby Girl scoops Lewis off of my desk as I rise to help her to the leather seating area. As they settle, my administrative assistant enters my office with a young redheaded woman behind her. I stride over to my desk as I gesture for them to sit in the guest chairs opposite.

Isla is pregnant and will take an early leave, followed by maternity time off after she gives birth. I've met with quite a few replacements for her role. But no one reaches my expectations. Gladys met with Isla's suggestion and recommended I meet with her. After Human Resources did their checks, I agreed since her resume and references were impressive.

As we take our seats, I notice the woman glances at my wife and children.

She smiles at them and nods as she waves her fingers at Leith, who watches us intently.

"Oh, don't mind us. Do carry on with your meeting," my wife says with a smile.

The woman nods and shifts her attention back to me.

"Mr. Jackson, this is Katrina Roberts, my friend who I recommend as my replacement. Katrina, this is Mr. Lachlan Jackson, CEO of Jackson Corporation," Isla says.

Katrina holds out her hand and rises slightly from her seat.

"Thank you for the opportunity to interview with you, Mr. Jackson," she says in a soft Scottish lilt as she grips my hand firmly and looks me straight in the eye.

"You're welcome Ms. Roberts—"

"Oh, please call me Kat," she interjects with an amiable smile. Her green eyes twinkle like emeralds behind tortoise-shell frame glasses.

I nod.

"Do you need me any further, Mr. Jackson?" Isla asks as she rests her hand on her baby bump.

I scan her face to be sure she's all right.

"No, that is all for today. Call for one of the company cars to take you home. They can pick you up in the morning, so you can leave yours in the garage overnight," I tell her.

Isla expresses her thanks and turns to tell my wife good night before she leaves my office. I watch her make her way and decide I need to get this replacement situation settled. Like yesterday.

I turn my gaze back to *Kat* with the hope she proves capable.

"So, Kat, tell me about yourself and why you believe your skill set makes you suitable for the role of my administrative assistant," I say.

She sits up straighter in her seat and proceeds to answer.

An hour later, I escort her to the doors of my office and ask Gladys to see her to the lobby.

Kat extends her hand, and I shake it.

"Thank you, Mr. Jackson. I do hope I satisfy your requirements and hope to hear from you soon," she says with another firm grip. Then shifts her emerald green gaze to my right and smiles. "Nice to see you, Mrs. Jackson. Your triplets are adorable."

"Thank you, Kat," my wife responds with a brilliant smile that illuminates her dove gray eyes.

I shut the door behind Kat and stride over to the sofa. I drop down and kiss My Baby Girl's temple as I lift Lewis onto my lap.

"So, what do you think of *Kat* Roberts?" I ask.

My Baby Girl giggles.

"She's obviously extremely smart to have achieved a full academic scholarship to the University of Edinburgh. It's the most prestigious institution in Scotland, and one of the best in the world," she responds. She giggles and adds, "It's not my alma mater, Harvard, but it'll do! Plus, she has strong references and worked in the C-suite for other executives, and Isla knows her. Do you trust her opinion?"

I nod thoughtfully.

"Enough of work, time to get to the restaurant," I say, then bounce Lewis on my knee. "And you get to see your grands! Isn't that nice?"

Once again, The Trips laugh and wave their chubby arms in the air in agreement.

We bundle them up before we put on our coats and head out of my office.

"YOU'VE HAD us on pins and needles all day! Tell us your news!"

"Yes, don't keep us waiting any longer!"

The Moms make their demands as our fathers nod in unison.

I turn to My Baby Girl and pick up her hand. She grins and brings my knuckles to her lips to brush a kiss across them as she nods.

"We're sixteen-weeks pregnant with twin... Boys!!!" We announce together.

The private room at one of Lucien's eateries erupts with our parents' exclamations. The Moms jump up from their seats and pull My Baby Girl into their arms, then hold her at arm's length to eye her babies bump.

She's wearing a black cashmere turtleneck mini dress with black suede thigh-high boots. At this stage, her belly only protrudes slightly. So one wouldn't necessarily assume she's pregnant.

I can tell since her tits have already gotten bigger and her hips rounder. I shift in my seat to hide my twitching cock. My Baby Girl is one Hot Mama!

The Dads pull me in for hugs and claps on the back. My father puffs his chest out and grins like the Cheshire Cat.

"That's my boy! Five heirs in no time!" He says, elated by my virility.

Dad Morgan chuckles and adds, "You've outdone them all, son! And you're doing an excellent job with Lilias, Leith, and Lewis. You and Haley make us extremely proud."

My throat clogs with emotion so I can only nod without my voice cracking like a prepubescent teenage boy.

He claps me on the shoulder again as his platinum gray eyes fill with understanding.

"I'm sure the rest of our clan would like to hear the good news. How about we ring them?" Dad Morgan adds with a fatherly smile.

I clear my throat and agree verbally as I pull my mobile out of my trousers pocket.

We gather back around the table, and I entwine fingers with My Baby Girl. She glows with her face flushed from the excitement.

It's quick to get the others on the line since we told them we would call in advance. More squeals and shouts of surprise followed by congratulations fill the air. Malcolm and Starr—who have two sets of twins—concede to us with our soon-to-be mini clan of five.

I tease we have our polo team plus one and will go for the rugby team next.

My Baby Girl throws her head back and guffaws. As she dabs tears from her eyes, she levels me with a stare.

"Oh, I do not think so, Mr. Jackson! Fifteen? Huh! Five is the limit!" She retorts.

Everyone cracks up.

Then she adds, "Four boys and a girl…Just like me with The Big Four. God help Lilias!"

"You bet that's right!" Baz says as he chuckles.

I throw my head back and laugh. Tell me about it!

After a while, we end the call and order our dinner. The conversation stays on The New Twins—since Roger and Leonie have The Original Twins—mostly. Then it shifts to our parents' trip. Our evening ends with more hugs and warm wishes.

When My Baby Girl and I return to our penthouse flat, we change and bathe The Trips before we put them in their cribs. When she's sitting on our bed with her diary, I sit beside her and put a legal-size envelope on her lap. She glances up at me in surprise.

"Open it," I tell her.

"A surprise? For little ole me?" She teases, batting her eyelashes as she raises the flap. "Why, thank you kindly, *My Lord.*"

My cock twitches. But not yet, big boy.

She pulls glossy photos from inside and flips through them. I watch her face for her reaction. She glances back up at me questioningly.

"It's Aboyne Castle—our seat, if you will," I answer. Her mouth gapes into another perfect O. I press on. "It's been in our family since the early fifteenth century. My steward oversees its maintenance. It's too big for just me. So, I never had a use for it before since Jackson Castle is where the rest of my family resides in the country."

I pause and cup her chin as I sweep my thumb over her lush mouth.

"But now. Well… Our little family is growing, and we can use the spacious property as our primary residence and keep this as a pied-à-terre. Aboyne Castle is only forty-four minutes away by car to Aberdeen. So we can commute, even by helicopter, for a faster route. What do you think?" I say.

Tears that shone in her eyes as I spoke slip down her cheeks. I lean forward and kiss them, then cover her mouth with mine. She moans, and I swallow it up as I pull her beneath me.

Careful not to crush her with my weight, I plank over her body and hold her head between my hands. Our kiss deepens.

I groan when she wraps her legs around my hips and pulls down to cradle my groin against her soft mound. My cock hardens to steel instantly at her warmth and softness.

"I love you so much, Lachlan," My Baby Girl moans against my demanding mouth.

I lift for only a moment to stare deeply into her adoring eyes.

"I love you so much more, My Baby Girl. Forever and ever. You are mine, Haley Jackson. MINE!" I say gruffly.

More tears slip from her gorgeous gray eyes.

The tears spur me to take them away with an undeniable claiming of my woman, my sub, my wife, the mother of my children. My absolute everything. My Baby Girl.

"OMG, Lachlan! I *cannot* believe you hid this gem from me! It's incredible! Look at your fairytale castle, Lilias, Leith, and Lewis. You'll grow up here."

The Trips laugh and coo as much as I do from the sight of Aboyne Castle and its manicured lawns and rolling lands outside of our Sikorsky S-92 Executive Helicopter's windows.

The six-story castle made from Aberdeen granite features towers on one side of the center keep and battlements on the other. A granite bridge spans the stream that flows before it. The Jackson heraldic flag ripples in the wind from the highest point. Aboyne Castle is an impressive sight. And huge, as Lachlan told me.

"I didn't exactly hide it. Even with the five of us currently, it's a massive residence," Lachlan says. "But now here we are, home sweet home, My Lady."

He has our pilot circle the perimeter of the one

hundred acres, so we can see the castle and outer buildings from the air. Lachlan points to some, including the pool house, stables, greenhouse, and a whimsical Tartar tent—a folly within one of the gardens. Bridal paths crisscross the land, covering different terrains perfect for horseback riding. The sun glints off of the snow-covered buildings and parkland, making Aboyne Castle an enchanting vision.

When the helicopter sets down on the front lawn, we see the staff lined up at the castle's primary doors. The first person to step forward greets Lachlan with a warm smile.

"My Lord, so good to see you, sir!" The older man says.

"Mr. Wilson, you look well," Lachlan responds with a smile as he shakes his hand. Then turns to me and continues, "This is my wife Haley Jackson, Countess of Aboyne. My Lady, this is Mr. Wilson, the Steward for Aboyne Castle."

"A pleasure to meet you, Mr. Wilson," I say as I extend my hand.

He takes it with a bow of his silvery gray head as he returns my greeting. Then he gestures towards the rest of the staff. Mr. Wilson introduces me to the butler, the cook, the housekeeper, a maid, the head gardener, a groundskeeper, and the stable master.

I glance at Lachlan at the introduction to the stable master since I recognize him as a stablehand from Jackson Castle who helped me with Moonbeam.

Lachlan smiles and explains he had our horses brought over to the stables here and promoted him to the new position.

I nod in understanding.

Nanny Gail follows us as we enter the front hall. My head swivels from one side to the other and up. It's incredible and full of history, with portraits, coats of arms, and tapestries. My heart speeds up with excitement.

"Oh, Lachlan! This is magnificent!" I whisper to him.

He beams.

"Come, let's get The Trips out of their car seats and into their pram so I can give you a tour," he says. When I frown in response to a pram indoors, he grins. "The halls are wide, and we have lots of rooms to cover. And you, my darling wife, will not carry one of our seven-month-old babies at sixteen-weeks pregnant. No."

I can't disagree with him since the castle is ginormous, and I tire easily these days.

Over three hours later, we have lunch in the dining room while Nanny Gail sits with The Trips asleep in the bedroom closest to the primary one. I know Leonie will love to help me with the redesign of this historic property. Lachlan agrees wholeheartedly, then goes on.

"Not only a redesign. But you will need to meet with Mr. Wilson to hire more staff. The current staff can't handle our little family alone, especially once The New Twins are born. Who we have now are meant as more maintenance than day-to-day care. And if you would rather replace someone, do not feel obligated to keep them. This is our home, and I want you comfortable with every aspect of it. You are the lady of the house."

My heart swells with love for my husband. I smile at him and reach for his hand.

"Thank you, My Lord. Let's spend some time with the staff and add more before we decide to replace any, if necessary. They're already familiar with the property. And the cook made a wonderful lunch. If she keeps it up, we're good!" I respond with a giggle as I pat my babies bump.

"Whatever you wish, My Lady," he says, chuckling as he rubs it, too.

After lunch, we go to the library. The butler lit the fire when we told him we would retire here. The warmth and fragrant scent it gives off from the six-foot stone fireplace makes the sizable room cozy. Shelves loaded with books line the walls from floor to ceiling. A second story runs along three of the walls and has more shelves. The spiral staircase gives access to it.

Leather sofas and chairs with throws and tables with Tiffany lamps sit atop an Aubusson rug that almost reaches the edges of the hardwood floor. I can tell the library will be my favorite place, like the one at Jackson Castle.

Nanny Gail and the housekeeper bring Lilias, Leith, and Lewis to us. Bonnie and Bella trot along beside them with their feathery tails wagging.

I thank Nanny Gail and the housekeeper, then curl up on the oversized window seat with The Trips and their toys to watch the snow fall on the picture-perfect land-scape outside. Bonnie and Bella throw themselves down in front of the fireplace with their chew toys. Lachlan smiles at us, then turns back to work on his laptop at the ornate antique desk in the corner.

Tears of joy fill my eyes as I realize my desires are granted.

I married Lachlan—the love of my life and my fairytale prince.

We have our babies—Lilias, Leith, Lewis, and our twin boys—the first of the Jackson heirs.

I have my own little family to love forever in our castle.

My fairytale's happy ending is complete.

arris

HEY, bro, I'm sitting in the lobby.

A moment passes, then the three dots appear indicating Lachlan is typing a response appear on the screen of my mobile.

On my way down.

I scroll through my email while I wait.

"Mr. Steele? Mr. Harris Steele?"

A soft Scottish lilt says my name like I'm Bond. James Bond.

And like a Bond Girl, this one is stacked. Her prim librarian facade of low heels, stockings, a conservative suit with an A-line skirt and a waist-length jacket, pussy bow blouse, and tortoise-shell glasses fails to hide her bodacious body. Thick, glossy red hair pulled back in a no-nonsense bun. Hot damn!

As my gaze takes in her long legs, grip-worthy hips, ample tits, and lush mouth, her natural beauty takes my breath away. Emerald green eyes stare back at me, unaffected—dare I say bored—by my heated gaze.

I put on my most dazzling, panty dropping smile and mimic her Scottish accent in my deep baritone timbre.

"Aye, bonnie lass. And who might ye be?"

I think I see a flash of something in the depths of those intriguing emerald orbs. But it's gone in, well, a flash.

She squares her shoulders and peers down her nose at me.

Her attempt to show confidence only serves to push her delectable tits out.

I smirk.

Her eyes narrow slightly. Then her face blanks again. Lady Gaga's "Poker Face," anyone?

"Kat, Mr. Jackson's administrative assistant," she responds.

Oh, fuck me. Why does this one have to work for Lachlan? Damn.

The realization wipes the flirtation from my mind in an instant.

"Mr. Jackson asked me to escort you up to his offices as a call detained him," Kat continues. "Kindly follow me, Mr. Steele."

Without waiting for me to acknowledge her statement,

Little Kat pivots and walks towards the executive floor's elevator.

Okay, Little Kat may be Lachlan's admin. But the sway of her hips and her round ass call to me like a siren's song. I follow like she's the Pied Piper.

The alluring scent of her perfume fills my nostrils as we stand side by side in the elevator. I guesstimate her height at five feet, six inches in her two-inch heels since I tower over her by five.

Surreptitiously, I ogle her in my periphery. Wild thoughts of yanking the pins from her bun to free that red mane, hiking her skirt up, and hoisting her long leg around my hip as I drive my hungry ten-inch cock balls deep inside of her wet, willing pussy fill my head.

The ping of the elevator doors opening interrupts my sexy fantasy.

As I follow Little Kat, I adjust my burgeoning length. And avoid staring at her sexy strut.

She knocks on Lachlan's doors and opens them.

"You may enter, Mr. Steele," she says as she steps back.

"Thank you, Kat," I say with a nod. The taste of her name sweetens my mouth.

I step inside, and she closes the door behind me.

My hand drags down my face as I blow out a long breath.

Fuck. Me.

When I open my eyes, Lachlan stares at me with his head cocked as he continues to speak on the telephone. I shake my head and point to his en suite bathroom. He nods but watches me curiously.

Once inside, I fully adjust my cock, then stare in the mirror.

"Did that Little Kat crawl under my skin? Fuck… Am I doomed like my brothers by one glance?" I say aloud to my reflection. Then I grin. "Hell nah! Not this playa, baby!"

I chuckle as I shake my head to dislodge *that* unsavory thought, rinse my face with cool water, and stride from the bathroom.

***

Lachlan & Haley's Story Concludes For Now…

But can Harris get himself together? Or is Kat The One who finally manages to get under his skin and not just in the Alpha male's bed for one night?

Find out in the next STEELE World: STEELE International, Inc. - Jackson Corporation Crossover Series Book 4

Intrigue My Desires Harris & Kat Part I

Turn the page for the Steele Family and the Jackson Family, Author's Note, and the Preview of *Intrigue My Desires*

THE STEELE FAMILY

STEELE INTERNATIONAL, INC

Multigenerational, multibillion-dollar business luxury real estate development and management corporation

Headquarters & Family's Primary Residences:

The STEELE Tower, New York City

A modern, gray-tinted glass fifty-seven story mixed-use skyscraper on southwest corner of Fifty-Seventh Street and Fifth Avenue within Billionaires' Row

Global Offices:

- The United States of America (New York City, New Jersey, Chicago, California, Miami, Las Vegas)
- The Caribbean (St. Maarten, St. Barth's, St. Lucia)
- The French & Italian Rivieras (Nice, Cannes, Positano, Capri)
- Monaco (Monte Carlo)
- The United Arab Emirates (Abu Dhabi, Dubai)

STEELE FOUNDATION: A STRONG AND SUPPORTIVE HOUSE

Builds and manages attractive, affordable housing for urban, lower-income families

Available for download at **bit.ly/STEELEFamily**

THE JACKSON FAMILY

JACKSON CORPORATION

Multigenerational, multibillion-dollar business fine dining,
distilleries, and vineyards corporation

Headquarters:

Jackson Town House, Aberdeen, Scotland

A landmark property built by the founders of Aberdeen granite
on Union Street; the second largest granite building in the world.

Global Offices:

- The United Kingdom (Aberdeen, Scotland; London, England)
- The United States of America (New York City, New Orleans, Miami, Chicago, Los Angeles, Napa)
- The Caribbean (Puerto Rico)
- France (Paris, Cannes)
- Monaco (Monte Carlo)
- Australia (Sydney)
- The United Arab Emirates (Abu Dhabi, Dubai)

JACKSON FOUNDATION: ENJOY LIFE RESPONSIBLY

Operates alcohol treatment centers for lower-income individuals and support for their family members

Available for download at **bit.ly/JacksonFamilyTree**

Author's Note

Thank you for reading Part III of Lachlan and Haley's sexy, sizzling romance! I hope you enjoyed the Happy For Now conclusion of their forbidden love affair. If so, I'd love to hear your thoughts, please share a review at **bit.ly/ CLBooksSI-JC3Review** and tell your friends.

Wait! What's up with Harris and Kat?! The epilogue gave lots of hints at what's brewing for these lovers...

Click below for the answers to their steamy, Alpha male playboy falls for The One billionaire romance in the next STEELE World: STEELE International, Inc. - Jackson Corporation A Billionaires Romance Series Crossover Book 4:

Intrigue My Desires Harris & Kat Part I **Click Here**

At **CharmaineLouise.com** take the *Four types of lovers. Which are you?* **Quiz** to match your Sexy Fantasy: sub, Voyeur, Dominatrix, or Dominatrix sub Switch.

Follow me on social media including my CLBooks Coterie Fan Club below or on your favorite channels below and subscribe to my newsletter at **bit.ly/ CLBooksNewsletter** for a **Free Book**.

Fulfill Your Desires.

xoxo

Charmaine Louise

bookbub.com/authors/charmaine-louise-shelton
facebook.com/CharmaineLouiseBooks
instagram.com/charmainelouisebooks
goodreads.com/charmainelouisebooks

**STEELE International, Inc. - Jackson Corporation
A Billionaires Romance Series Crossover Book 4**

Intrigue My Desires Harris & Kat Part I

Click on the link below or visit books2read.com/u/
mg7wVK to get your copy.

Intrigue My Desires Harris & Kat Part I

Books in the Series:

Tempt My Desires Lachlan & Haley Part I

Tease My Desires Lachlan & Haley Part II

Grant My Desires Lachlan & Haley Part III

Intrigue My Desires Harris & Kat Part I

Decode My Desires Harris & Kat Part II

Honor My Desires Harris & Kat Patt III

A Trilogy of Desires Lachlan & Haley Parts I-III

A Trilogy of Desires Harris & Kat Parts I-III

Series Extras

Series Playlist

Visit CharmaineLouiseBooks.com for the complete list.

COMING NEXT: INTRIGUE MY
DESIRES HARRIS & KAT PART I
STEELE INTERNATIONAL, INC. -
JACKSON CORPORATION A
BILLIONAIRES ROMANCE SERIES
CROSSOVER BOOK 4

"Tilt your chin towards the corner over there. I want the light to cross the planes of your gorgeous face... A little more... Just... Right there! Now, hold still and allow me to capture your beauty."

My muse-cum-lover preens as my brush skims across the canvas before me. Her nipples pebble as though the soft sable tip caresses her flawless, porcelain skin. Sky blue eyes twinkle when she moves them to catch a glimpse of me at work.

I tsk at her, and a small smile plays at the corners of her Cupid's bow mouth.

We continue in silence for the next hour until I notice her shoulders shake from the exertion to maintain her position for an extended period of time. With a sigh, I finish one last stroke to the curvaceous hip on the canvas before I release her.

"Relax, My Beauty. We are done for now," I tell her as I

cover the canvas with a tarp. My preference to keep the unfinished work hidden mars her lovely face with a scowl. "No, you cannot see it yet."

"Oh… You're so mean to me!" She huffs and crosses her arms beneath her ample bosom. The move only serves to present them to me like a platter of tantalizing treats. "Well, I can't see. So, neither can you!"

She wraps the white silk sheet around her like a toga as she rises from the red velvet chaise gracefully. A glance over her shoulder as she sashays towards the ancient stone stairs drives me from my stool.

My long legs make short work of the distance between us.

My Beauty squeaks when I grip her hips and hoist her over my shoulder with ease. A firm smack to her rear makes her yelp and flail her arms and legs. Her tiny hands pummel my broad back, to no avail. Another round of smacks, and she drapes her torso over my shoulder in complete submission.

"Good, girl," I murmur as I carry her to the bed at the center of my studio.

She bounces on the feather mattress when I toss her to the middle. The silk sheet slips open to reveal her naked beauty in all its mesmerizing glory. The thatch of dark hair at the apex of her thighs glistens with her arousal. She notices my lust-filled stare and covers her mound as her porcelain cheeks flush a contrasting crimson hue.

Quick as lightning, I grab her wrists and pull them from her treasure trove to place them above her head. One hand pins them to the mattress while the other parts her thighs. A single thick, calloused digit breaches her slick folds.

Her back arches from the bed as a moan escapes her lips.

Rhythmic thrusts that graze the textured patch and stroke her inner walls have her writhing beneath me. A second digit has her panting. A tweak to her swollen bud, and she screams my name.

My mouth crashes over hers as I plank above her. Our tongues dance, and I swallow her moans greedily to capture every piece of her—beauty and pleasure. A shudder runs through me when her fingernails rake along my bare back.

Her dainty fingers reach between us, eager to unleash my turgid member.

Both of us groan at the carnal contact as her hand fists my erection. Her gentle tugs do not suffice to quench my lust.

With a primal growl, I take control and slam deep within her slippery core. Her warmth engulfs me from tip to base. My eyes roll to the back of my head.

My hips snap of their own accord as I drive her into the mattress. She meets each thrust with one of her own as her core flutters along my length.

The sounds of our carnal passion resound off the stone walls of my studio to soar towards the ceiling high above us. Through the open windows, the sea crashes to the shore in time with my thrusts. Her cries match the seagulls in their quest for food.

The base of my spine tingles. Three final snaps of my hips, and I roar my release. It ignites another climax for My Beauty. She keens her pleasure as she bows from the bed. I collapse atop her, and she winds her arms and legs about me.

I roll to my side, still intimately connected to my lover. She cuddles against my chest as my fingers draw circles around the two dips above her round derriere.

With the release of my creative and carnal passions, my mind returns to the request—rather demand—my father sent to me. I am to meet him along with my younger brother in the city tomorrow.

Undoubtedly, it's another of his threats. I will attend. But nothing he says will change my mind. Nothing.

I shake my head to rid it of the sense of impending doom. With a sigh, I roll My Beauty onto her back to lose myself within her welcoming embrace once again.

* * *

"Hello, Father, brother."

I nod at each of them when I enter my father's office.

My brother greets me with a sorrowful smile.

"Glad you can join us," my father responds gruffly. His dissatisfied scowl takes me in from head to toe, not at all pleased with my attire of a smock shirt, trousers., and paint-stained brogues. "You could not find an appropriate suit? Never mind. Sit."

Once I'm seated beside my brother, our father settles

behind his massive wooden desk. My artist's eye takes in the ornate carvings appreciatively. A master craftsman's finest work.

"Have you come to your senses and will take your proper place as the next to run our family's company?"

My father's question draws me from my musings.

I glance over at him.

We stare at one another for a heartbeat.

I look away first.

He sighs.

"With all due respect, Father. We have had this conversation many times before. I intend to follow my passion. I do not care to follow in your footsteps," I respond as I bring my gaze back to his angry one.

My brother cringes beside me. He knows the roof is about to blow off the building. Again.

Surprisingly, our father remains silent. He studies my face for any sign of a change of heart.

I remain steadfast and hold his gaze.

He rises to tower over me.

"From this day forward, I disown you and no one will speak your name ever again. Your presence erased from this family's history completely. As I speak, your *studio* is being destroyed and your harlot removed. Leave this city with what you have at this moment. Do not let the sunset find you here. Never return. Contact none of us again. Ever. Do you understand?"

His pronouncement sends a chill through my very soul.

The sense of doom comes to fruition.

I scan his face, hoping to find a crack in his countenance. Nothing. I turn to my brother, and he glances away from my imploring gaze. My eyes shift back to my father. He stands indomitable and raises his hand to point at the door.

"Leave now, or I will have you escorted from the premises," he commands.

I never guessed my father would go so far as to banish me. To obliterate me from our family. Ruin my dreams.

I open my mouth to implore him. But as he rounds the desk with an expression of such detestation, I flinch. Then suck in a breath when he grips the back of my shirt and lifts me from the leather chair.

Forcefully, he pushes me towards the door.

I stumble before I catch myself.

One last glance over my shoulder reveals his imposing figure glaring at me and my brother's stiff back as he stares straight ahead. No remorse. No sympathy.

"Goodbye, Father, brother."

***

Click the Link Below or Visit books2read.com/u/ mg7wVK For Your Copy

Intrigue My Desires Harris & Kat Part I

I dedicate this novel to those who believe in fairytales and dreams that can come true.

Fulfill Your Desires.

xoxo
Charmaine Louise

WELCOME TO CHARMAINELOUISE — THE SENSUAL LIFESTYLE

GLITZY. GLAMOROUS. STEAMY.

CharmaineLouise New York, Inc. invites you to indulge in *The Sensual Lifestyle* through **CharmaineLouise Books** and **CharmaineLouise Intimates**. CLBrands immerse you in *Sexy Fantasies* with CLBooks contemporary romance novels and give you *Sexy Under Things & Loungewear* with CLIntimates.

Charmaine Louise Shelton the Founder, CEO & Author of CLNY loves all things classic, elegant, feminine, and of course with an erotic edge! Favorite outfit of choice is a cashmere cardigan, leather pencil skirt, and seamed silk stockings with stiletto heels. Sexy Fantasy Type: sub with a dash of Voyeur. When not writing and designing, Charmaine Louise travels and spends time with her Maltese buddies, ZIGGY and Jynger.

CharmaineLouise — *The Sensual Lifestyle*

~ Visit online at **CharmaineLouise.com**

~ Subscribe to **CharmaineLouise Newsletter**

~ Find us on Facebook **@CharmaineLouiseNewYork**

~ Instagram **@CharLouNY**

CharmaineLouise Books *Sexy Fantasies* launched summer 2020. Sizzling, contemporary romance with your soon-to-be favorite Alpha Doms, Powerful Billionaires, and the women they lust after and love for second chances, insta-love, enemies-to-lovers, and more.

Want to chat it up and share your thoughts with other CLBooks Lovers? Read our blog, join our Charmaine-Louise Books Coterie Fan Club and follow us on my author pages and social media to be in the know about the book release dates, exclusive content, giveaways, contests, and more!

~ **Purchase your eBook and paperback novels from my Author Page by clicking here!**

~ Read and subscribe to our blog *The World of Sex*

~ Connect on **Amazon Author Page**

~ Goodreads Author Profile

~ <u>BookBub Author Profile</u>

CharmaineLouise Intimates *Sexy Under Things & Loungewear* debuted in 2003. Inspired by the sensuous sirens and sylph swans of the past and present, the hand crochet cashmere and silk collections are for the sexy: hence, the line names Ginger — Bombshell; Diana — Showstopper; Jackie — Timeless; Lena — Classic. Also known as The Movie-Star from Gilligan's Island; Ms. Ross The Boss; Mrs. Kennedy Onassis; Ms. Horne.

Do you thrive on seduction and being sexy lounging at home? Read our blog and follow us on social media to receive the tips, the latest additions to the collections, private sales, and more!

~ Read and subscribe to our blog *The Art of Seduction*

~ Find us on Facebook **@CharmaineLousieIntimates**

~ Instagram **@CharmaineLouiseIntimates**

Fulfill Your Desires.